ST. MARTIN'S

MINOTAUR

MYSTERIES

THE HAIRS ON THE BACK OF MY NECK STOOD UP.

Amy pulled the screen door open and pushed the front door inward. I followed her in.

"Dad!" she called.

No answer. There was an acrid smell in the air. . . . strong enough to make my eyes water. We went into the living room, with old-fashioned wicker furniture and bamboo blinds. . . . That burning, choking smell was even stronger. We headed toward the kitchen. Something was sticking out of the half-open bathroom door. It was a man's foot. Looking around the door, I saw him sprawled face down on the floor in his Hawaiian shirt. One outstretched hand seemed to be reaching for a small plastic funnel-like apparatus on the floor next to him. My mind registered that it was an asthma inhaler at the same time that I realized the man was totally still, his stretching hand too stiff for sleep. Amy gasped and pushed past me to look.

ST. MARTIN'S PAPERBACKS TITLES BY LYNNE MURRAY

Larger Than Death
Large Target

LARGE TARGET

LYNNE MURRAY

St. Martin's Paperbacks

LARGE TARGET

Copyright © 2000 by Lynne Murray.

Excerpt from *At Large* copyright © 2001 by Lynne Murray.

Library of Congress Catalog Card Number: 99-089839

ISBN: 0-312-97537-6

Printed in the United States of America

St. Martin's Press hardcover edition / April 2000
St. Martin's Paperbacks edition / July 2001

St. Martin's Paperbacks are published by St. Martin's Press, 175 Fifth Avenue, New York, NY 10010.

10 9 8 7 6 5 4 3 2 1

To my beloved cats, past and present—
any one of whom, if presented with this page,
would sit on it rather than read it,
which keeps everything in proper perspective for me.

ACKNOWLEDGMENTS

I deeply appreciate those who helped me with this book:

My father, Channing Wayne Murray, is no longer among the living, but his perspectives on military and civilian cultures shaped this book, not to mention my childhood—the poker-playing incident with the officers was a true tale from my erring youth.

Michael Mitchell Murray, my wonderful brother, who kindly checked my Southern California routes for accuracy.

Adam Goldberg, a true friend, who is always ready to look at the big picture.

Christopher Rankin, who graciously consented to be my part-time muse.

Roberto López and Phillip Guilbeau, who checked the Spanish for embarrassments.

Keith Vickers, who generously shared insights into chess openings and tournament views from a Master's perspective.

John A. Miller of Orloff Press, who talked me down out of my tree on at least one occasion, a service which he points out the fire department in many areas no longer provides.

Lajon Webb, a former USN Radioman, who valiantly checked my manuscript for civilian blunders.

My agent at Writers House, Michele G. Rubin, who has managed to be delightful, insightful, dynamic, and re-assuring, each at the appropriate moment.

My editor at St. Martin's Press, Joe Veltre, who provided thoughtful perspective and creative feedback that very much enriched Josephine Fuller's fictional existence.

JP, without whom this particular story would not have been written, and certainly not set in San Diego.

I take full responsibility for all factual errors, invented places, and flights from reality that have crept in as side effects of the tale-spinning process—or what my father used to call "living in a dream world."

LARGE
TARGET

A woman of my size is supposed to be invisible—a factor that often proves useful in my line of work. My job is philanthropic troubleshooting. Such inquiries have to be discreet to be worth anything at all. As a woman weighing over two hundred pounds, my very existence bothers some people to the point where they erase me from the landscape. They look, and turn away. So I do my job, go home, take off the please-ignore-me black polyester pantsuit, and put on my preferred red silk lounging pajamas.

My name is Josephine Fuller and I make my living as an investigator of sorts, judging the worthiness of candidates for the charitable grants of Alicia Madrone, a woman whose personal fortune exceeds the gross national product of several small developing nations.

It was a June Sunday in San Diego when I went back to work—one month after my best friend, Nina, was murdered. She was a second mother to me. My own mother had been dead two years when I first met Nina, selling plus-sized clothes from her Pike's Place Market store in Seattle, looking like the kind of blond cherub Renaissance painters adored. She lived her life as a woman of size who never apologized or compromised. I was a miserable fifteen-year-old when we met and Nina taught me how to be a confident large woman. It wasn't right that she should be gone from the world. Rather than consolation, it seemed a kind of twisted irony that I had inherited her cat along with her worldly possessions. Worse yet, I had a yearning for her grieving lover. I just wanted everything back the way it had been. Leaving Seattle wouldn't bring my friend back to life. But if I buried myself in my work at least I could avoid thinking about it for a while.

So I escaped. Mrs. Madrone welcomed me back with an assignment to make some confidential inquiries in San Diego. I brought the cat; in the depth of grief I couldn't bear to part with him. I wound up in a Point Loma house party trying to blend into the wallpaper, hoping to discreetly discover for my employer whether a friend's daughter was, to put it bluntly, insane.

I took a cab from the San Diego Airport across the Coronado Bridge to Mrs. Madrone's rarified hideout— a Southern California version of an Italian villa built around a fountain in a tiled courtyard. It functioned like a small hotel, though most of the guests were traveling executives in the Madrone corporate empire. Once in the room, I opened Raoul's cat carrier and checked on the tranquilized gray Persian. He was snoring. I left food, water, and litter within easy reach.

The top floor had been customized for Mrs. Madrone's wheelchair with ramps and hardwood floors. They hadn't done anything, however, to accommodate her personal assistant's lean height. Ambrose had to duck his immaculately barbered red head to lead me through the door to Mrs. Madrone's private apartment. His laser-blue eyes hadn't relaxed in the mellow San Diego afternoon. He acknowledged the June climate to the point of wearing all white cotton, a shirt with a banded collar and trousers that looked vaguely Edwardian, as if he planned to take his coffee break with Vita Sackville-West. He showed me into a room bathed in sunlight, the central heating cranked up hot enough to grow orchids. I'd been in enough conversations with Mrs. Madrone by now to expect to sweat.

She wheeled her chair around to face me. She had been looking out over San Diego Harbor's turquoise waters. It had been over a month since her attendance at my friend's funeral, a gesture that both touched me deeply and surprised the hell out of me. As pale and drawn as ever, from her once-blond gray hair to her barely pink lips, her sharp dark eyes held an element of anxiety that I had never seen before.

"Sally Rhymer and I were at school together," she said. "She and the admiral are divorced now, she won't be at the gathering this afternoon. But Sally is worried about her daughter—little Amy. That's how I think of her, though she's a grown woman with a child of her own. Ambrose will give you the information. Amy has begun spending time away from her husband and young child to work with dying people. This, uh, calling . . . Does that sound sane to you?"

"I don't know. Is it a religious thing?"

"If so, it's something she picked up recently," Mrs. Madrone said, classifying religion with communicable diseases.

She waited for further comment.

"I'm no expert," I managed to say.

"It's common sense I'm hoping for here," Mrs. Madrone said, worrying a thread on her sweater sleeve. "Go talk to her, see what you think. She'll be at her brother, Dwight's, house. Sally is coming over in the morning. We can hear your impressions then." She turned her chair toward the window to signal that our business was done. Mrs. Madrone never wasted words.

On the way out, Ambrose handed me an information

packet, including a map and the keys to Mrs. Madrone's silver Lexus. He gave me brief instructions about how to deactivate the alarm with the key chain remote to keep the car from yelping. It did anyway, of course, sounding like an annoyed bloodhound.

Dwight and Colleen Rhymer lived at the northern end of the Point Loma peninsula, up from the Naval Training Center. Parking the car near their house, I mentally thanked Ambrose for suggesting that I borrow the Lexus. The silver status symbol slipped right in and looked at home with the cluster of high-priced Detroit and foreign metal parked in front of the house. Ambrose was usually right about these things.

A black Lincoln Town Car with a "Two Star" vanity license plate was parked on two gravel strips with grass growing between them, an old-fashioned driveway that ran alongside the house to a just-visible backyard cottage.

A deeply tanned, coltishly thin woman greeted me at the door, peering out from under brown bangs that hid her eyebrows. She wore a casually elegant white tank top with gold shorts roughly the same color as the heavy gold-link chains around her neck and wrist. She smiled inquiringly at me. Behind her I could hear music, a Frank Sinatra ballad, competing with a babble of party voices. I wondered if the woman in shorts was wary of me. Standing on her doorstep in a turquoise raw-silk blouse and skirt I must have looked as though the missionary's wife had dressed up one of Gauguin's South Sea island ladies and sent her round to distribute pamphlets. The pearl comb holding my hair up and the matching pearl-with-seashell earrings put me over the top. I was way overdressed.

"Oh, yes," she said, standing aside and beckoning me in. "Mrs. Madrone's assistant called and said you'd meet Amy here. I'm Colleen Rhymer, Dwight's wife."

"Beautiful house you have," I said, stepping into the foyer and taking in the cathedral ceilings and polished wood floor that continued up a winding stairway to the next level balcony. Any reply she might have made vanished, drowned out by the deafening roar of an airplane that vibrated the Venetian blinds with the force of a minor earthquake.

"*Amazingly* inexpensive, too—and every twenty minutes or so I'm reminded why." She made a sardonic mouth and raised her eyebrows even farther into her bangs.

I laughed sympathetically, and she beckoned me along the hall. "Still, this is paradise compared to most of the places Dwight has been stationed." We passed mounted color photos of battleships, aircraft carriers, and fighter jets to a back bedroom. "You can put your things here if you'd like."

I left my purse on the bed with my sweater over it. I lingered, looking out the window where a flagstone patio gave way to a few cactus plants bordering the backyard cottage.

"Did the property come with an extra house?"

She raised her eyebrows up under her bangs again. "Yes, we can have our in-laws come and visit *forever* if we want to. Except that wouldn't be wise because we do have weapons in the house. Come on, let's put a drink in your hand so you'll fit in."

Either she was always sarcastic, or sensed a kindred spirit. Or maybe Colleen Rhymer was so over-the-top angry today that she was letting off steam in front of total strangers and she simply didn't give a damn. I liked her already.

She led me past a carpeted dining room where a few guests were grazing at a buffet. I followed her into the kitchen. A tall, stout man with lizard-tanned skin straightened abruptly and shut the kitchen cupboard. His startlingly pale blue eyes glared at us. He turned on his heel and left the kitchen.

"My father-in-law, the admiral," Colleen Rhymer said with a wave and slight bow, seemingly introducing me to the man's retreating backside. "An hour ago he switched from beer to diet soda with great public fanfare. But he has to splash some bourbon into the soda every half hour or so. Come on, you'll want to meet Dwight."

I took a can of soda from an ice chest and followed her into the living room. It was a bit early for alcohol. Dwight was even taller than his father and substantially leaner, but still a teddy bear next to his thin wife. He had the same ruddy complexion, a bit less sunbaked, and the same silvery-blue eyes. I knew he was a navy officer. His dark hair was regulation short and his polo shirt and madras pants had the ironed look of a uniform. Everything this man owned would be a uniform of some sort. He shook my hand, only making eye contact for a distractedly polite second. His nails were bitten to nearly nothing. He kept glancing past me, over my shoulder across the living room. I was invisible already.

Of course maybe he was staring at his father. The stocky white-haired admiral had parked his soda and picked up a Minicam. He was now down on the floor aiming it up the skirt of a young woman, who was cowering like a gazelle before a predator. Watching this, I realized that she was perhaps the only woman here, other than myself, who hadn't been forewarned not to wear a skirt. A man about her age, who must have been her date, pulled the woman out of camera range. He looked out of place in this gathering, from his shoulder-length hair tied in a short pigtail to his Corona sweat-shirt and drawstring pants.

"Dad, get away from her. You've totally forgotten how to talk to a lady. This is the only language you understand." He aimed a desert-booted foot at the admiral's head.

"Don't even think about it, sonny," the admiral said, not even glancing at the foot suspended over his head. "You're not man enough to protect a hot little filly like this."

"Wait, Brad," Dwight called, "let me get a gun and we'll shoot the old geezer." A few guests laughed, but most continued their edgy migration around the admiral to a deck that looked out over the flagstone patio below. Those who remained in the living room seemed inter-ested in the admiral's floor show, or so comfortably seated with drinks and food that they didn't care to move.

The young man with the pigtail must be Omar Brad-ley Rhymer, the younger son. His date chose this mo-ment to make her escape and he turned to follow.

The admiral was only momentarily discouraged. He got up on his hands and knees, held the camera to his eye and panned slowly around the room at knee level, "Looking for decent legs." He muttered in a gravelly undertone, "Doesn't anyone wear those hot pants any-more?"

"Only hookers," one of the women muttered.

"Women haven't done that in years, Ron. You're dat-ing yourself!" one of the men called out.

"Damn right, I'm dating myself till my honey gets here tomorrow. But I'll be happy to accept any candidates to help me make it through the night."

"Colleen, sweetheart, you should cut him off," a woman nearby said quietly.

"If only I knew how." Colleen sighed.

I didn't realize I was becoming a target till I noticed the admiral kneeling in front of me. He swung the camera from my sandals to my calves before he fell back on the floor in hilarity. "Look out, boys, the Zeppelins have landed! Is the party over? Maybe I can make the fat lady sing."

There was a sprinkling of chuckles and a few gasps. A silence fell over the room, but the admiral didn't notice. "I'm making some movies to keep me company tonight. And you're no use at all, darlin'. Be a sport and help me up." He reached a hand up, and caught me behind the knee. I almost went down on the floor with him. As I regained my balance, he groped up the back of my thigh to brace himself.

"Back off," I said, firmly.

"Thinks she can get coy," he brayed, gripping my skirt for purchase and holding out the Minicam with the other hand.

"No." I shook the can of soda with a thumb over the hole and aimed it at his eyes. The spray at close range startled him enough to send him back on his rear while I jerked my skirt from his grip.

"Whoa!" the admiral exclaimed, shaking his head and looking around as if he weren't quite sure how he had landed wet-faced and back on the floor.

Several guests applauded as I retreated into the kitchen. A woman handed me a dampened dish towel and took my dripping soda can. "Here, honey," she said, "clean yourself off and I'll get you a new one. We all enjoyed that." I mopped up the spilled soda from my clothes and arms and thanked her for the new can, although when she went back to the front room, I left it unopened on the counter next to the folded towel.

A glance over my shoulder showed me the admiral, his face flushed, was being helped to his feet by a red-haired, red-bearded man with a traditional Santa Claus build, untraditionally dressed in a Hawaiian shirt.

I went through the front room. Pigtailed Brad Rhymer was just disappearing out the door with his whimpering girlfriend. Standing over the buffet was a square-built, African American man in his late fifties, his coppery brown head bald, his eyebrows gray, and his face furrowed. He was layering a cold-cut sandwich, moving with measured pace, as if the sandwich would explode if not properly assembled.

Colleen came back in with a plate of cookies that she put on the buffet. "Hello, Admiral Coffin, can I tempt you with some dessert?"

"No, thank you, dear, I'm watching my sugar intake." He stopped and pointed to a chair at the edge of the buffet table, "It looks like that young woman with Brad forgot her purse. They just left a moment ago."

"Thanks for letting me know." Colleen picked up the purse. "I'll keep it for her so it doesn't get lost."

As he went past, Admiral Coffin leaned toward Colleen and said in a low voice, just loud enough for me to hear, "I see Stewart Meade is on watch tonight. Where's Freddy?"

"Freddy's out of town on family business," Colleen said. "Damn it! Dwight and I have friends who'd like to stay but *he's* already driven every woman under forty out of this party because he literally—can't—keep—

his—hands—off." The last few words were delivered through clenched teeth.

"Freddy usually keeps ol' Genghis Ron in line," Admiral Coffin said, unexpectedly looking my way to meet my eyes with a brief, efficient nod that did double duty as sympathy and as close to an apology as I could hope for. He flicked his eyes back to Colleen. "Say, isn't Ron's girlfriend some relation to Freddy?"

"Right, Lani is Fred's niece."

Admiral Coffin nodded again and took his sandwich back to join the party.

Colleen stood for a moment surveying the buffet. Then she noticed me. "You didn't think you'd have to fight off the host's father at a house party, did you?"

"Well, no, but—"

"Try living here sometime. The old goat can't resist copping a feel if he goes past me in the kitchen. I thought Dwight was going to kill him when he caught him grabbing at my butt while I was setting up the buffet. I don't even want to talk about the precautions I have to take when I want to shower. The man is out of control." She suddenly seemed to come to herself. "I'm sorry, you wanted to see Amy. She might have left. Her husband will know. He's down in the rec room." She pointed to a carpeted stairwell that led off the foyer.

I went out to the hall just as Ron Rhymer came in from the kitchen. I glanced back to see him sprawl in the chair next to the buffet. The red-bearded Santa, who was apparently the admiral's sitter, Stewart Meade, followed him closely and pulled up a folding chair to the edge of the table. He rearranged a few dishes and set a bottle of Wild Turkey between himself and the admiral, who immediately pushed his glass forward so that Meade could pour him a generous shot.

Both men wore nearly identical aloha shirts. Meade's was green, the admiral's navy blue.

I lingered just outside the door. I'd had enough of the admiral, but I was curious.

"My wife—my ex-wife—used to tell me I was an alcoholic," the admiral remarked to the world at large.

"She must know you better than we do," I muttered too softly to be heard.

"You know what I told her?" he said, turning to Meade. "Sure, Sally, you can have a divorce if you feel that way, but I'll be damned if I'll talk to some jerk of a shrink."

Meade pushed a plate of chicken wings at him. "Eat something, Ron."

"Little Lani knows better than to talk back to me. Hell, I might even hang on to her after my Thai connection comes through." He laughed so hard for a minute I thought he would choke. Meade leaned forward in a conspiratorial crouch and tipped another splash from the bottle of Wild Turkey into the admiral's drink, moving the corners of his mouth in a most un-Santa-like twitch. I wondered what Meade was up to. A chill fell over me as if someone had turned the air conditioning down twenty degrees.

The carpeted stairwell led down to a low-ceilinged room that appeared to be deserted. A pool table dominated the space and the hanging lamp over it was unlit. A plate-glass window let in filtered sunlight. Outside a few people could be seen standing on the flagstone patio or sitting in lawn chairs.

A clockwork click came from the far end of the room. In the dimness beyond the pool table, a man sat across a card table from a girl perhaps nine or ten years old. Between them was a chessboard. A chess clock with two dials was the source of the click. Advancing into the room I could hear its faint ticking. The man moved a chess piece and tapped a button on top of the clock. His timer froze and the girl's clock started ticking. I crossed the room and stood a few feet off. Neither of them looked up.

The file from Ambrose had told me that Amy was married to Ivor Russo, an assistant professor of biology at a local university. Amy was under thirty. Her husband looked about forty, which seemed old for an assistant, tall and hatchet-faced with round silver-framed glasses and an untamed mop of curly gray hair. The girl must be their daughter, Stefanie. Round faced, her dark hair as curly as her father's, she bent over the board, concentrating with an almost tangible attention. At last she reached out to move a white piece. She used it to push aside a black piece, grabbing it up and hitting the button on her side of the clock.

As the man's clock began to run, the little girl looked up and said, "Did you want something?"

The man appeared to notice me for the first time. He glanced at the chess clock, moved a piece and put his hand across the top, pressing both buttons, freezing both clocks and stopping the ticking. "Let's adjourn for a moment, Stef." He gave his daughter a significant look and she grinned devilishly. "She wants to hold any conversation when my clock is running." He raised an eyebrow at her. "That's a strategy right up there with the old face-your-opponent-into-the-sun, kid."

The girl shrugged broadly, "Hey, Dad, if it works . . ."

"You're a better player than that," he said, standing up and reaching out to ruffle her dark curls. "I'm Ivor Russo." I introduced myself and we shook hands. "This is my daughter, Stefanie."

I told Russo I was looking for his wife.

"You appear to be in good health. I hope you don't have a relative in the hospital," he said.

It was such an odd question that I hesitated before replying. "I need to talk to Mrs. Russo about the Feather Heart Project."

The little girl watched this interchange with mild interest. "She's at Rio Oro Hospital with some woman who's dying," she piped up. Clearly death was not a taboo subject.

"Sorry you missed her. Mrs. Madrone's assistant did call to say you'd be coming over, but Amy got an emergency call to the hospital so she took our van. Stef and I are getting a ride to a blitz tournament pretty soon. I could give you directions. Or if you don't mind waiting a few minutes, I'm sure Duke can swing past the hospital on the way to the tournament and you can follow us. We've got plenty of time if we pack up and get ready to go now."

Stef waved her notebook at him. "I've got it all here." She started to pack up the clock and pieces.

The overhead light snapped on and we all flinched at the sudden brightness. "Chesssssss . . ." a familiar voice rasped in disgusted tones. I turned to see Admiral Rhymer wander past on the other side of the pool table. He fumbled with the sliding glass door but finally managed to get out.

Russo watched his father-in-law walk unsteadily onto the flagstones. I couldn't tell if his expression was amusement, tolerance, or veiled contempt. "My friend Zane loves military strategy," he said. "When he learned my father-in-law was an admiral, he had all these tactical questions he wanted to ask. I had to tell him the old guy hates games."

"I take it the admiral doesn't play chess."

"He told me he played it as a child but ever since he saw real combat, the fake stuff is too pathetic for words." He shrugged. "Frankly, I don't think he was ever that strong a player."

"And he wouldn't want you to beat him," I said.

For the first time Russo looked carefully at me. Behind his thick glasses he had green eyes with laugh lines at the corners. "Nobody likes to lose," he said.

Outside, the admiral proceeded through the knots of people on the patio. Some responded to his loud greetings. When he staggered, some turned away in embarrassment, some laughed. Meade came up and took the admiral's arm to steady him, holding the bottle of Wild Turkey in front of them as if it were a lantern lighting their way. The two men disappeared behind the cottage door.

"Ready to roll, kid?" Ivor said to his daughter.

Stefanie Russo looked up at me with an unsettling calculation in her gaze. "Want to come to the chess tournament? The hospital is boring and we could use more women players."

"Does your mother play?"

"She used to, but now she's too busy."

Ivor cast me a sharp look, perhaps for asking the wrong questions about his wife.

"Well, I'll have to say no, thanks," I told the girl. "You look like you're pretty good and I barely know how the pieces move."

"Better yet." The kid was incorrigible. "I could spot you a queen. Maybe we could make some side bets. Make it interesting."

"All right, you," Ivor said with mock sternness. "No sharking in your uncle's rec room, save it for the tournament."

"Look!" Stefanie called out, tapping on the glass door. "There's the Birchmeister! Let's go!"

A very thin blond man of medium height tapped at the glass from outside. The sun had gone down. The rec room stood out like a cell of light against the twilight of the backyard. Ivor Russo slid the door open and when the man stepped in, he began to laugh.

The blond man had a long narrow face, deeply tanned over still visible acne scars. He looked a bit like an Afghan hound. The resemblance was increased by the leather cap helmet and goggles he wore. The twilight outside had concealed his World War I flying ace costume—a leather bomber jacket, long scarf, and the sort of headgear favored by Amelia Earhart and Charles Lindbergh.

"My God, Zane, where did that get-up come from?"

"Catalogues and the Internet," he announced. "You can get anything on the Internet." A long blond braid poked incongruously out of the leather helmet. "I came with Duke in the van," he announced.

Ivor began to chuckle. "*Duke* let you ride in his vehicle in that outfit?" he asked in disbelief.

"He let me in but he wouldn't talk to me. Well, he did say I was a disgrace to my species, whatever that might be," Zane said with a smile that made him look like a teenager, though he must have been in his twenties. "Duke told me someday he was going to make me pay. After that he wouldn't even respond to questions, so *I* had to do all the talking."

Ivor shook his head and turned to his daughter. "We'd better get him out of here before some of the admiral's guests spot him and shave his head."

Stef giggled.

Zane seemed totally unabashed. "Duke is parked out front."

Ivor introduced me to Zane. "If you want to go with Stef and Zane I'll meet you out front after I say goodbye to Colleen and Dwight."

"I have to go up and get my stuff anyway," I said.

Stef and Zane disappeared out the sliding door chatting. "Do you think he'll ever open with anything other than the Nimzovich?" I heard her ask as they went out.

"Let's ask him," Zane replied.

Stef giggled again and I could hear Zane's laughter even after they were out of sight.

Ivor shook his head as we headed for the stairs. "Zane is a brilliant student and a master chess player.

But this army-navy-surplus fixation he's got is dangerous. When somebody asks what branch of the service
he's impersonating, he says the Royal Canadian Lem-
mings. He really was born in Canada. But people take
their military uniforms seriously in this town."

"I doubt that the lemming joke would be very popular
in Canada either. I take it he's never served in the military?"

Ivor laughed. "Your average drill sergeant would eat
him for breakfast."

Upstairs Colleen seemed more relaxed. The crowd
had thinned out. She shook my hand warmly. "I'm sorry
you can't stay longer. Anyone who sprays soda in the
admiral's face is my kind of woman. Not that I'll let
anyone quote me on that." She involuntarily glanced
around for eavesdroppers.

Dwight stood next to the dining room table turning
the leaves in a small, leather-bound book. I looked
again. It was the New Testament. An odd choice for a
naval officer. Or perhaps not—with a father like his, he
needed all the help he could get.

Zane and Stef were talking outside a van that had
pulled up to the curb in front of the house. It had a
handicapped parking sticker in the window. Ivor opened
the passenger door and introduced the driver, Duke,
who leaned across the passenger seat to give me a brisk
handshake. Even in the dusk it was clear that his shoulders and arms were heavily muscled.

Just behind and above his seat, a folding wheelchair
was mounted on a rack. When Ivor explained that I
needed to follow them to the Rio Oro Hospital, Duke
simply said "Sure" in a low, gruff voice.

Ivor got in the front seat, while Stef and Zane clam-
bered into the back. I nearly jumped when a figure in

the shadows moved. Someone was already in the van, crouching just behind Duke's seat as if trying to hide there. *"Buenos noches, Juan"* Stefanie greeted him.

His *"Buenos noches, señorita"* was a little muffled, almost as if his Spanish was worse than hers. Zane had fallen silent; despite his earlier bravado, he seemed intimidated by the brisk, guarded Duke. Aside from Stef's greeting, everyone else ignored Duke's shadowy companion.

3

I followed Duke's van a few miles north to the entrance to the Rio Oro Hospital. Duke flashed the van's lights and drove on. I parked and went through the darkness to the twenty-four-hour nightmare zone of the hospital. Signs directed me to the intensive care unit on the second floor.

My knees felt rubbery going up in the elevator. Hospitals meant death to me and the loss of my mother's unconditional love. I had been thirteen on my first and last visit to a hospital not long before she died. Her death had plunged me into two years of hell. My father escaped into his government service work and traveled even more than ever. I was stranded on Vashon Island in Puget Sound with an aunt and uncle who regarded me as an embarrassing plus-sized problem they had inherited. My memory is that it rained for two years straight. Then when I was fifteen, I met Nina, a fat woman who was undeniably beautiful and who made it a point to let me know I was great just as I was. I believed her, because her existence proved it was possible.

Now Nina was dead too. I felt like turning and walking out of the Rio Oro Hospital. But walking away wouldn't bring back my mother—or Nina.

It was a slow Sunday night in intensive care. Behind the heavy swinging doors, a few staff members at the hub of the unit were watching *Casablanca*—silvery images on a portable TV with the volume turned way down. I asked for Amy Russo, and a black woman in dreadlocks, lab coat, and surgical scrubs pointed me toward one of the open bays of the unit that radiated like spokes off the hub of machines and desks at the center.

A large, dark-haired woman sat at the bedside of a white-haired elderly woman who lay in a nest of tubes, wires, machines, and monitors. The young woman sitting in the chair seemed almost rudely healthy with pink cheeks and abundant flesh. We could possibly wear the same dress size so I had a pretty good idea how much free advice Amy Russo must get—I shuddered to think of the kind of abusive remarks the admiral alone must throw at her.

I introduced myself softly. "I need to talk to you for just a few moments, Mrs. Russo."

"Okay." She glanced up and appeared to finally grasp that I was really there. "Please, call me Amy." She took a deep breath, as if to disengage from her communion with the comatose figure on the bed. "We'll go in the lounge. Just give me a minute."

As she turned back to the patient, an angular nurse in polyester uniform and prune-lipped expression approached me clutching her clipboard as if it were a weapon she was just itching to use. She pushed her pelvis up to the bed rail and made no effort to lower her voice. "If you're not a family member, I'm afraid you can't be here. Besides, there's no room."

"We were just going." I gestured to the woman in the lab coat and dreadlocks. "That lady there directed me to Mrs. Russo."

"Well, no matter what *Doctor* Johnson says"— clearly, Dr. Johnson was not entitled to full doctorhood in her book—"I can't have you bothering Mrs. Hogan."

"Only you and family members get to do that," I said recklessly. Who could have predicted that hospitals would bring out my aggressive side?

She ignored me as if she had already effectively thrown me out. She turned to Amy. "You have been warned before."

"We're just going to the lounge," Amy said.

The woman marched away to give Dr. Johnson a piece of her mind, pointedly twitching her tightly trousered ass in displeasure. Amy said softly, "She has a very small aura."

I had to smother a wild burst of laughter. "Almost as small as her brain." Amy managed a little wider smile and my barely stifled laughter earned us another nasty look over the shoulder of the clipboard lady. I cast a guilty glance at Mrs. Hogan in the bed, but she was beyond noticing.

Amy stood up and nearly sat back down again. She seemed exhausted. She patted Mrs. Hogan's hand and murmured a few words to her before we went out.

I hadn't realized how much the swoosh of the respirator bothered me until the heavy swinging doors closed behind us. I followed Amy into a deserted waiting room nearby. A wall-mounted TV set muttered to itself almost inaudibly—in color. Not *Casablanca*. Flickering from the screen and a puddle of light around a reading lamp next to a reclining armchair gave us enough illumination to talk.

"Doesn't being here, around dying people, depress you?" It was getting under my skin already.

"Sometimes." She looked at me as if from a distance. I wondered if she really had been somehow brainwashed. Despite the family resemblance, Amy's pale blue eyes were soothing, like looking into the heart of a sapphire. She also had her father's easily sunburned skin.

"You must get outdoors sometime," I said, "because you've got a sunburn there."

"Oh, my husband and I take our daughter to the beach and on hikes, sometimes. to the desert or the mountains. Of course, every time we stop, they take out a portable chess set, so I always bring a book." She smiled.

"That's right, your daughter seems like a very gifted player."

She nodded. "We're very proud of her. But what was it you wanted?"

I launched into my cover story about a foundation that was considering a grant to the Feather Heart Project.

"Oh." She looked back toward the intensive care unit a little wistfully. "You want to talk to Lance Feather, not me. I just sit with people. Excuse me, but I have to go back—"

"Doesn't that take you away from your family?" The minute I asked it I regretted it, but she turned back to me for an instant.

"My family—"

"Amy." A voice from the hallway interrupted us. "We just came from the airport."

We both looked up as a man and two women came into the lounge. Amy stood up and greeted all three of them with a hug.

She introduced me to Mrs. Hogan's son and daughter and daughter-in-law.

"Amy, I'm sorry, I didn't mean to get off on the wrong foot. Could we talk later?"

"Call the Project tomorrow," Amy said.

I left her holding the daughter's hand and listening as she talked. I glanced back before rounding the corner to the bank of elevators and I saw them begin the long walk back to intensive care. Once the hospital doors closed behind me, I breathed a deep sigh of relief. I couldn't imagine what would motivate someone to go in there on purpose, and I was going to have to rethink my approach to Amy Russo because we hadn't exactly hit it off.

I found my way back to Coronado Island and Mrs. Madrone's establishment after a couple of miles looking for the right freeway. A message from Ambrose informed me that Mrs. Madrone expected a report at nine o'clock the next morning.

Raoul's carrier was empty. When I went into the bedroom he yawned at me with shaggy disinterest from the middle of the bed. I stepped out of the sandals and stripped off the cola-spotted skirt, which was going to go to the cleaners. I decided to take a shower in the morning and used a washcloth to swab off my legs, although it seemed as if most of the cola had gone onto the admiral. Raoul watched with mild interest as I put on a purple silk robe, which made me feel comfortable in San Diego at last. I wondered if the drugs were making Raoul drowsier than usual.

When I first met him as a half-grown kitten at Nina's apartment, she had told me, "He can say his own name." Indeed, when I opened the suite's half-sized refrigerator, the now-hulking tomcat strolled in, stretching, to join me standing in front of the open door. "*Row-wul*," he said with a certain degree of urgency as I poured some milk into a glass to heat for cocoa and into a dish for him. He had his without cocoa.

It wasn't that late. I put my cup on the coffee table

in front of the sofa in the suite's front room, took a deep breath, and called Mulligan. He had been Nina's lover, they had planned to marry. When I first met him, she was already dead. I didn't know how much of our intense mutual attraction was genuine, and how much was grief. It scared me as much as it drew me. But I felt a rush of excitement when he answered the phone.

"Hi, I'm in San Diego."

"I guess that means I can't invite you over for dinner this weekend. You've been putting me off for a few weeks now, Jo. Is that a hint? Do you think we should put each other on hold for a while?"

"No." It came out so quickly that I sat back in startled shock. I had felt a surge of panic as if he had proposed pumping all the air out of the room. I stood up and walked back and forth the length of the phone cord to dissipate some of the tension that just wouldn't go away.

"So where are you staying? Give me your number."

I sat down on the sofa and read the number to him from the phone. Raoul hopped up on my lap and put his front feet on my shoulder.

"How's the cat?"

"You must be psychic, or can you hear him? He's lying on my chest purring." I held the phone up to Raoul's throat and he obligingly purred into the receiver.

"Lucky stiff. Well, I'll leave him to it. Good night."

I headed for bed and Raoul soon joined me. A few words from Mulligan and I couldn't seem to lie still. After I turned over one time too many I heard the cat thump down onto the carpeted floor and trot into the next room for a quieter sleeping surface.

"Tell me about it," I muttered, "Can't sleep with 'em,

can't sleep without 'em." I turned back in the other direction as if that would help.

Not long after 7:00 A.M. I awoke to Raoul's steady, suggestive purr next to my ear. He placidly settled down to a bowl of dry cat food while I made myself a cup of coffee. Leaving him grooming himself in a patch of sunshine near the terrace door, I went out for a walk. The sunshine was diffused with a haze off the water. The woman in the minimart where I bought groceries told me that was called the June gloom and it would probably burn off by noon. I said that sounded pretty good to me, having just arrived from the Pacific Northwest where the sun usually gave up the field to fog and rain clouds.

When I got back at a little after eight and the phone was ringing, I knew it would be Ambrose.

"So, is Amy Russo crazy?"

"I don't know yet. I finally found her last night, sitting with a dying lady in the hospital. We didn't get to talk for more than a minute before we were interrupted. She told me to call her today over at the Feather Heart Project office."

"Those people. I'm still looking into them. I haven't come up with any solid evidence but there are some hair-raising rumors. Of course, that could just be jealous competitors."

That idea gave me pause. "You mean there's competition for your death-counseling dollar?"

"I'll give you details later, Jo. Mrs. Madrone's friend is here early."

"I've got to check one thing and I'll be right up." I called the Feather Heart Project and talked to a woman with a gentle, cooing voice. She told me that Amy had been at the hospital most of the night. The old woman died at dawn. Amy had left word she would be at the office around noon.

After dashing on a little makeup, I regretfully put on an employer-acceptable linen pantsuit the color of oatmeal. It was already warm enough for shorts and a tank top and getting warmer. I decided to come back and change before going out to meet Amy.

I went up to the penthouse. Mrs. Madrone was not far from the door waiting for my report. "Well?"

I started to explain but she held up a hand. "You'd better tell Sally. Ambrose?" She gestured to the terrace door, shut against the gentle morning breeze off the ocean.

Ambrose strode over and slid the door open.

Mrs. Madrone wheeled over, but paused at the edge. The runners of the sliding glass door were sunken so that she could wheel onto the terrace, but she was so easily chilled, I doubted she often went out there.

She gestured me to go on. "Sally?" she called. A woman in white turned from where she had been leaning against the railing. "This is Josephine Fuller. She's done good work for me in the past."

Sally Rhymer turned away from the railing at the far end of the balcony. She had been studying the yachts moored in the marina below. I would never have placed her as Amy's mother by her looks. Like Mrs. Madrone she was in her early sixties with platinum blond hair framing a round face. She was only a shade shorter than my five foot eight inches and her two-inch heels made up the difference. The brisk way she walked and the nervous energy she radiated gave me the idea that she spent a good portion of her waking hours in some kind of intense sporting activity. She wore a white summery dress, modest white pumps, and a broad-brimmed straw hat. She looked like a politician's wife. Well, she had been.

She looked so crisp that I went to surreptitiously wipe off the sweat before we shook hands but it was too late. She gestured to an umbrella-shaded table where a pitcher of lemonade had been set out. She pointedly picked up a linen napkin to dry my sweat off her hands. Then she sat in one of the chairs, poured me a glass of lemonade, and picked up her own glass.

It was very early for lemonade, but she had done enough laps around the terrace by now that she probably needed to rehydrate. She lowered her sunglasses with a modestly polished pink fingernail and gave me *the look*, assessing my competitive threat on the current meat market as calibrated to the micron according to the latest Woman's Jungle Predator Standards. Her expression told me my stock wasn't trading too high with her today.

"You spoke with my daughter yesterday?" She had a lovely southern accent that softened her words.

I sat down across from her. "Yes, ma'am. I met her last night, but she was too busy to talk. We agreed to meet again at noon today." Before she could attack my lack of information, I decided to start to gather more. "There is one thing I wonder, though."

"What do you wonder?" She was not quite offended by my audacity.

"Just this, ma'am." I felt like Joe Friday on *Dragnet*. "Why don't you talk to her yourself?"

Mrs. Rhymer managed a wounded bird sort of flutter with her hands. I began to suspect even Joe Friday might have had a problem getting the facts out of her.

"My daughter has refused to talk to me for over a year," she said reluctantly.

"Why is that?"

"She resents my advice. Even as a young child she took in injured animals and stray puppies. But . . ." She raised her lemonade glass and swallowed. "Lord knows Amy was never a beauty." She put down the glass and leaned forward. "She favored my ex-husband. All my children did. The man is built like a cracker barrel." Her eyes flickered over me, checking for blood. I was intact, but I'd be willing to bet her husband and kids had a few scars.

"I fail to see what Amy's dress size has to do with her working with the dying."

"I don't know! But I worry about her. She was never popular as a child." She paused, hoping that would explain everything. I raised my eyebrows and waited. Mrs. Rhymer continued a little uncertainly, "I thought no one would ever marry her."

"But someone did, and Ivor Russo seems like a great guy."

"Well, yeeees." She made it into several syllables. I really loved the accent. It could turn a yes into a maybe or a flat-out no before you quite knew what was happening.

"Amy's husband, Ivor, is a little strange but he's been marvelously patient with her about her weight. I wonder if there's something wrong. I mean with their relationship. I'm so worried that this Lance person is preying on my daughter. Maybe he's driven a wedge between Amy and her husband."

It would have been a waste of time to point out how even the athletic and elegant Mrs. Rhymer could lose a husband. She was well aware of that.

I took a deep breath and asked gently, "Does Amy seem to be on worse terms with her husband and daughter?"

"I believe I told you earlier that she refuses to speak to me. I hope you can find out what's really happening. I miss my granddaughter."

I wanted to suggest that she try an abject apology for meddling in her grown child's affairs, but Mrs. Madrone was paying me to do the meddling, not to express my opinion. "I'm on my way now to talk to her at more length. I'll let you know what I find out." I said. Sensing the interview was almost over, I polished off the lemonade.

"Thank you so much." Sally Rhymer's face assumed a guarded look. "Please don't tell Amy that I asked you to talk to her." She almost seemed afraid for a moment.

"Of course not." I folded up one of the napkins and blotted the condensation from the lemonade glass off my hands. But she had already dismissed me and gone back to contemplating the harbor.

Mrs. Madrone watched me through the door anxiously. It was the closest I had ever seen her to uncertainty.

"I'm on my way over to the Feather Heart Project," I told them both. "I'll call as soon as I know more."

Mrs. Madrone waved a slender hand in dismissal and actually rolled her chair out onto the terrace to talk to her friend, who had already sprung to her feet and was pacing along the railing.

Ambrose escorted me out. At the door he handed me a couple of folders. "When you've got some extra time after talking to the Rhymer people, here's another little job. No rush, but before the end of the week we need you to check up on a grant approved by your predecessor."

"You mean—I wasn't the first?"

"What, in the job? No. Why?"

"No reason. I just never thought of it before. Um, so, did she—I'm just assuming it was a she—get fired or quit?"

"Really, I can't say. Does the fact that someone did the job before you somehow spoil it?"

"No, of course not." But the fact that I might be easily replaced gave me a little shudder.

4

The Feather Heart Project was located in a small shopping mall near the airport. As I skirted downtown on I-5 an airliner flying over the freeway appeared to come stunningly close to scraping the roof of my car. So that was the famous Lindbergh maneuver. I had heard that pilots needed a special license to fly between the downtown buildings to land at the San Diego Airport. But staring up and counting the rivets as the plane thundered over drove home the skill involved.

The mall was an older one built decades ago. It boasted a liquor store as its drawing card in the center of the arch. A local chain dispensed chicken and tacos on one end of the horseshoe and a video rental store did a brisk business on the other. Along the half circle, vacant stores embarrassed their neighbors like gaps in a sad smile.

The Feather Heart Project seemed deserted as well, with whitewashed windows. But as I pulled into a parking spot nearby, a man came out and locked the door behind him. He was tall and thin, dressed in a polo shirt and white cotton pants. He was very fair skinned, scarcely tan at all by Southern California standards. His high forehead was gradually eroding his frizzy pale blond curls, yet he wore no hat. With his crest of hair and long limbs he gave the impression of a heron or maybe an egret. Could this be Lance Feather? Before I could speculate further, the man climbed into a green Saab and drove off.

I had a rash impulse to follow him. But I expected Amy Russo to arrive at any moment. I moved my car into the parking place the Saab had vacated, directly in front of the Feather Heart sign. I wondered what the other mall tenants thought of the place. No other words followed the logo—a line drawing of a feather on one side of a primitive scale and a heart on the other— tacked up over what had been a beauty salon sign. They might have been selling feather boas, valentines, or black market donor organs.

I rang the buzzer next to the whitewashed glass door just for something to do. Nothing. I waited. The phone inside rang and the answering machine interrupted on the fourth ring. I leaned on the wall of the store. I hadn't dug into my stored clothing for shorts when I quickly packed to come on this trip. The cotton blouse and pants I had decided to wear had seemed lightweight when I packed them in Seattle, but not here. I vowed to find some clothes more appropriate to the climate as soon as I could get a few hours to shop. I turned my mind to what I wanted to ask Amy.

Maybe if I could keep her talking, the real situation would become clear. The Feather Heart operation looked odd, to say the least.

Amy pulled up in a Dodge van. She saw me waiting and was in full apology as she opened the door and got out of the van, long before I could even make out a word.

"Sorry, I overslept. Stef has some summer school classes. My husband took her in and they let me sleep. Did you wait long?"

"Only a few minutes. I just missed one of your co-workers." I described the man.

"That's Lance."

Her mother was afraid of what strange hold Lance had on Amy. I examined her for signs of infatuation. She didn't blush or smile fondly or linger over saying his name. She wore white cotton overalls with no blouse under them and a red cotton blazer that might have come from a waiter's uniform store—I would have to ask her, it looked great. Her hair was wet and her cheeks flushed and she looked like a teenager rather than the mother of a nine-year-old. Putting aside the idea of an affair with Lance, I wondered if she had just come from a warm bed with her husband in it. Those college professors worked irregular hours.

"Well, I did finally make it," she said, as if reading my mind, "Ivor only came back and woke me up because he doesn't have a class to teach today." She smiled and I smiled back. Her blue eyes were as amazing as ever. She wasn't exhausted as she had been the previous night. If her mood was from less sleep and more sex, I was willing to try that prescription.

Amy unlocked the office door. The Feather Heart Project occupied a long narrow space. The linoleum floor and mirrored wall remained from its beauty parlor days. Several large plants in baskets lined the wall and our reflections moved through a small reflected forest lit by the daylight through the whitewashed windows and a faint flickering of color at the far end of the room.

"That's funny. Lance usually turns his computer off when he goes for the day. He left it on with the screen-saver program running. That's not like him. I've never seen him in a hurry."

Amy turned on the light. Three desks were set up

like boxcars. Not much money had been spent on decoration. The first two desks were thrift-store metal. A blond-wood shoji screen blocked off most of the desk at the far end of the room from view. I went back to look while Amy fiddled with the answering machine sitting on the front desk. Its red blinking light signaled a message.

The computer behind the bamboo screen was sitting on a tall Japanese *tansu* chest, all brass binding and small drawers. Instead of conventional office furniture, a Swedish modern leather recliner sat in front of the computer and a leather folding chair sat within conversational range. I heard the faint sound of the recorded message being played and then silence.

"That is the most impractical office setup I have ever—" I turned to see Amy almost literally slumping over the answering machine, her face pale with shock. She fumbled for the chair behind the desk where she stood. If I hadn't leaped to her aid and guided her into the chair, she might have missed it and sprawled right down on the floor.

"What is it? Do you feel ill?"

"No." She looked at me wildly. "It's my father. I need to go to my brother's house. My father called here. He never does that. Something is wrong."

"What did he say?"

She gestured at the answering machine, as if afraid to touch it. I rewound the tape and played it. The actual words were so faint that I had to lean close to hear them under the heavy background sound of traffic. But it was unmistakably Admiral Rhymer's gravelly voice. "Amy. I'm alive. You will receive further instructions, I'm being . . . held—" and the receiver was audibly hung up.

The silence that followed gave me a sinking feeling.

I tried punching in *69 to see if the telephone would redial the last incoming number but a recorded message told me that was impossible.

"Can you call your father's number?"

"I can't remember it—I have to look it up." She fumbled a little notebook out of her purse, looked up a number, and dialed. "No answer."

She hung up. "I'll try Dwight." Before she finished dialing she stopped. "No, they'd be at work. Would you come over there with me? Something is wrong."

"Of course, but do you have a replacement tape to put in the answering machine?"

"No—I don't know, why?"

"We need to preserve the recording. There might be information on there that could tell an expert where he is." I didn't say anything about the police being the people to do this. At the moment it seemed as if that would upset her more.

She gulped convulsively. "I don't . . . know . . . where there's another."

"We'll just have to leave it empty. Let's go to your brother's. I'll drive. You can give me directions." I wasn't about to let her get behind the wheel. She had gone from pale to a sort of sickly flushed color. She didn't say much else but directed me on the quickest way to Point Loma. We passed a nondescript apartment complex on the way and she said dully, "My brother Brad lives there."

I slowed down a little. "Should we stop and get him?"

"Brad? Right. Like he'd be of some use. No. It's Monday, everyone should be at work. Not that anyone knows what Brad does."

"You don't know what your brother does for a living?" I asked.

"Not really. I'm kind of afraid to ask in case it's—maybe I don't want to know." When we arrived at Dwight and Colleen's house Amy took a deep breath, "The Lincoln is there." The Town Car was in the driveway beside the house just as it had been the night before. I parked on the nearly empty street in front of the house.

We walked back toward the rear cottage. There were no small sounds of human habitation. The cottage door was slightly ajar behind its screen door, which was not latched.

It wasn't terribly hot yet, but the haze had burned off as promised and it was warming up. "Is the cottage air-conditioned?" I asked Amy, wondering if someone might have left the door ajar to catch a breeze.

"It is." Her voice betrayed her puzzlement. "But usually he just puts a couple of fans on." She looked at me and the hairs on the back of my neck stood up.

I couldn't think of anything to say.

Amy pulled the screen door open and pushed the front door inward. I followed her in.

"Dad!" she called.

No answer. There was an acrid smell in the air. I couldn't identify it. But it was strong enough to make my eyes water. We went into the living room, with old-fashioned wicker furniture and bamboo blinds. The floor was cool tile. That burning, choking smell was even stronger. We headed toward the kitchen. Something was sticking out of the half-open bathroom door. It was a man's foot. Looking around the door, I saw him sprawled face down on the floor in his Hawaiian shirt. One outstretched hand seemed to be reaching for a small plastic funnel-like apparatus on the floor next to him. My mind registered that it was an asthma inhaler at the same time that I realized the man was totally still, his stretching hand too stiff for sleep. Amy gasped and pushed past me to look.

5

Amy slipped back around the corner to lean against the wall.

"It's not Dad," she said, putting her hand to her mouth. "It's Stewart Meade."

I looked again. I had thought at first it was the admiral. The man's head was not visible from the doorway. But once I leaned farther into the bathroom I saw the red hair. Up close it was liberally streaked with gray. It was Meade wearing a green aloha shirt. Now that I thought about it, Admiral Rhymer had worn a blue shirt. I reached a hand down to touch his hand. It was cold. The fingers stiff.

I straightened up and dug in my pocket for a tissue to wipe my face; it was hot and the strangely stinging air brought tears to my eyes. I breathed through my mouth while I made a quick circuit of the cottage looking for signs of another victim. There were no obvious signs of struggle or a search effort except in the farthest corner of the bedroom where a Mosler GSA Class 5 Security filing cabinet stood—all four drawers open and empty. I recognized it as identical to the one in my father's home office, part of his ties to the civilian portion of the intelligence community. The navy probably did things a little differently but the admiral's security clearances must be functional.

On the floor in front of the cabinet was a single sheet of paper with Top Secret printed on it in red letters two inches high. I didn't touch anything, but I noticed there was a paper clip on the sheet of paper. Nothing was clipped to it.

I turned away from the safe and surveyed the room. It was remarkably clean and tidy despite the liquor bottle and glasses on a table between two big easy chairs. There was no evidence of smoking, no visible ashtrays, not even a bag of potato chips. Like the main house, the cottage was decorated with color photographs of ships and airplanes. A plastic model of an airplane, with what looked like a radar dish on its nose, sat in a glass case. A brass tag identified it as a Wild Weasel.

The admiral's bedroom was even tidier than the front room, with everything hung up and properly put away. I didn't want to see any more.

Amy stood in the front room where I had left her, staring at Meade's prone form. "Come on, let's make some phone calls." I took her elbow and we made our way out of the cottage. I led her over to a couple of wooden slat chairs on the flagstone patio. We sat down. It was a great temptation to sit in the pleasant sunshine and not think about what we had just seen. I took a deep breath and dug the cell phone out of my handbag. After the initial talk to the police switchboard, I handed Amy the receiver to give them the address and particulars.

Amy handed me the phone back when she had given the directions. She was entitled to be shocked. She knew the dead man we had just seen, and her father was missing. I was a total stranger and I was feeling dazed myself. Then we sat waiting for the police.

"Exactly who is the man back there?" I gestured to the cottage. "I saw him drinking with your father last night."

"Stewart Meade." Amy glanced over her shoulder as if expecting someone to emerge from the cottage door. "When Dad retired a couple of years ago, Meade went into business with him."

"I wonder what killed him," I said, thinking out loud. "There were no signs of violence and he had that asthma inhaler in the bathroom with him."

"He must have had a heart attack. I don't know much about him except he's my father's old friend from the navy, but I have seen him use that inhaler before. Asthma doesn't kill you though, does it?"

"Even if a heart attack killed Meade, that still doesn't explain why your father is missing or why the records safe is open." I looked at her with a sudden thought. "Last night at the party your father said something about a Thai connection."

She shook her head. "I never listen. I was glad to leave early last night. Dad is always gruff, but once he gets drunk he picks on me. I wonder where he is now."

"Good question." The whole situation made me jumpy. Although, for all we knew, the admiral had argued his friend into a heart attack and then wandered off with some drunken idea of scaring his family with a fake kidnapping. I was willing to think the worst of him based on first impressions.

"Oh my God!" Amy suddenly jumped and I flinched as well. "I need to call. Could I use your phone?"

I took a deep breath. Her sudden yell had set my heart pounding. I handed her the cell phone again and Amy called her husband, explained the situation and arranged for him to get their van and pick up Stef at school. Then she called Lance Feather, and reached the woman who answered his phones. I could hear the cooing, soothing voice expressing concern even a few feet away.

When she hung up I asked, "How did you get into the job of hanging out at hospitals?"

Amy sighed. "I had a miscarriage nearly two years ago. I couldn't seem to get over losing the baby. I thought I would go crazy. My husband was kind, but I think he was a little relieved that we didn't have all that extra expense. My family just pretended it didn't happen. Finally, I went to Lance's workshop on grief and it helped."

"So he does the stuff like Elisabeth Kübler-Ross and Stephen Levine. I've seen all those books on dying and grieving and so on."

"I don't know about any books. I couldn't stand to read about it. But Lance understood when I told him about the people in the supermarket."

"The, uh, people in the supermarket?" That did sound irrational but I tried not to blink at it.

"It was like someone had ripped a hole in the world and I could see suffering I never imagined before. They could see me too. Strangers started coming up to me standing in the produce aisle and telling me they had a parent that was dying or their husband was sick. Like there was a mark on me that drew them to me. Lance said if I got involved in helping other people, I'd feel better. He was right. Ondine really understands because of how she is herself."

"Was that Ondine on the phone just now with the soothing voice?"

"Yes."

"What do you mean, 'because of how Ondine is'?"

Amy sighed. "Well, I guess you could say she's psychic. She *sees* things . . . you know?"

I felt an odd lurch of fear to be having this conversation outside of a cottage with a dead body in it. "What about you? Do you ever, um, see things?"

Amy looked at me in alarm. "No. Never. I don't think I could handle it. But Ondine can take it. I think she almost likes it."

"I'll bet she does." I tried to keep the cynicism out of my voice. I hadn't yet met Ondine, but I was starting to get a glimmer of her aura already.

I raised my head at an odd sound. Amy looked past me toward the house and flinched violently. I turned too and saw the young man with the pigtail and the young woman he had dragged out of the way of the admiral's prying Minicam. They were standing just outside the sliding glass door to the rec room.

"You said he'd been on the scene of abductions," she said accusingly.

"I honestly believe he has," the young man said, "but you know that stuff is classified."

Today they were both clad in shorts and T-shirts. They appeared to be in midargument, clearly not having seen Amy and me.

"But—you saw him. I only just asked about the Bermuda Triangle. He said he'd get right to it and he put his hand up my ski-i-irt," she wailed.

"Amber—you've got to get past this, otherwise how can we—"

"Brad!" Amy got up and walked toward her brother.

Brad saw us at last. Both he and Amber froze like cornered prey. "Oh, uh, hi, Amy. Amber left her purse here. We had to leave the party so fast yesterday. Dad got on her case—"

"You didn't check in the cottage, Brad." Amy said.

It wasn't a question. She half rose, as if to block the way.

"No, we didn't even get into the house. I thought Colleen might be home. She sometimes takes Mondays off." He suddenly seemed to notice that Amy was upset. "What's wrong?

"I got a call from Dad—he's been kidnapped. We just found Steward Meade dead in the cottage there. We called the police. They're on their way."

"We've got to go," Brad said instantly. He hugged his sister and planted a kiss on top of her head. "Come on, Amber." This time he had no need to drag Amber. She followed him with alacrity.

"Did you notice that Amber was carrying a purse?" I asked Amy.

"It could be a different purse."

I was pretty sure it was the same purse I had seen Colleen holding the day before, and the sound I had heard just before turning to see Brad and Amber could well have been the sliding patio door closing.

"Look," Amy said.

We got up and went to meet the two uniformed policemen who were getting out of a squad car and walking up the drive.

6

Dwight arrived not long after the police. We went into the house while the yard and cottage filled with police and homicide technicians. Dwight took the first two policemen on a room-to-room tour of the house. I explained, first to a couple of uniformed policemen and then to a plainclothes detective, what I had seen. They solemnly took the tape of the admiral's phone message. I didn't see Amy and assumed she was telling her story at the same time in a different part of the house.

Colleen arrived as the police and Dwight were standing in the front room, agreeing that the main house showed no signs of disturbance or entry. I wondered if I had really heard the sliding patio door just before Brad and Amber appeared. I hadn't actually seen them come out of the door. I didn't think I had misheard but I decided not to say anything for the moment.

I went into the kitchen and found Amy sitting, staring at her hands. I asked her where the coffee was and she shrugged. I found some Kona Roast in the freezer and a fresh filter in the coffee machine, which was soon hissing and sputtering. The phone rang. Both of us looked at it. No one else was going to answer it.

I picked up the phone. "Rhymer residence."

"Who the hell are you?" It was a woman's voice, in full fury. "You're not Colleen? Are you one of Ron Rhymer's hookers? Put Stewart on the phone immediately. Pour water on him, whatever you have to do to wake him up."

I refrained from saying that there wasn't enough water in the known universe to do that. "Just a sec." I covered the receiver. "Amy, this is some lady who appears to be very angry at Stewart Meade."

"That would be his wife," Amy said, wearily getting up to take the phone. "This is Amy Russo. Hello, Martha." She nodded unconsciously as the woman on the other end of the line protested vigorously. She held the receiver away from her ear and the little complaining voice was audible across the room. Dwight came in with a homicide detective in tow and snagged the phone out of her hand without so much as a word exchanged. It was the most brother-and-sister-like thing I'd seen around this family since I arrived, though I sometimes have trouble telling those things, having been an only child.

"Dwight Rhymer here, may I help you?" He listened for a second. The detective who had accompanied him into the kitchen waited patiently. "Martha!" Dwight said, clearly interrupting. Obviously Martha had mastered the art of continuous speaking without noticeable pauses for breath. "Martha! Goddamn it. Your husband is dead!"

Everyone, including the policemen, stopped and stared.

"Dwight!" Amy said, "You're supposed to sort of lead up to it."

He covered the receiver. "*You* wanna have another try at leading up to something with Martha?" Amy shook her head. Dwight listened a little longer, then said, "No, Martha, I am not kidding. I would not kid about a thing like that." He raised his eyebrows and rolled his eyes in a gesture he must have picked up from his wife. "Martha! There's been a terrible accident, and Stewart . . . Damn it! Martha! Here, let me put the police on the line."

He gave up the phone to a plainclothes detective, who shook his head pityingly and began to scribble notes on a small pad while talking. Eventually he dispatched another policeman to go talk to Martha.

Colleen had taken over dispensing coffee and I was beginning to wonder if I could leave soon. The detective in charge got the details of where I was staying, Mrs. Madrone's name made the expected impact. I headed for the front door when I saw Ivor drive up in the Russos' vehicle with Stefanie, who looked distressed and even younger than her nine years. Following Ivor closely was a van with a handicapped parking sticker. I recognized the van and Duke driving it from the night before. When Ivor got out onto the sidewalk, he went up to the van's window and exchanged a few words before Duke drove off. Then Amy saw her husband and daughter and ran down the front steps to embrace them as fervently as if she had feared they had been kidnapped too. I realized it was the first time I had seen mother and daughter together. They came into the house. Amy retired to the living room and I glimpsed her sitting on the sofa stroking Stef's hair and talking to her quietly.

Ivor stopped in the foyer and looked around awkwardly. I realized he was holding a folded up cardboard windshield screen, the kind people put on the dashboard to keep their car seats from heating up in direct sun. I went over and said hello.

"Thanks for bringing Amy here," Ivor said. "She's upset enough that she probably shouldn't be driving.

Fortunately, Duke was able to drive me over to get our vehicle. This was on the outside of the windshield, under the wipers. I folded it up to keep the kid from seeing it. I guess I should give it to the police, what do you think?"

I looked and did a double take, staring at the stenciled letters on the accordion-folded cardboard. One of the policemen saw them as well and came over the minute Ivor unfolded the screen. The cardboard was printed with a cartoon sun but what looked like spray-painted stenciled letters read:

$1 MILL FOR ADMIRAL & FILES & TAPE
DO NOT CALL POLICE. RAISE $ WAIT.

The policeman reading over my shoulder whistled in amazement. "Hey, Gordy, lookit this."

Too late not to tell the police. Ivor surrendered the sign without protest and went into the living room to explain to the detective in charge.

I was about to check with the police and leave, when a yellow Mazda Miata sports car pulled up to the curb and a young woman got out. She wore a bolero jacket over a tight blouse and a cotton miniskirt the same yellow as the convertible. Her skirt was short enough to cause a riot when she got out and began to haul luggage out of the Miata with a stunning disregard for the crowd of police cars, crime scene barriers, and indeed the coroner's van, which had just driven up.

"Girlfriend of the admiral?" I asked Ivor Russo, who had come back out minus the cardboard sign, to stand behind me in the open doorway.

"Yup," he said. "Her name is Leilani. They weren't

married." I noticed the past tense, but I wasn't sure Ivor
had used it on purpose.

"That's why I asked them not to sleep together under
our roof," Dwight said, coming up to join us in the
doorway. Neither seemed eager to go down to help with
the luggage. He and Ivor exchanged glances.

It was usually the parents who were telling the kids
not to cohabit rather than the reverse. Suddenly, it occurred to me to wonder why a retired admiral was reduced to living in the cottage behind his son's house.
The night before I hadn't paid much attention, assuming
that the admiral slept wherever he passed out because
he was too drunk to go home. Now Dwight was saying
that his father lived in the cottage. Yet Colleen had earlier mentioned firearms as a first line of defense against
unwanted houseguests of the father-in-law variety.

Colleen had half turned to go back toward the
kitchen, but she stopped to watch Leilani's struggle with
the luggage and the volunteers who materialized to help
her.

With a jangle of bracelets and a clatter of high heels
she arrived at the door, her luggage carried by one of
the policemen and a neighbor who had dropped the hose
he had been applying to the sidewalk in front of the
house and rushed over to help. Looking around at the
faces that turned to her she giggled a little. A couple of
uniformed policemen wandered around from the backyard. A few more seemed to arrive every few seconds.
Either she was broadcasting pheromones at a distance
usually only projected by cats in heat, or the male grape-
vine was alive and well.

Her skin was the color of long-steeped Darjeeling
with a touch of milk. She had the classically admired
features: small nose, large doe eyes and sensuously full

lips that curved into an appreciative smile as she basked in the warmth of a crowd of admirers. Her body, too curved for the modern starvation standards of beauty contest or show business, was excessive in exactly the areas to merit maximum male attention. Her perfume was subtle—even I leaned forward to catch a whiff of it. She stood a moment to let everyone appreciate her. She was very good at this.

"Don't stare," she announced, posing just a bit. "I'm Puerto Rican and Chinese and Hawaiian with maybe a little dash of the white-bread missionary position. My auntie says not to talk about it, but everybody asks." I could almost hear a sigh from her audience.

"Is Ronny here?" she asked petulantly, glancing around as if someone might have him concealed.

Dwight shook his head impatiently, and muttered "No."

"Oh, good—I can cheat!" she said with a wicked smile that sent a shudder of anticipation through the room. She whipped out a pack of Virginia Slims. "I promised him I'd quit, see? But I just gotta cheat a little sometimes. Don't tell, now. Promise?"

Everyone watched in fascination as she fitted a cigarette into a pearl-and-gold-plated holder. She must have been in her early twenties. Probably still got carded every time she bought those cigarettes, just so the clerk could hold her there a little longer.

Dwight Rhymer stood aloof from the hypnotic trance that had engulfed the room. He had not brought out the New Testament again but I thought I noticed him putting a hand on his breast pocket a little furtively and I wondered if he was touching his Bible for strength. Colleen had moved to stand at her husband's elbow, almost touching him, but not quite. Her eyes met mine for a moment and I could see her satisfaction that this walking female hormone was not swaying her husband into the same abject pool of drool as the rest of the room. Ivor had put one arm around his wife and another around his daughter as if waiting for an opportune moment to escape. Amy had reached across her husband to run her hand along her daughter's arm.

I wouldn't have guessed the scene in the foyer could escalate until Leilani began twitching out of her bolero jacket. Somehow there were now five or six policemen within sight of this drama. Three of them moved forward involuntarily to help her. When her blouse was revealed to be lace, the tension level in the room shot up a few degrees while the fabric was inspected for transparency.

"Did someone tell her about the admiral?" I asked Colleen.

The room fell silent as Leilani turned her doe eyes on me. But a rougher voice spoke from behind her through the open door.

"Yeah. Where the hell is the admiral?"

7

A brown-skinned man leaned in through the door-frame. He wore a subdued T-shirt and tan shorts. Short and squarely built, he looked as if he could change a flat tire without a jack.

"Freddy!" Stef Russo broke free from her parents and went to hug him.

"Uncle Fred," Leilani said in a subdued voice, eyeing him cautiously.

"Stewart Meade is dead and Grampa's missing!" Stef said as she hugged the man in the doorway. He looked over her head at Ivor, and gave the girl a little shove toward her father.

"Come on, kid." Ivor nodded to Fred as he pulled his daughter out the door. Amy followed.

"I'm glad you're back," she said, patting Fred's shoulder as they went past. "We missed you."

Fred stood back to let them through the door. The neighbor who had been watering returned to his hose. The policemen who had volunteered to carry Lani's bags suddenly remembered they had other duties. In short order, I was alone with Dwight, Colleen, Leilani, and her uncle.

"Okay," Fred said in the silence that followed, "who screwed the pooch?"

Everyone stared at the floor as if incriminating pictures were imminent.

Colleen broke the tension by turning to me like a

good hostess, "Josephine Fuller, this is Fred Luna, the admiral's driver. Lani, Freddy, come on in, would you like some coffee or something stronger—it's been quite an afternoon. Anyone else?"

Lani looked at Colleen uncertainly, then at the floor. With the change in audience, her self-assurance had melted away.

Fred took her arm. "You can't stay here, Lani. The police are working in that cottage." He easily hefted the luggage the other two men had carried. "Go tell your aunt what happened. I'll see you at home in a little bit. Commander, Mrs. Rhymer, you know where to reach us if there's any news." Fred exchanged nods with Dwight Rhymer and followed Lani down to her Miata.

I noticed that Lani had dropped her bolero jacket just inside the door. I picked it up and went down the steps to where Fred Luna was stowing the last of the luggage in the sports car. Lani was in the driver's seat, head down, numbly staring at the ignition. "Uncle Fred, what will we do?"

"We'll fix it. Don't worry. But you better behave. Listen up. People are going to watch you. If you make the admiral look bad, you'll live to regret it."

I cleared my throat and they both jumped a little. I held out the jacket. Fred took it, folded it neatly, and put it on the seat next to Lani. He said something in Spanish that went way faster and further than my one hundred-word vocabulary.

Lani wiped her eyes with her knuckles and sniffled. "You know I don't understand that stuff, Uncle Fred."

He shook his head and slapped the side of the car. "Get going and don't get lost on the way home, girl. Got that?"

"Okay." She ran her hand across her eyes again,

started the engine, and drove away. Watching the car disappear around a corner, Fred took out a cigarette and lit it. He took a deep drag and blew it out before he looked at me. "Believe it or not, she's a sweet kid, but—" He took another lungful of smoke and spat it out. He shook his head.

Then he looked at me and smiled. The transformation was astounding, from a middle-aged man suddenly he became a mischievous boy. I could see the likeness to Lani that the lines and extra flesh on his face had hidden. I could also imagine him hanging out and getting into trouble with the admiral. "So. You must be one of Amy and Ivor's liberal university friends, huh?"

"I work for Mrs. Madrone. Her friend Sally Rhymer was worried . . ." I stopped, realizing I was telling him a lot more than he was giving back in return.

He smiled. "Sally Rhymer is a classy lady. You know the admiral?"

"Well, I threw a drink on him yesterday, but I can't say I know him well."

"Okay." Fred chuckled, then gazed at me solemnly. "But do you know who he is?"

"No. You're saying there's more."

"A lot more. He's not a desk-jockey admiral. He flew combat missions in Vietnam. He has one of the most distinguished records under fire of any man of his rank alive. It was a great honor to be able to drive him, and frankly I was happy to retire and take a job working with him."

"So why did he retire?"

"Politics." Fred looked at his cigarette disdainfully. "The circles he was traveling in, you can do your job, but if you miss the minute when the wind shifts, you can get trampled in the stampede. He was a good man.

A capable leader, but they cut him out of the loop." He shrugged his heavy shoulders. "Nothing left to do but retire."

"How long has he been retired?"

"Two years."

"And how long were you driving him?"

"Eight years before he retired."

"So it wasn't his drinking problem?"

"He always drank, who doesn't? But now it's a problem." He had sucked the cigarette down in record time and lit another off the glowing end.

"Did it jeopardize his security clearance?"

"And what would a young lady like you know about a thing like that?"

I shrugged. "I'm asking because that Mosler records safe in the cottage was open and empty except for a sheet labeled Top Secret when we found Stewart Meade's body."

Fred stopped in midpuff and looked at me with raised eyebrows. "When *you* found the body?"

"Amy and I found the body."

"You are full of surprises." He dropped his cigarette in the gutter, kicked it down the storm drain, and turned to look at me. "So. You saw Meade. What do you think?"

"He was halfway in the bathroom so I couldn't see. There was no blood visible and he was reaching for an asthma inhaler."

Fred snorted in disgust. "What a way to die."

"When I saw him last night he was holding up a bottle of bourbon and leading the admiral out to the cottage."

"You were here last night too? Okay." Another long

silence. I felt irritated. It was his turn to give me some information.

"Who is Stewart Meade to the admiral? Everyone said he was keeping an eye on him."

"Well, you saw him, did he need someone to keep an eye on him?"

"Oh, yeah." We both laughed a little at my instant, heartfelt response.

"He's an old buddy of the admiral's. They're in business together. He took over for the weekend keeping the admiral out of trouble. To tell you the truth, I don't think he was up to the job. I gave him a couple of pointers." He shrugged. "For what it was worth."

"Stewart's wife seemed to think he and the admiral had some hookers in here when she called this morning."

"Martha Meade? Yeah. She would think that." He cast a look up at the Rhymers' house.

"Can I ask one more question?

"You can ask."

"The admiral drives that Lincoln Town Car, or you drive for him?"

"I drive for him."

"He bought that Mazda Miata for Leilani?"

"Yeah, so?"

"Well, if he can afford all that, why is he living in a cottage behind his son's house? Why doesn't he get his own place?"

"He did. It burned down. They're rebuilding. But it will take another six months or more. The admiral travels enough on business that he stays here in the cottage when he's in town. He was going to Thailand in a couple weeks."

"With or without Lani?"

Suddenly, Fred grew deadly still. "What have you heard?"

I wished I hadn't said anything, but I forged ahead. "Something about a Thai connection coming through and whether or not he would take Lani."

"Well, then you know more about it than I do." But he looked suddenly very sad. He seemed to notice for the first time that his cigarette had burned down to a stub. He dropped it in the gutter, took another from the pack in his pocket and looked at it. Then he put it back again. He turned to me brusquely. "Any other questions?"

Before I could answer, a car with an official press pass taped to the window drove up and a man in a sport coat and jeans got out. He was carrying a notebook and had a camera strung around his neck. The neighbor rolling up his hose called out something to him that I didn't catch. The man with the notebook went over to talk to him. After exchanging a few words with the neighbor, the reporter started toward us.

Fred gave him a dark look that set him back on his heels, and headed for an Isuzu Trooper parked in the driveway behind the Lincoln Town Car. I followed, and said in a voice I hoped the reporter didn't hear, "Wait. How can I reach you?"

"I'll reach you."

I gave him a harsh look. He looked back and laughed, jumped into the vehicle, and drove off. I noticed a sticker on the back window reading University of South Vietnam, School of Modern Warfare, Class of 1969.

My impression was that while Fred Luna might be capable of anything, I would have bet money he wasn't involved in the admiral's disappearance. I couldn't help myself from watching his sport utility vehicle round the corner and even watching the corner for a second. What was I thinking? If I really wanted to question someone who worked for the admiral, it wouldn't be too hard to find out how to reach him.

Not that I did want to question him.

Necessarily.

The reporter was coming out of his trance and targeting me now. I headed for the Lexus, using the remote to open the door as I approached, hoping it wouldn't yelp at me, which of course it did. A blue sedan slid into the parking place I had vacated. I paused long enough to see two men in dark suits and ties getting out. Either the Mormons were making house calls, or the intelligence community had arrived.

It was after five when I reached the hotel. At the front desk I picked up mail, which consisted of a large envelope from Ambrose with a note clipped to the top saying "Call me."

"Okay," I said to the air in the elevator. I didn't open the envelope on the way up.

I didn't look forward to telling Ambrose about the body in the cottage and the admiral's disappearance.

I let myself into the room and looked around. The maid had come and gone, emptying the trash and tidying up. No sign of Raoul. Could he have sneaked out when she was cleaning? The terrace door was shut. "Raoul?" An answering, *"Raw-wul!"* from the far reaches of the bathroom. Then a solid whump as twenty pounds of cat hit the tiles. A second later Raoul strolled out the bathroom door, licking his chops, his tail held as high as a gray ostrich feather. I glanced in and noted the empty space on the sink where I'd left the cake of complimentary mink oil complexion soap. Good thing I'd unwrapped it. Bon appetite, Raoul.

I poured a glass of ice water from the fridge and sat on the sofa in the living room part of the suite, pulled the phone over, and opened a pad of paper on the coffee table in front of me. Raoul was up and sitting on the pad before I could find a pencil to write with. Ambrose's answering machine took the call and I doodled on the pad while Raoul tried to trap the pencil with his gray paws.

Ambrose came on the line as soon as I started to leave a message. I pictured him near the machine screening calls. I briefly outlined the major events of the day.

"So some contractor named Meade has been murdered and the admiral is missing?"

"Stewart Meade is definitely dead—murdered—I don't know. It sounds like the admiral is being held for ransom." I explained the recorded message from the admiral and the writing on the cardboard sun screen on Ivor's windshield.

"Hmmm. Let me put you on hold for a minute." After less than a full minute he came back on the line. "Come on up. But we should make it brief. Mrs. Madrone was about to retire early. I think all this worrying about the Rhymers is wearing her out."

I went straight up to the penthouse and Ambrose took me to a room I hadn't seen before. It must have been the anteroom to Mrs. Madrone's bedroom because she came out escorted by a disapproving Lupe, the night nurse, who was tucking a cashmere shawl around her shoulders and giving me a make-it-snappy glare.

It didn't help that I'd been glancing around looking for Mrs. Madrone's lilac point Siamese, who for once was nowhere to be seen.

"What are you looking for?" Twisting her head sideways, Mrs. Madrone shot an accusatory glare at Ambrose, who had lingered, holding a notepad and pen. "Are you sure she's ready to go back to work?"

Ambrose passed the look on to me with an arched eyebrow for emphasis.

"Sorry," I stammered, gathering my scattered wits. "I

guess I was looking for your cat. I haven't seen him here in San Diego but he was always with you before." I bit my lip realizing too late that if something bad had happened to the cat I would only be increasing her distress.

But Mrs. Madrone smiled. "Oh, Prince is around somewhere. He does periodic inspection tours."

"I inherited my friend Nina's cat and I brought him along," I explained.

"You should leash train your cat. Prince prefers a leash to a carrier. He screams like the damned in hell when you put him in one of those cages. I'm not about to have him addicted to tranquilizers. We travel so much."

She shot me a cautionary glare and I wondered if someone would be testing Raoul's litter box for drugs. She cleared her throat. "Ambrose told me Ron Rhymer has disappeared," she prompted.

I gave her a capsule history of my day.

I wouldn't have thought it possible for Mrs. Madrone to turn any paler. Her eyes focused on an arrangement of Meissen figurines on the mantel of the unlit fireplace. While I waited, I wondered if they were fastened down to give the porcelain shepherdesses a hope of surviving here in earthquake country. I noticed that Lupe was keeping a weather eye on her employer, assessing whether she needed medical intervention. At last Mrs. Madrone took a deep breath. "Josephine," she said at last, "this is really something I should do, but since you were there and you can answer her questions, would you mind calling Sally Rhymer about this? She may have heard it from the police, but—"

"Of course, I'll call her."

"Ambrose will give you her number." Mrs. Madrone

turned her chair and Lupe had her out of the room within seconds.

Ambrose accompanied me to the door, where he took a moment to thumb through the leather notebook to an address section at the back. He copied a number on his notepad, tore off the sheet, and gave it to me. He didn't appear to regret not being the one to make the call.

Sally Rhymer answered the phone immediately as if she'd been waiting for a call. I explained briefly about how Amy and I found Stewart Meade's body, the admiral's phone call, and the ransom demand. There was a long pause. Had she set down the receiver? I hoped she hadn't fainted. I heard a sound in the background that it took a moment to identify. Then I realized she was laughing. Laughing as if she hadn't heard such a good joke in a long time.

I couldn't help but say, "I'm sorry, I don't know if you heard me correctly. You know Stewart Meade is dead."

Another pause. "Yes, of course." I could hear her take a deep breath. "You're right, that is a tragedy. How is Amy taking it?"

I thought about that for a moment. "She seems to be in a state of shock."

"Well, of course she would be. That's why I can't see the girl spending all this time in hospitals. She was never good in a crisis. Josephine, you are going to keep looking into this for me, aren't you? Just to make sure those strange people aren't taking advantage of her when she's even more vulnerable."

"I'm still looking into it."

"Good. Thank you for calling me about this. Keep looking and I'll be glad to hear whatever else you've found tomorrow at lunch. I'd better call Dwight. At least I have one responsible offspring."

I put down the phone. I didn't know what to make of Sally Rhymer.

There was a knock at the door. I opened it to find Ambrose. I was a little startled. Showing up unannounced was not his style. "I wanted to make sure you really were all right," he said by way of explanation, looking me over for signs of shock.

"I'm fine. Really. Did you want to come in?"

"Just for a minute. Did you call Mrs. Rhymer?"

"Yes."

"How'd she take it."

I told him.

"Hmm." He raised his eyebrows. I could see he was noting it for further study, but he made no comment. "Your news was so distracting that I forgot to remind you about the other envelope I left for you at the desk." He ran his hand over his beautifully cut red hair. I had never seen him so close to flustered. "I know you're involved in the Rhymer situation but we do still need you to update the information on this grant renewal. There's an official deadline in the way the grant was set up. We need a follow-up report. Your predecessor recommended the grant. The question is, should it be continued or changed—is it being used well? The usual sort of thing."

Trust Ambrose to notice when I had totally forgotten about something. He had given me the folders when I first arrived in San Diego and I hadn't thought of it since.

I opened the envelope. It contained a report, signed H. H., recommending that Mrs. Madrone make a grant to a sculptor named Magda Sobel.

"Do you think you could fit in a visit to this woman? Maybe after lunch tomorrow?"

"Sure." There were directions to the studio, including a map. Ambrose was always thorough.

"You're sure you're up to this? We could get some-one else to—"

"Don't worry, I'm fine. What about you? You actu-ally know these people, right? Admiral Rhymer and Stewart Meade?"

Ambrose smiled kindly but distractedly. "Well, they're not close friends of Mrs. Madrone who show up all the time. I did meet Admiral Rhymer at one of her social functions, but not Stewart Meade. I just don't like having Mrs. Madrone so directly involved."

"I'll just start drafting a report for tomorrow."

"Good idea. We need to document everything." I didn't think he was suggesting I start updating my ré-sumé. But the unspoken idea was floating around.

I realized a little extra effort might be in order. I had been toying with the idea of visiting the Feathers at home and suddenly I found myself telling Ambrose, "I'm going to go ahead and see Lance Feather tonight."

"*If you feel like it.*" Ambrose paused, as if torn be-tween getting more information sooner and counseling caution. "Do be careful, though. They check out okay so far in California, but I'm getting some funny prelim-inary reports on the Feathers. Nothing but rumors so far. But call me when you get back so I know you got in safely."

I blinked in surprise. "You think Lance and Ondine Feather are dangerous?"

"If I really thought so, I would advise you not to go there. They might have, uh, helped some of their clients along a little sooner than necessary back in Arizona, but

I've never heard even a whisper that they've done anything to anyone who wasn't already on life support to begin with."

"Well, that sets my mind at ease."

"I'm telling you to be careful is all."

I closed the door thoughtfully and went to call the Feather Heart Project. The woman whom I'd talked to in the morning answered again.

"We spoke earlier, and now I'm trying to get in touch with Lance and Ondine Feather. I was with Amy when she called you from the Rhymers' house. I don't know if you are aware of what happened with Amy's family today, but she was quite upset."

"Upset! Jeez! I'm upset and I only saw it on the news. Poor Amy. Oh, I forgot to say, I'm Ondine. Lance should be home any minute. Do you want to come for dinner?"

"If it wouldn't be too much trouble I'd like to come right after dinner. I have a couple of responsibilities here to take care of first." I scratched under Raoul's chin and he began to purr like an outboard motor. He seemed to have amused himself pretty well while I was gone. I cautiously took him out on the terrace to watch the sunset. But he squirmed out of my arms, headed for the railing and started climbing down to the deck below. I scrambled to grab him and haul him, protesting, back inside.

He leaped out of my arms and stalked away once I closed the sliding door. The price of forgiveness was to pick up the can opener and a can of cat food. I fed him and took out some turkey, which was doing a decent pastrami imitation, and made it into a sandwich with tomato, mayonnaise, and some very serious multigrain bread. I hadn't realized how hungry I was until I got close to the refrigerator. I liked deli sandwiches but not pickles. This way I didn't have to throw away a perfectly good pickle or remember to ask not to get one in the beginning. I also didn't have to look for hidden pickles, which were an unpleasant culinary surprise in my book. My ex-husband, Griffin, was always happy to take whatever pickles appeared on my plate from the first date onward. I didn't think there was much chance of training Raoul to do this. It was odd how I never thought of Griff although I had adored him during our six years of marriage and followed him around like an enthusiastic St. Bernard puppy, carrying his camera gear, patiently holding light meters and making arrangements of whatever variety he needed. Somehow that moment when I stood in a hotel lobby at dawn and saw him come in and passionately kiss another woman broke my heart like a cracked plate. I had turned my back on Griff. I had to.

I wondered if Mulligan liked pickles.

I left Raoul licking a paw and running it over his head and ears in postmeal grooming contentment.

9

Lance and Ondine lived in a trendy little pocket of expensive-looking shops and apartment buildings in a neighborhood east of Encinitas. It was probably more picturesque in daylight. I parked on a street with no sidewalk and dodged up a winding path among eucalyptus trees that shielded the home from prying eyes.

The Feather's house had a tile roof. It looked dark inside with only a porch light burning. But I recognized the green Saab in the driveway from this morning at the Feather Heart Project. The morning seemed a thousand years ago now.

"Hi!" The owner of the sweet voice who threw the door open was a very pale, delicate woman with a head of hair so curly and blond that it looked like a dandelion gone to seed. She had something of the same delicate stemlike look about her. Lines around her pale mouth and gentle hazel eyes testified that she was in her late thirties at least, maybe older. Although her face showed no sign of mature caution at opening doors into the night when total strangers knocked. "You're Josephine?" she cooed.

"Yes. You must be Ondine, I recognized your voice."

"Come on in. Lance is here. We were just sitting, listening to music and meditating. It helps when you have to deal with death and stuff all day." She turned and led the way in. Once I crossed the threshold I could hear the music—a tinkle of chimes like the sound a

chandelier might make in the early stages of an earthquake a few seconds before it begins to rain down broken glass.

No chandeliers here, though. The light was provided
by a series of glass bowls, each filled with a different
shade of oil: red, blue, yellow, and transparent. A burning wick floated in each bowl. The walls were hung with
huge color reproductions of Tibetan art; I recognized
some of the demons reputed to besiege the souls of the
newly dead as they travel between incarnations. A niche
held another oil lamp burning in front of a statue of the
jackal-headed Anubis, the Egyptian god of death. I'd
have to check. I seemed to recall that he was involved
in weighing the feather against the heart of the recently
deceased—which would explain the feather, the heart,
and the scale in the crude sign above the storefront office.

The man sitting cross-legged on the low sofa was the
one I'd seen in the parking lot. I had not seen him close
enough to appreciate the magnetism of his calm hazel
eyes.

He held out an arm and Ondine slipped down to join
him on the sofa, which was low and strewn with puffy,
earth-toned pillows. He did have more sense than to
gesture me down onto any floor cushions or the large,
folded futon. I could have got down easily enough, but
getting back up would have been awkward.

Unhurriedly I looked around until I spied a solid,
normal-looking wooden chair in a darkened corner.
"May I?" I asked, lifting it slightly.

Lance nodded. I hauled the chair over to a conversational distance and sat down. Looking from one to the
other, I realized. "You're brother and sister?"

Lance laughed and Ondine made a sort of chirping sound.

"You thought we were a couple?" Lance said once he stopped laughing.

"Amy just mentioned Lance and Ondine Feather."

They both smiled and none of us said anything for a while. Sometimes people will feel moved to fill a silence, but I got the impression the Feathers would win the wordless sitting contest easily. I wasn't quite sure what to ask them. I didn't have a clue yet where anyone fit in. Most of the time that was what I liked best about working for Mrs. Madrone—each assignment so far had been a puzzle that could have fit together a number of ways. Right now I was working on the edges, trying different ways in.

"Did you know that Admiral Rhymer called the Feather Heart Project Office this morning?"

"No!" Both of them said it in chorus.

"Ondine was here," Lance said thoughtfully. He turned to his sister, "You didn't talk to him, did you?" Ondine shook her head, her eyes even wider. "We're hardly ever there, but if Ondine is out doing errands or something, the line here forwards over there to the answering machine as a backup."

"I knew you were going to meet Amy there," Ondine said thoughtfully. "Her father must have called the storefront number directly. It is listed in the book after the main number, but usually nobody's there. Sometimes we only go in every week or so to pick up the mail. I just retrieve any messages on the tape from this phone. If it's an emergency, they can page Lance by pressing a number."

I told them I had given the tape with the admiral's message on it to the police, and they both nodded thoughtfully. Neither of them asked about the content of the admiral's message.

I didn't mention the ransom demand.

"So the admiral wasn't in the habit of calling Amy on either number?"

"I can't remember the admiral ever calling Amy." Ondine said. "He didn't seem to treat her very well. She said she wanted her little girl to get to know some of her relatives, and the admiral was at least kind to his granddaughter even if he sometimes insulted Amy."

"Do you know if Amy ever brought her daughter along to sit with people in the hospital."

Both of them shook their heads immediately. "Never," Lance said, "that would be inappropriate even if the hospitals allowed children under the age of sixteen to visit terminal patients, which they usually don't— unless they're relatives."

I nodded. That made sense. "When I talked to Amy's daughter, she said the hospital was boring. I wondered if she spoke from experience."

Lance shrugged.

Ondine examined me with almost childlike interest. "I went out and bought a paper today. They said the man's death was being investigated and the admiral was missing. Is it true Amy found the body?"

"Yes." I didn't mention my being there at the time.

"Wow. I found a body once." Now Ondine was leaning forward, eager to share. Lance looked at her fondly. "It talked to me."

"Huh?"

"I *hear* things. Well, sometimes I *see* things, but mostly I just *sense* things."

"Oh, right, Amy mentioned that you were . . . uh, psychic?" I wasn't sure if that was the right word.

Ondine nodded. "I guess. Anyhow, I found my friend's body after she killed herself. And she talked to me."

"You don't mean that you revived her with CPR or something?"

"Oh, no, she was way *trés* dead. But she and I were real close, see? So she, like, y'know, told me why she did it? I just sat there and she explained all that. Till someone came in. Then she kind of left."

"How old were you?"

"Fifteen. We were both fifteen." Ondine nodded brightly, and Lance straightened up slightly, although he continued to lounge on the pillows. He looked at me assessingly. "The thing was," Ondine said a little more sadly, "that she kept coming back."

A chill went down my spine. "Your friend who killed herself? Came back?"

"*Kept* coming back. But my mother made her stop."

Score one on the sanity scale for Ondine's mother, but I was curious. "How'd she do that?"

"Took me to a psychic healer."

"Really?" I said inanely.

"Yeah. And you know what the healer said?"

"No, what?" I was totally at sea, not even sure when we had left suburban San Diego and entered the Twilight Zone.

"He told me next time she came, I had to *tell* my friend to stop coming back." She laughed a little uncertainly and the nearest candle flickered. "Smart, huh?"

"Very. And ethical, too. When you consider he could have charged more for some sort of ceremonial exorcism type thing."

Lance's eyes on me sharpened unpleasantly at the mention of money but Ondine nodded. "For sure. He even said he could do that, but we should try the simplest way first."

"And it worked?"

"It did," Ondine said with a wistful smile. "Now I see where it was my fault too for hanging on to my friend. I mean, I should have let go. Unfinished business and all like that."

Lance smiled at his sister. "Ondine," he said, "would I be a total pig if I asked you to get us some tea? It's my turn to talk, after all."

Ondine turned to him as if the request were a surprise and I wondered if she usually waited on her brother. "You can't help being a pig, Lance. You were just born that way. Do you like raspberry leaf tea, Jo?"

"That would be fine."

As Ondine had padded on bare feet back to the kitchen, Lance stretched forward like a crouching cougar across his low pillows. "You have a drawing effect on Ondine. She listens to people on the phone talk about their problems, but in person she can be quite shy. This is the most she's opened up to someone about her life in months, years maybe."

"Really?" I could see why she might not be encouraged to open her mouth, judging from what came out when she did. "Maybe it's the whole situation, the death at Dwight Rhymer's place, the admiral kidnapped."

Lance cocked his head in skepticism. "Not likely. We're no strangers to death, and Ondine knows Amy, but we've never met Amy's family, except Ivor. I think Ivor keeps the daughter away from us, what's her name?"

"Stefanie."

"Stefanie." He hardly knew her name, let alone that everyone called her Stef. "We haven't even met Amy's daughter. Her relatives seem to think Ondine and I are a bad influence." He smiled and shook his head at the thought. We sat in silence for several seconds, then he took a breath and changed gears. You could almost see his lecture light click on. "You saw a side of Ondine tonight that isn't usually on display, but frankly I think it's healthy. Our culture makes death into this commercialized service that hospitals shield you from at great personal and financial cost."

So Lance could charge to put the personal into it? I managed to amend this to ask, "Where does the Feather Heart Project fit into that?"

"We're here to help heal the fear our culture has of death. We shun real death, put it in a hospital, and let the professionals deal with it. But all the popular art forms circle around it like vultures—soap operas, monster movies, murder mysteries." He had dodged the question but he circled back to it as well, irresistibly drawn. "Here we have in front of us the great opportunity to confront the reality of life. One example is the use of actual corpses for charnel-house meditations in India—"

"Sri Lanka."

"I beg your pardon?"

"Charnel meditations are illegal in most countries. But Sri Lanka makes it available to some serious Buddhist monks."

"How did you know that?" I had startled him out of his lecture and he was staring at me as if I had suddenly grown a few feet and begun to spout fire.

"I traveled in Sri Lanka a few years ago with my ex-husband. He was covering a story about an anthropologist who was studying unusual meditation techniques. The practice of using corpses as meditation objects is very controversial these days. There are no charnel grounds anymore. What you're talking about only happens now when the government gives certain Buddhist monks permission to go into morgues to conduct their meditations."

"Um. Yes." Lance regarded me with the caution of a rooster startled off his usual perch just before crowing. "Well. You can see the parallel with our modern society, which *is* a charnel house. I mean, here is this *golden* opportunity to study death, disease, and decay all around us and we just step over it on our way to Disney World."

I sighed. "You know the primary point the monks keep in mind at all times during charnel meditation?"

"Uh. No." He decided to throw away his all-knowing mask for a moment and leaned forward. "What *do* they keep in mind?"

"The mantra for that is 'I too will come to this.' "

"Sounds a little selfish." He seemed disappointed. "When they could be studying the universal," he added.

I made a mental note to amend my living will to specify that this couple was not to be let into the same hospital with me during the last hours of my life or at any point immediately after its cessation.

I was silent for a while. I crossed my legs on my wooden chair and waited. So did Lance.

At last he took a deep breath and looked up at me with a flicker of very businesslike comprehension. "Mrs. Rhymer sent you, didn't she?"

"What makes you think so?"

"Well, you've been sticking pretty close to Amy and her relatives. Mrs. Rhymer doesn't approve of the Feather Heart Project. Did you know Amy was named after Amelia Earhart? Her parents never forgave her for being a chubby kid and that goes very deep. They see her as an underachiever and she is very, very hurt. That's why she doesn't talk to her mother and only barely speaks to her father."

"But she talks to you. Why?"

"Well, she doesn't talk much. When she first came to our grief workshops she hardly said a word about herself—as if she weren't even there. She talks in cryptic little bursts about how she's been a disappointment to her mother or how her father stopped noticing her when he saw she wasn't going to be an asset to him in public life. I asked her to help me when we first started the project out here—"

"When you say 'out here'—did you used to have the project going somewhere else before?"

"Yes, the project was at a southwestern facility in New Mexico and also in Arizona." If Lance saw anything suspicious in the question, he didn't show it. "At any rate, we have found it works best in some situations to use a male-and-female team."

I glanced toward the hall where Ondine had vanished. "Why not work with your sister?"

"Ondine doesn't have the stamina to spend hours like that. Besides, she says things that scare people. Amy is very good at just sitting quietly with people."

"And you pay her for that?"

"Not much, but we try to compensate her for some of her time."

"Who pays you?"

"Well, not the bereaved families. We have supporters. I give lectures and workshops. People give gifts. We are able to help out just a few who need us. Here." He extracted a business card from his breast pocket and handed it to me. The card was simple in the extreme.

Lance's name and two phone numbers conservatively printed on heavy cardstock.

"The bottom number is our personal line here. If you ever find you need to talk about anything, just call."

I looked up to see Lance observing me solemnly. I wondered about Ambrose's rumors of misconduct. I wasn't sure what to ask next.

"Ondine and I may be the closest thing Amy has to friends outside of her family," Lance remarked.

"What does her husband Ivor think about all this?"

Lance sighed. "Ivor won't speak to me—hates my guts." He leaned forward to emphasize his point. "When I call to talk to Amy, he holds out the phone, and says, 'It's my hated rival.' It's a joke but he wants me to hear it. He doesn't cover the phone. Once I ran into them down by the harbor. Amy stopped to say hello. Ivor just kept on walking. I'm not kidding. Amy had to run to catch up to him. None of Amy's family approves of our work."

Lance leaned back and put his arms behind his head, a little posing there, like a New Age centerfold. "*Our* parents, on the other hand, are *thrilled* that I'm affiliated with universities and hospitals, despite my rather unorthodox background. They thought when I was a teenaged motorcycle gang member that I'd end up dead or in prison before I was thirty." He pushed one sleeve up nearly to the shoulder and showed me a fading skull and crossbones tattooed above the crook of his elbow.

"Most appropriate for a death worker," I commented.

He laughed. "Well, I don't show it to clients unless they show me theirs first. I was pushing the envelope during those years. I think I wanted to meet death in person from a very early age. It's as if I always knew I was meant to do this work."

"*I* always knew," called out Ondine, bringing in a tray with a simple brown ceramic teapot and three small, round Japanese cups. "I wanted to be a taxidermist when I was ten."

Herbal tea falls into three categories—the sweet lemony or minty kind, which I often like; the kind that cleans your sinuses at ten paces, which I avoid; and the kind that tastes vaguely of something wholesome but not generally regarded as edible.

Ondine had brought a steaming pot of brew that tasted as if a few dry stalks of herbs had dipped their roots in hot water for several seconds. I made an earnest pantomime of drinking what seemed to be barely liquefied steam and managed to scald my tongue despite all efforts to sip conservatively.

I had asked as many questions as I could muster so I took my leave soon after that. Lance waved politely from where he had already settled back on his cushions and half lowered his eyelids. Ondine barely glanced up from contemplating the steam rising from her cup. There seemed to be no other appropriate flat surface in the room, so I left my own nearly untouched teacup steaming on the floor next to the chair.

10

When I got back to the hotel room, I poured myself a glass of wine and sat down with Raoul curled up on the bed beside me. I gave in to temptation and called Mulligan. He answered on the first ring. His voice raised my temperature but I found myself suddenly unsure of what to say after hi.

"So how's that cat?"

"He's okay. Probably bored."

"You should have let me know before you went. Next time you have to go out of town, you can leave him with me."

"Okay."

I asked about his work in the security end of the telephone company and he told me he was making a case for theft of telephone company equipment against a computer hacker. "What about you? How's it going down there?"

"Well, it looked like a simple matter of just giving my opinion in a family dispute. But I found a dead body this morning and a man I talked to last night seems to have been kidnapped."

Silence at the other end of the line. Then I heard him take a breath. "Are you all right, Jo? What happened?"

I explained. Telling him about it brought home to me the horribleness of it, just a few months after we had lived through Nina's death. Of course, he would be thinking of Nina, his lover, now dead. What made me feel worse was that I hadn't thought of Nina all day. In fact, it was one of the first days when I hadn't thought of her a lot. Stewart Meade's death and the action at the admiral's house had driven her from my mind. That was part of why I went back to work to begin with, but all of a sudden I hated it.

"Jo?"

"Sorry. What? I guess I got spaced out."

"I said, are you sure you're all right?"

"I think so. As right as any of us can be after what we all went through the past few months. I'm trying not to get too involved in this whole mess." I suddenly wondered if he interpreted that to mean I was trying not to get too involved with him.

"Just take care of yourself, okay?" he said.

"I will. You too."

We said good night on gentle terms. When I dialed the phone, I had thought it would be nice to talk to a simple, honest man who had no hidden agenda or odd quirks. But now I was starting to feel like an unstable eccentric by contrast. I went to sleep with that thought in mind.

I woke up an hour or more before the alarm. The early edition of the San Diego daily was outside my door. The newspaper played the story down, putting a small paragraph on the first page with a picture of Stewart Meade and his death in the Point Loma cottage where he was a guest. The story mentioned Admiral Rhymer's disappearance but not the ransom demand. The article tactfully concluded that the police "suspect foul play." I didn't know anyone used that phrase anymore.

I turned to my report. I halfway agreed with Sally Rhymer about Lance and Ondine being a questionable influence on Amy, but I had no hard evidence. Ambrose didn't answer my call. I wondered if he was out or had simply turned off the machine. I left a message asking if his research had turned up anything concrete on the Feathers before they arrived in California. I was pretty sure, though, that giving the Feather Heart Project money would not help. After that I intended to chase down the woman sculptor who had received the grant under my predecessor. So when the phone rang at seven-thirty, I was printing out a discreetly edited set of my notes for the lunch with Sally Rhymer.

I took the last page out of the printer and answered the phone, expecting Ambrose.

"Hello, Josephine?"

It was Amy. I recognized the shell-shocked tone of her voice more than anything. She didn't sound a whole heck of a lot better than she had the evening before.

"Jo, I don't know you well, but—Ivor has been taken down to the police station."

"You mean arrested?

"No, but—could you come out to my place? There's been another note and I need to talk to someone."

"I'll be right over."

I called again and this time reached Ambrose, who said he hadn't got any more information about the Feathers. He noted Amy's address and number and observed dryly, "I'm sure Mrs. Rhymer will be glad you're looking out for her daughter. But unless someone else turns up dead, I wouldn't advise being late for lunch."

"I understand. I'll be there."

It took an hour to reach the Russos' little bungalow near the university in San Diego where Ivor worked. It wasn't that far away but the rush hour traffic was fierce on the access roads as well as the freeways. The Russos lived in an old-fashioned California house—squat, one story with a low pitched roof stretching out over a front porch. Big square beams framed either side of the steps up from the street. The walls would be thick and the rooms small with high ceilings. A house built to stay cool without air conditioning. There were no cars parked out front. No sign of the Russos' Dodge van.

Amy let me in and we walked though the dim living room. It was already in the low eighties outside. There was an air-conditioning unit in the front window but she had not turned it on. An open window in the front room sent a breeze down the hall to the kitchen where the back door was open and a screen door latched shut. A fan aimed at the room in general picked up any breath of breeze and passed it along. The most distinctive feature of the living room was three tables occupied by chess boards featuring games in progress. Two were on card tables and a third on a student desk in the corner.

Amy saw my double take. "Ivor and Stef are usually analyzing something. This month I think they're looking at Capablanca's greatest hits."

Her words were flippant but Amy avoided my eyes. "Come on in the kitchen." She led the way down the hallway. At the back of the house, the kitchen unexpectedly had a skylight and rows of herbs in the window, even a couple of scraggly tomato plants climbing a trellis and reaching for the window. I looked out the screen door and saw a lemon tree in the backyard.

"Thank God this happened after Stef got off to school. Ivor went in early and dropped her off. I don't usually need the car." She sat down at the kitchen table and I sat next to her. "My husband found a message in the fax machine at work."

"At the university."

"Yeah." Her voice broke, and she started to cry. "The police are blaming us. Why would we do something so insane? Let alone evil and awful."

I patted her shoulder. "Take a deep breath and tell me what happened."

Amy took a shaky breath, "They have a departmental fax machine in the Life Sciences Department. Usually the secretary puts the messages in each professor's mail box, but when Ivor goes in so early he just picks up his own." Now she was crying in earnest.

I looked through my purse and found a packet of tissues and offered her some. She took a few sheets and wiped her eyes and nose. When she seemed a little better, I asked if she wanted a glass of water or anything. She shook her head. "I should be offering you something," she said.

"I'm fine, but tell me what was in the fax Ivor found?"

"It was a deadline for the ransom. This Friday. Ivor called me and I called Dwight. They've been expecting a call to Dwight. They put equipment on his phone to trace it. I don't think they expected a call to come to me and I don't know where Brad is."

"Your brother Brad hasn't been seen since right after we found the body?" I asked, although I could guess the answer.

Amy made the kind of gesture usually used to shoo away small insects, "Oh, Brad disappears all the time. We don't even really know how he supports himself, although he seems to survive okay. It's Ivor I'm worried about. The police took him in for questioning. They think he has something to do with this because he found the other message on our van windshield and now this.

How could they single *us* out? We're not even that close to Dad."

"The kidnappers might be worried about the call being traced. And Ivor's fax number at the university is a matter of public record, right? I mean, if they knew your husband taught there and what department?"

"Life Sciences."

"So anyone could just call up and ask for their fax number. That's probably what they're checking now to see if any unusual request for fax number happened recently."

"It's in the college catalogue," Amy said.

"Okay. So they wouldn't even have to call up. Let's see. How did you find out about this?"

"Ivor called me."

"Where did he call you from, work or the police station?"

"Work. But he said he was going to go to the police station rather than talk to them at work."

"Okay. But he wasn't calling to say he'd been arrested, was he?"

"No." She sat bolt upright. "What was that? Did you hear that?"

We both sat silent and I heard it as well. A tapping on the back door. I went to the door and stopped a few feet short to see a grubby-faced man with a halo of unruly hair tapping on the doorframe, pressing his face against the screen door, which suddenly seemed an awfully frail barrier.

(11)

Amy come up behind me, wiping her eyes with a tissue. When she saw the man, she giggled. "Brad!"

Now that she said it, I recognized the round face, which was covered with stubble. The ponytail had obviously come loose and scrambled into a nest of tangles. "Amy! Let me in."

She moved around me to let her brother in. "Bradley, what is the matter with you? You look like you've been sleeping in the gutter."

He came in and sat at the kitchen table bar. "Close. I slept in my car last night." He ran his hand over his face a few times, "Do you have some orange juice or something?"

"Sure." She went to get a carton from the refrigerator. "Would you like some too, Jo?"

"Sure, thanks. Why did you have to sleep in your car?"

He looked at me askance. "You were at the party. What are you doing here?"

Amy interrupted. "Don't you know what happened?" She set glasses on the table and poured the juice. "Stewart Meade is dead, Dad is missing. Jo is here because I asked her to help me. Ivor had to go down to the police station because someone sent a ransom note to him at the university."

"Yeah. I know. I mean I heard about all of that except Ivor. It's going to be okay." For a moment Brad's face twisted as if he were fighting off a strong emotion. He took a deep breath and drained the orange juice in one long swallow. "My neighbors said the police were all over my place. I don't know what they think, but some-one must have told them I had some reason to want to get rid of Dad. That's why I'm sleeping in my car." He glared at me accusingly.

"Your name didn't come up when I talked to the police. But the way he was acting at that party, lots of people wanted him out of there. And there is the little matter of the ransom, if someone could pull it off."

Brad and Amy exchanged glances. It seemed to give both of them a little more strength. Brad shook his head. "You don't get it, do you?" He shook his head and rolled his eyes at Amy. "She doesn't get it." He turned back to me. "Look, whoever you are, in our family there was one motto—'*Good enough*—' "

He looked at Amy significantly and they recited in unison, " '*Is not good enough.*' "

"I see. So, nothing is good enough." I said.

"Basically." Brad continued, "Amy and I have elected not to join the best and brightest down in the spotlight where the admiral lives. Our mere existence as a fringe element in the family is a mild but constant irritation to both our parents—one of the few things on which Mom and Dad have always agreed and continue to agree, before and after their divorce. I make it a point to come around and scrape a few handout crumbs off the table just to irritate the old man. Our father would be delighted for me to simply vanish from the earth and the only reason he does not include Amy in that wish is that she has presented him with a grandchild. Of course, it is a female grandchild, but what the heck, it's all he's got."

"Brad!"

"Well, you know it's true. You of all people, Miss Amelia Earhart Rhymer Russo, should know that the admiral never counts women as really mattering unless he's forced to."

"It's not fair to bring that up, Brad." Amy sat at the table with us. She picked up a stray grocery receipt that had been shoved between a salt and pepper shaker and began to pleat it nervously. By saying her full name Brad had embarrassed her to the point where she wasn't willing to meet my eyes.

Brad emptied the last of the carton of orange juice into his glass. "Dwight has elected to play the admiral's game by the admiral's rules and look where it got him."

"Has he always been a Jesus freak?"

Brad laughed, but his laugh had a bitter ring to it. Amy looked at him plaintively. "See, even a total stranger can see it. Or did you tell her?"

"I didn't tell anyone anything about Dwight or you."

"Well. That's something. But you don't have to say anything at all to read it in the local newspapers. The admiral's youngest son, yours truly, has a police record."

"What for?" I asked.

Brad ran a hand over his face and through his disheveled hair. "I've got to get some sleep. I'm running on empty."

"You can sleep on the sofa in the den," Amy said gently. "You want me to get you a blanket and pillow?"

"I know where they are. I may take you up on that in a little bit." He turned back to me. "Amy's always been the good kid. Maybe when people gossip about her they'll be merciful and say that she's a wife and mother who does volunteer work at local hospitals."

Amy shook her head. "I don't care what anyone says."

"Then there's the born-again naval officer. Old Dwight is hoping Jesus will save his career." The sharp edge of Brad's voice could have drawn blood. "Still, I will grant Dwight, he hasn't been tempted by the bottle. He's only a failure when you measure him against the admiral, and that must hurt worse than ever now that the old man is camping out in his backyard, throwing out a trash basket of booze bottles every day and still acting like he's God's gift to everyone. Frankly, I wouldn't be surprised to hear that Dwight and Colleen kidnapped the old man, just to get some peace of mind and to dry him out."

Amy looked up, startled. She made a small sound but stopped herself.

"You've thought of it too, haven't you?"

Amy shrugged, "I couldn't see them killing Stewart Meade."

"Do we really know that Meade was murdered?" Brad directed this question at me.

"I have no idea. The newspaper said the police suspect foul play."

"Well, maybe he got in the way. This counseling drunk people is not for the faint of heart."

I was more skeptical. "You're actually entertaining the thought that your father was spirited away to a home-grown detox program and Stewart Meade died trying to stop it? That's a pretty aggressive intervention."

Brad turned and examined me with his pale blue eyes. "You know, it's been real fun swapping theories.

But just exactly who the hell are you? And whose side are you on?"

I explained without mentioning any names that I was representing a foundation that was looking into the Feather Heart Project for a possible grant. Of course, I totally left out Sally Rhymer's part in it.

"So you could actually get money for that death watch thing, huh, Amy?" Brad sent the orange juice container sailing into the trash and put his feet up on the kitchen chair next to him. "If that happens you'll have to rethink the whole concept. I mean, isn't the idea not to make any profit?"

"You should talk," Amy said, turning her mouth down against a smile. "I don't see you getting paid for all that UFO research." Plying her brother with orange juice seemed to revive her spirits.

The front door slammed and all three of us jumped. A moment later Ivor came striding into the room. "Is there any beer left?"

"Beer for breakfast?" Brad made a face at Amy. "I thought we were the ones with the problem-drinker genes," he said, but very softly.

Amy went to meet Ivor. "Are you okay, honey? I thought you had classes later today."

Ivor moved her gently out of the way and opened the refrigerator. He pulled out a bottle of beer. He didn't even look at Brad or me but unscrewed the top and took a long thirsty swallow. Brad looked a little wistful, but the tension in his shoulders the moment Ivor marched in suggested that he was not going to make demands on Ivor. He had already surreptitiously removed his feet from the kitchen chair. The bottle emptied, Ivor set it on the counter, wiped his mouth, fell into the nearest chair and belched softly.

He looked around at us. "Canceled—or rather suspended," he said. "The department chairman didn't cancel my classes, but he's getting someone else to cover them for the week. Told me to take the time off to get things sorted out. Obviously, getting hauled out of there by the police was not good for my image as an educator. I'd still be at the damn police department except the kidnappers called Colleen at work and she informed the police. They dropped me to go bother her for a while."

Amy stared at Ivor in amazement. "They called Colleen at the real estate brokerage?"

"Yep. After they told me it was going down Friday, they told her what kind of cash to bring and they were going to tell her where to take it when she turned them down."

"What?" Amy was horrified.

Ivor shook his head and reached out for his beer bottle. He upended it, without getting more than the dregs. "She said we don't have the money," Ivor concluded, putting the bottle aside, a little mellower now, whether from the beer or the chance to let off steam.

"She's right." Brad said cheerfully. "I don't have gas money for my car half of the time. Dwight and Colleen could mortgage their house. You guys are renting but even if you had savings, none of us could come close to any million dollars cash. It's cold-blooded of her to say so, but she's right. We don't have that kind of money."

I was fascinated. "Did Colleen make a counteroffer?"

Ivor's lips thinned into a straight line. "She told them we might be able to access the admiral's own funds if we could talk to him to get him to authorize it. But she wasn't going to do anything till she knew that he was alive."

"Smart woman!" Brad leaned his chair back until his head touched the wall and whooped with laughter. "That Colleen is some hard-ass negotiator."

"It's not her father!" Amy exclaimed. "What right does she have to say yes or no?"

Brad shrugged. "Hey, they asked her, she answered. She just told them the truth."

"Her work phone was unlikely to be tapped, just like the fax at Ivor's office was unlikely to be tapped," I said.

Ivor looked at me for several seconds. "Anyone want another beer?" Brad agreed eagerly, Amy shook her head, and I turned one down as well.

Brad took the bottle with a relieved look, as much at being accepted as for the beer. "Wow," he said. "If the admiral *is* alive he'll be loving this."

Ivor's brow clouded instantly and his eyes went to Amy, whose face had fallen. "Of course he's alive, Brad. Consider someone else's feelings for a minute. Your sister happens to care about your father." Very softly, as if to himself, he said, "God knows why."

I emptied the last few drops of orange juice from my glass. "So did the kidnappers hang up on Colleen or vice versa or what?" I asked with what I hoped was a casual tone.

Ivor nodded at me. "She told them to call back tomorrow and put the admiral on the line. We'd better figure out how much we can offer."

Brad shrugged. Amy looked thoughtful.

"Would the admiral's money be enough?" I asked.

Ivor shrugged. "If he were here, he could scrape up some more, call in some favors. The thing is, none of us know much about his finances. His ex-wife might have known up until a few years before the divorce, but he's not telling her now and I'm sure he doesn't confide in Lani. I think Stewart Meade would have known at least where most of the admiral's money was located. But he's dead. The admiral knew some important people but they're not flocking round to help us in our hour of need. Maybe they'll talk to Dwight. I don't even know who to ask. Hell, if Dwight and Colleen borrowed against their house and the admiral put in the word to turn his assets into cash we might be able to swing most of it."

Amy turned to me. "Why don't you ask Mrs. Madrone?"

Now it was my turn to stare in amazement. "How did you know I worked for Mrs. Madrone?"

She laughed a little wildly, then put her hand over her mouth. "You just told me, Jo." I returned her smile uneasily.

Brad raised his eyebrows at me and shook his head. "You've got to watch our little Amy."

"I'm sorry, Jo." Amy said, "I don't want to get you in trouble. I just know Mrs. Madrone has the Madrone Foundation and she is an old friend of Mom's. It's a typical Mom kind of way to get at me so she can see Stef more often. If her rich buddy Mrs. Madrone is getting ready to throw money at the Feather Heart Project, why not help Dad? That woman is a billionaire. Tell her we only need a million dollars to save Dad's life."

"Maybe less than that," Brad murmured, "After Colleen does her stuff."

At that moment the front doorbell rang. Brad picked up his beer and went to answer it. He came back with the young man I had last seen dressed as a World War I flying ace. "A friend of yours, Ivor," Brad said, sitting back down at the table.

"Have you all met Zane Birch?" Ivor asked by way of introduction.

Today Zane wore his long blond hair in a loose ponytail that reached halfway down his back rather than a braid. He had swapped the aviator outfit for khaki shorts and a T-shirt that read, I'd Rather Be Mating—at the Golden Triangle Chess Club. His lean, scarred face and too-sharp blue eyes made him look older and more careworn than his early twenties. He was holding a foil-wrapped casserole dish in each hand.

"Hi, guy," he said to Ivor, who nodded mournfully back. "Hi," he said a little uncertainly to everyone else. "Here." He held out the casseroles to Ivor.

"You can put them on the table," Ivor said.

"They're both vegetarian, but the one with the C on it has cheese. In case somebody's allergic to that." He stopped at the thought. "My mom helped me make them. All you have to do is heat them up. We made two in case you wanted to take one to, um, like your brother's."

"Thanks, buddy," Ivor said. He peeked under the tinfoil of the nearest casserole. "Want some beer?"

Zane blinked in surprise. He had seemed like a playful anarchist when I first saw him in his Red Baron getup. Today he seemed painfully earnest, like a kid trying to comfort an adult.

"Thank you, Zane," Amy echoed as she put the casseroles in the refrigerator. "Maybe some coffee or tea if you'd rather."

Zane shifted nervously from foot to foot. "No. Thanks."

"Did you know Stewart Meade?" I asked.

Zane turned to look at me sadly. "The man who died? No, I never met him."

"You might have seen him, a big red-bearded man going into the cottage in the backyard with another older man, both of them wearing Hawaiian shirts."

Zane shook his head. "No. Sorry. There were a lot of people in that backyard and it was getting dark. I didn't pay much attention."

Brad and Amy were looking at me strangely, but there was something about Zane that I couldn't quite fathom.

"Look, I've got to go. My moped is still in the shop. You'll never guess who I rode over with." A tentative smile split his thin face. "It's the same person who's going to play World War Two with me."

"Who's *that*?" Ivor asked in surprise. He got up and put his empty beer bottle into the sink. "It can't be a chess player." He glanced at me and explained, "Most chess players don't like other board games. *Maybe* backgammon. But Zane likes these crazy military strategy games." He punched at Zane's arm but missed by a few feet.

Zane flinched even though Ivor's fist never came close. "Oh, it's, um, Duke."

"Duke Dufrane!" Ivor exclaimed. Everyone fell silent. Even I couldn't imagine Zane getting cooperation from the gruff driver of the van I'd met at the admiral's house. "Duke is going to play war games with you?" Ivor shook his head in disbelief.

Zane smiled sheepishly. "I don't know if he'll get through the Battle of Britain without rolling out of the place in disgust, but he said he could kick my ass at anything. So I said as long as he was giving me a choice of weapons, I chose World War Two."

I had a question. "So this guy is waiting outside? He never comes in?" Everyone stared at me in a way that made it instantly clear I had made a faux pas. "What did I say?"

Ivor explained patiently, "You must have noticed that our house is quite old and it's not wheelchair accessible."

"Oh, sorry. I should have noticed. I didn't mean to be insensitive."

"Of course you didn't," Zane said gently.

"Uh, Zane." I thought, since I had been forgiven, I had better ask my question before I managed to step on more toes. "Who is the Spanish-speaking guy who was in the van night before last?"

"You must mean Juan—he's sort of an attendant for Duke, though he doesn't speak all that much Spanish or any English. I think he speaks an Indian dialect. Duke learned to speak his language when he met him down in South America. Speaking of wheelchair inaccessible—Duke takes him back from time to time to visit his family. He said mostly Juan and his brother have to carry Duke but he likes it down there and he can swim and lie on the beach." Zane turned around to go out.

"I'm surprised Duke talks about it that much," I said. "He seems so gruff."

Zane smiled wickedly. "The trick to getting him to talk is to get him angry—then he'll talk for quite a while." Zane said his good-byes and left.

Ivor was still shaking his head when I left a few

moments later. All I had to do was go ask my employer for a million dollars ransom money. I was beginning to see another side to the Rhymer family. I wondered if it would cost me my job.

12

It was late midmorning and the traffic had eased off as I drove thirty miles up the coast to Carlsbad, where I followed the directions turning onto Highway 78 and heading east, away from the beach over which the faint mist had almost burned off. Sally Rhymer lived in a gated condominium community on a hilltop on Hospital Road, which struck me as a poor choice of street names for a retired person of a certain age, but go figure. The security guard was expecting me and after consulting my driver's license, he buzzed me in, gave me directions to Mrs. Rhymer's unit, and pointed to the visitor's parking area. The gate slammed behind the Lexus. I drove past a couple of tennis courts on my way to park.

Mrs. Madrone's usual daytime nurse, Constancia, let me in and pointed me toward the dining room, which was around a corner. It was a large condo with vaulted ceilings. I crossed the entryway where a skylight illuminated the green patina of a bronze Etruscan horse—its legs stretched into elongated sticks, wasp-waisted like a horse in a killer corset.

Mrs. Madrone and Sally Rhymer sat at either end of a burnished oak table in an informal dining room. A window along the length of the room let in light and a view of a private, shaded patio with flowers in planter boxes. It looked like an elegant place to breakfast alone but I got a strong sense of shame from Sally Rhymer. Mrs. Madrone was as matter-of-fact as ever but it was clear that having her friend see her in this place embarrassed Sally.

Lupe, whom I usually saw at Mrs. Madrone's in the evening, had just brought in a plate with sliced fruit. Ambrose came through a door that must lead to a kitchen with a bottle of chilled white wine. He poured glasses for Mrs. Madrone, Sally Rhymer, and himself. He said hello and set out a glass for me but I asked if I could get some soda as I was going to have to drive soon. Ambrose murmured "Quite right," and went into the kitchen to find some. No doubt there was some sort of catering effort going on behind that door. I would have liked to have followed Ambrose back there, but I knew I would have been kicked right back out again.

I took a place at the oak table, which would have comfortably seated six. My bet was that there were leaves in storage that would expand it to seat twelve.

Mrs. Madrone looked at me expectantly. "Is there anything you can tell us about the kidnapping that we haven't learned from the news?" she prompted.

I gave them a brief but thorough account of discovering Stewart Meade's body, the admiral's absence, and the open safe. Sally Rhymer still hadn't said anything. Indoors, with the noon sunlight filtered through the room's picture window, the air chilled against the oncoming afternoon heat, she seemed to shrink in on herself. I wasn't the only one who didn't want to be here. She looked as if she wanted to be on the other side of the window glass, moving and doing something. But unlike Mrs. Madrone, who was running her finger distractedly along the edge of her place mat, Sally hardly moved.

"Did you know Stewart Meade?" I asked.

A muscle under her eye twitched slowly, deliberately,

she met my gaze. "Not well. He was a defense contractor—one of Ron's buddies." Something in her voice made me realize that she was looking at me with new interest. I had graduated to human status in her eyes from her previous view of me as a distastefully large young woman whom her friend insisted on employing. Now I actually had some power over her. I could almost see her debating whether I was worth cultivating.

Ambrose came back with a lemon-lime soda for me and refreshed the ladies' wineglasses, then he sat down and began devouring the fruit and crackers and cheese which none of the rest of us had touched. This was the kind of ladies' lunch where the food was a decorative toy.

Sally Rhymer cleared her throat and continued. "Ron and I divorced five years ago. While he was still in the service we entertained a great deal. But this Stewart was part of a whole set of people he saw primarily with his slut."

The last word hung on the air like puff of exhaust. "But you know Fred Luna?" I had to ask.

"Oh, yes." Sally took a deep breath and she seemed pleased to hear the name. "Fred is such a character. But he's been good for Ron. You don't get to be an admiral's bodyguard without some special skills. Ron's first driver had been a navy SEAL. When Ron lost his first driver he asked for Fred."

"What happened to the first driver?"

I expected her to say something about a transfer or retirement, but her face grew solemn. "It was terrible—a traffic accident of all things. He was a pedestrian victim of a hit-and-run driver. Very sad. So Ron needed someone in a hurry and Fred's record came to his attention. Fred's a war hero. He did two tours of duty in

Vietnam in the army. After the army, he didn't like civilian life, so he enlisted in the navy. He was a bit of a handful. They didn't quite know what to do with him. He was working in munitions when his commander brought him to Ron's attention. He drove Ron for eight years and then retired so he could work for him in civilian life. I envy Ron his friendship with Fred. Fred can be a troublemaker but he was perfect for Ron. They understood each other."

"So you don't blame Fred for bringing Leilani around?"

"It was hardly Fred's idea." She shrugged her muscular shoulders. "What can he do? It's a disgrace to his family but he can't pick a fight over it. At least I could leave Ron and get alimony but poor Fred is stuck working for him. He could never find another job that paid like that. A retired naval non-commissioned officer. A man with his attitude." She paused delicately. "Pride is a very expensive commodity, Ms. Fuller, not everyone can afford it."

I knew that better than she did. Constancia brought in clear soup and fussed a little at Mrs. Madrone for not eating. Evidently both she and Lupe were monitoring what Mrs. Madrone ate today. We all had some soup. It was Thai style with lime, green onions, and hot pepper. Very good.

"I have a few more questions, Mrs. Rhymer, but they'll keep till after lunch."

"No. No. Please, I know Alicia has to go to some kind of board meeting later and I have a tennis lesson at two. As long as it isn't graphically distressing, by all means, please finish."

I was struck by the every-muscle-clenched attitude that Sally Rhymer assumed with this. It looked like a recipe for indigestion to me, but it also reminded me of Amy's frozen reaction to this crisis. Maybe it was some sort of stoic, military domestic thing. Zen and the Art of Dysfunctional Family Life.

Lupe came in, cleared away the soup bowls, and put down plates of grilled sole and a bouquet of spring vegetables hiding among sliced new potatoes.

Contrary to popular myth, as a large person I don't eat conspicuously more than smaller people. But this luncheon was so sparse and both Mrs. Madrone and Sally Rhymer were scarcely eating at all. I have to admit I cleaned the plate very quickly. Ambrose did the same and we settled down to watch Mrs. Madrone and Sally play with their food. Constancia brought a sauce boat and ladle to the table—too late for Ambrose or me. She and Lupe appeared to have a good-cop/bad-cop thing going to get Mrs. Madrone to eat. Now she gave her a stern glance and muttered a few words to her, which caused Mrs. Madrone to actually begin to eat some of the food. I had never seen anyone bully my boss before, so I enjoyed that.

I didn't care to be observed marveling at the other women's poor appetites, so I continued my report. "The kidnappers called Colleen at work at the real estate office. She basically told them no."

"What?" Sally looked up from pushing a shred of carrot around her plate to stare.

"Exactly what Amy said."

Ambrose coughed and raised his napkin to his mouth for several seconds to mask what must have been a chuckle.

"She said the family couldn't afford a million dollars and wouldn't pay anything until they had proof the admiral was alive."

Mrs. Madrone smiled. "She has a point. Why pay anything for a dead body? Even Ron wouldn't want that."

I cast a careful eye on my boss. "Amy asked if you could help. I only told her I worked for a charitable foundation, but she not only guessed that it was the Madrone Foundation, she suspected Mrs. Rhymer would be involved as well."

"Why not?" Mrs. Madrone was not surprised. "She's an intelligent young woman. She knows Sally and I were at school together, it's not such a stretch of the imagination." Mrs. Madrone pushed her plate away as if it contained some pain she could rid herself of.

"Don't worry about it, Alicia," Sally said, with a tightness in her voice that sounded close to tears. "This is not your problem. If it wasn't for the children and my granddaughter I'd hang Ron out to dry. Lord knows that's what he did to me."

"Well, maybe there's something we can do," Mrs. Madrone said thoughtfully. She turned to me and I saw the kind of candor in her sharp brown eyes that might have looked like ruthlessness if I hadn't known her better. Come to think of it, maybe it was ruthlessness. "You can see my problem here. I'm besieged with appeals as it is. Only the most urgent personal pleas ever reach me. That's what my staff is for. Ambrose and Jo, you handle the matters that need my personal attention. If it were known, even if not widely, that I would pay ransom, no one close to me would have a shred of safety or privacy left. Let me talk to some advisors. We deal with several companies throughout the world in areas where kidnappings are an occupational hazard of executive daily life. I'm sure we have some experts on retainer. Ambrose will call you later today."

"Mrs. Rhymer, I realize the situation with your daughter and the Feather Heart Project has kind of got lost in this crisis, but I do have a suggestion."

"Yes?" Now a spark of curiosity lit Sally's eyes. She looked more approachable.

"Your granddaughter is clearly enthusiastic about chess. She goes to lots of tournaments with her father. These events are open to the public. I think you might consider attending one just to get to know her better and encourage her. I can let you know where she's playing next."

"I'd like that," Sally Rhymer said. Mrs. Madrone nodded as well, and murmured something to her friend that I didn't catch.

We left it at that and I went on to my next task, seriously considering stopping somewhere on the way for a drive-through fast-food supplement to the luncheon.

After leaving the secured community on Hospital Drive, I took a few minutes to find a drive-through taco stand so that by the time I drove east on 78 past Ramona, I was feeling much more nourished.

As I drove I couldn't help thinking that two years earlier the mysterious H. H. had made this same drive and filed the report recommending the grant. Now I would be updating it. The thought made me feel very replaceable. The small town I was looking for was on the edge of the Anza Borrego Desert State Park. Summit City, which was unaccountably well below sea level, boasted a population of less than five-hundred. Magda Sobel had her studio and a small shop here. It didn't look like the kind of community that could support an art gallery.

It wasn't hard to find the shop. It was in the heart of the three-block-long main street of Summit located between a barbershop that was closed despite an Open 10:00 to 3:00 sign and a secondhand store that only opened on Saturdays. It was early afternoon, but the temperature was in the high eighties. The town looked as if it might close down for a siesta.

But Magda's shop had an Open sign. The cramped window displayed a woman's sculpted hand emerging from a cube of metal mounted on a velvet display stand and beckoning customers into the store. The inside of the shop was lined with similar pieces of steel with human features trapped in them. A torso appeared to be surfacing after taking a dip in a pool of liquid metal. A face was just fighting its way out of the metal. A full head and shoulders had emerged to sit on a pedestal. The faces were all women and most of them resembled the woman who stood behind the counter fussing with a drip coffeemaker. She had a high forehead, large green eyes, a sharp blade of a nose, and a slightly receding chin. It was easy to recognize her as the subject of the sculpture because her silver-gray froth of hair was almost the same color as the metal in which it was frozen in all those portraits. I gestured to the nearest sculpture. "Are you? . . . Is that?. . . ."

"Yes." The woman said patiently, "Those are the works of Magda Sobel and I was the model. I also work in the store here." She stopped. Clearly there was more.

I held out my hand. "Hi, I'm Josephine Fuller. I'm doing my master's thesis on women artists in contemporary society."

She nodded politely and asked where. I told her UC Berkeley, hoping sincerely that she didn't know anyone there. I decided that the questionnaire I had put together would be best coming from a dreadfully idealistic graduate student. Older people always like to disillusion the starry-eyed young. Perhaps this woman would burst my bubble with some useful information. "Are you an artist too?"

She looked at me sadly and shook her head. "I was," she whispered. "At least I thought I was."

"May I interview you too, Ms.—" I made it a question.

"Hayworth, Helen Hayworth, please call me Helen."

"Thanks, people call me Jo. I wanted to interview Magda Sobel, but your input would be really helpful too. It's just a few simple questions. It won't take much time."

The pale woman thought a little more. "You'll have to catch Magda when she comes through for her coffee after lunch. She'll be anxious to get back to work. Here." She reached around behind her, snatched the carafe of coffee and shoved it at me. I took a step backward to keep from being burned. "Give her that. She'll want a cup. She can be a little intimidating but—"

"Helen!" A loud but husky voice with a vaguely European accent came from the back room behind the counter.

Helen half turned and squeaked like a trapped rabbit. "She's here."

I grabbed the handle of the carafe before Helen dropped it. I looked past her as she bustled back to the room behind the counter to find cups. You could see all the way through the open back room of the shop, out the rear door to the walkway behind it. The back of the shop opened on a cactus garden and a cement walkway to a small house behind the store.

Coming up the walk, through the back room and into the store, was a tall, very muscular woman with short-cropped salt-and-pepper hair, hawklike nose, high cheekbones, and a jutting jaw. With her piercing gray eyes she bore a certain resemblance to a bird of prey. She looked a little like the sculptures also, not in her features but in the fierce expression. Model or no, Helen, who was meekly handing Magda her cup, looked about as ferocious as a baby bunny.

Magda Sobel's clothes were still gritty from a morning's work. She wore blue jeans that had faded nearly white and an equally hard-used blue chambray work shirt. Tendrils of wet curls shot with gray crept out of a rusty bandanna whose original color was unknowable.

I introduced myself and explained about the survey. Magda held the cup out expectantly in front of me. I looked at the carafe in my hands and poured. I get a little bleak in the morning before coffee myself, but this was well past noon.

I set the carafe on the counter on a stack of flyers. Helen retrieved it and poured coffee into two more plain white china cups. She pushed one toward me, but neither of us drank. We both watched Magda sip her black coffee.

She pulled up a wicker chair and sat down. Magda gestured to me to sit. Helen dragged a wooden stool from behind the counter and placed it near Magda's chair. I perched on it while Helen retreated back to lean on the counter. "Oh, yes." She looked at Helen with sudden warmth in her gray eyes, "*Liebchen,* magnificent coffee, as always." Helen sighed with relief. Magda looked at me frankly. "When I tasted Helen's coffee, I knew I had to taste Helen. You understand." She chuckled.

I said, well of course I did understand. But I found myself putting down the cup I had raised to sip some of the coffee. Helen blushed a little and lined up some of the flyers and cards on the counter more evenly.

"When I tasted Helen's cooking." Magda continued, leaning back expansively, "well, then I knew I had to have her in my life forever. The rest is herstory."

I thanked the gods of deception that I had run off a little questionnaire when I pondered possible cover stories. Jo Fuller, Grad Student, wanted to know about Women Artists, Feminism, and Survival. All yes-and-no questions. The few numbers thrown in centered on

How do you finance your art career? Give percentages. Sales of artwork? Grants or scholarships? Teaching art? Jobs outside of the art field?

Magda snorted at that question. "What about ninety percent living off your loved ones? Would you believe this sweet woman came up the road two and a half years ago to interview me for a foundation grant?"

I sat speechless for a moment. Helen Hayworth. This must be my predecessor H. H. standing behind the counter, fingering the steel statuettes that held the flyers down. She looked at me a little too narrowly when I blinked, so I must have reacted visibly. Magda didn't seem to notice. She rattled on oblivious, "Helen's foundation gave me a grant. Eventually I also got Helen. We lived nearly two years on that grant, which was not meant to support two. Fortunately, Helen had some savings."

So that was where H. H. had gone, why the job had been open for me.

Magda talked on, a little louder, as if sensing that she was losing me. I straightened up on the stool and made a few notes on my clipboard. I looked up to see Helen examining me a little too intently.

"The money has gone. No one else has helped us," Magda went on. "We go to the galleries in La Jolla and Carlsbad and sell nothing. If I sell a large piece tomorrow we could live for six months. Or Helen might have to go to work for the fast-food place again like last month and a few times last winter. We close the store when she works. It's a pity. She would sit and draw nicely and sometimes people come in and buy her sketches. This one sells more than me. They don't sell for much. Small sketches but very pretty. You should interview her."

"Oh, yes, I'm going to, just a few more questions."

"Five more minutes, I can't waste the daylight. I'd invite you to my studio but you'd just get in the way." She stared at me with sudden focus. "Unless you'd be interested in modeling. Perhaps a nude. You're a healthy girl, interesting body." She raked me up and down with a brusque, assessing glance.

Great. Now Helen was starting to look distinctly peeved.

"Oh, gosh. No, thanks. I've got so much work to do just getting my thesis together. I've got twelve more artists to interview before I get all the data."

"Who?" Magda's full concentration hit me like a floodlight on a migraine sufferer.

She threw me off for an instant, but I took a deep breath. "I'm sorry," I said primly, "but the nature of the study requires that I keep the participants anonymous. You must understand that."

"No. I don't." She narrowed her eyes. "*I* don't care if you use my name—no, you *should* use my name. We need every scrap of publicity. These other artists, perhaps they aren't even serious competition if they're that fragile." She stood, put her coffee cup on the counter, and began to rock back and forth from foot to foot, clearly impatient. I closed my notebook and thanked her.

"Well, you caught me at a free moment, I could do no less. Now I must go back to work or you will depress me."

I was spared the trouble of thinking up a reply to this as Magda squared her shoulders and marched out without another word.

Helen and I stared after her. The atmosphere was a little chilly after Magda's inquiries about nude model-

ing, but when I put a fresh form in my clipboard and
Helen realized I meant to interview her as well, she
thawed considerably. "Would you like me to freshen
your coffee?" she asked. "Or would you prefer some
tea?"

"Yes, tea, please, if you'll join me."

"Okay. We can sit over here on this bench." She took
my untouched coffee, dumped it out, and poured from
a carafe of hot water into a teapot.

We moved to a bench at right angles to the counter.
The bench was a stone slab supported by a full figure
of Helen, stretched out like Atlas, bearing the slab up
on her back, shoulder, and arms, seeming to pant with
effort. Helen poured us cups of tea, peppermint by the
smell of it, and brought them back to the bench. We sat
so that she could see the door, but the street outside was
deserted, so it didn't seem too likely we would be interrupted by customers. I asked Helen the same questions and from her answers it was clear that Helen had
worked more jobs outside the fine arts, including teaching high school. As she started to relax more I finally
managed to ask, "So, what were you doing for a living
when you met Magda?"

"I came around Magda's studio like you with a bunch
of questions, although I didn't have a clipboard or a
questionnaire. I was working for a foundation that gave
grants to women. Magda was much poorer then. She
used to haul her pieces around in the back of a rusty
station wagon. She received a grant, at my recommendation. The grant allowed her to display all this work,
to have this space. Magda's devotion to her art inspired
me to give up my comfortable job and to just paint. Of
course, our personal relationship made it difficult for me
to travel, which my job required." She watched me care-

fully as she talked. Magda might be so far out of the closet she was practically across the street, but Helen appeared to only reveal herself as much as seemed diplomatic. While Magda acted the wildly eccentric artist, Helen would deal with customers at their comfort level.

"Do you ever miss your old job, travel and all?" I tried to put myself in her place. If I took up with Mulligan and settled down in Seattle I might feel similarly marooned.

"Sometimes. I always stayed in very comfortable surroundings but it was lonely. Here in Summit, we're just part of the community. It's close enough to the desert here that people mind their own business. I liked the people I worked for, Mrs. Madrone was very nice. You've heard of her, of course."

The Madrone name was a public institution. I took a chance. "Oh, she's a friend of Mrs. Rhymer, isn't she? I know her daughter, Amy."

That was true after a fashion, but Helen came at me out of left field. "Oh, do you know her from Weight Watchers?"

"No. I didn't even know she went to Weight Watchers."

Helen squinted at me as if she could hardly believe this possible. "How strange. I taught at her high school a few years before I went to work for Mrs. Madrone. Amy was very shy, but her mother made a point of telling all the faculty that her daughter was seriously dieting. Weight Watchers was the last one I remember."

"She never mentioned dieting to me," I said.

Helen shrugged. "Like I said, it was the mom who kept us up-to-date on Amy's latest diet. I never noticed that the girl lost much weight—or if she did, she always seemed to gain it back."

"That's not surprising, the odds are about ninety-five percent against any diet producing lasting weight loss."

"Oh?" Helen wasn't interested.

"I met her mother and she did seem controlling."

"To put it mildly." Another thought occurred to her, and she smiled broadly. "Of course, Mrs. Rhymer kind of shut up about everything after Admiral Rhymer ran off with that exotic dancer."

"Ouch."

"It definitely took the wind out of her sails." Helen put her teacup down. "Sally Rhymer is apparently moving on, herself. The last I heard she was consoling herself with a young lover. Probably her tennis pro."

"That would explain why she's so enthusiastic about her game. Anyway, whatever her parents did, Amy and her husband seem pretty happy."

Helen sniffed. "I never met Amy's husband," she said with crystal clear disinterest.

"They have a nine-year-old daughter, who's great, and they're doing pretty well," I said. I wasn't sure that was true.

"Goodness, I was teaching Amy in high school a little over ten years ago. She must have dropped out of college her first year to get married."

"Right. I think she did."

Helen sipped her tea, refreshed by a little light gossip, and we went down the items on my questionnaire. For all our talk about the Rhymers she hadn't mentioned the kidnapping. It seemed she didn't follow current San Diego news very closely.

I saw a frown form on Helen's pale brow as she looked past my shoulder. "Do you know that man? He's been staring at us for a couple of minutes."

I turned round to look and saw Fred Luna. At that

moment he looked as if he were scouting locations for a hit by a South American drug cartel. His eyes flickered when they met mine but he made no other sign of recognition and did not move to come inside. He lit a cigarette and continued to examine the store through the window.

"You don't recognize him?"

"He does look familiar. Did he used to work for Admiral Rhymer?"

"Yes. He still does."

"Well, he appears to want to talk to you. I won't keep you." She blinked at me as if begging me to leave.

"Thanks for your help," I said, getting up to go. All the statues around the store gave it a populated feeling as well as a cemetery sort of quality. I was glad to be going back out into the sunshine.

Helen shook hands with me. "Good luck with your dissertation."

"Oh, thanks! It's just a thesis." She almost tripped me up on that one. I'd forgotten I was supposed to be producing something here. One of the things that had surprised me about the deceptive side of working for Mrs. Madrone was how little it bothered me to lie to strangers. Helen watched me go with only mild curiosity. I had no particular desire to go back and confess that I was working the job she had given up and I liked it a whole lot.

Fred Luna had his back to me when I came out but I could tell he was waiting for me to approach. It was all I could do not to look back and wave at Helen as I came up beside Fred and nodded to him.

He put out his cigarette and dropped the butt in the gutter. "So, what did your two little lezzie friends tell you?"

That wrung a laugh of surprise out of me. "You are the most politically incorrect person I've ever met."

"Yeah?" He gazed at me guardedly from under his eyebrows, "Well, that is because you have led a very sheltered life."

"If you say so."

"I do say so." He took out his pack of cigarettes, looked at it, then back at me, and put them away. "I followed you from Amy's to Mrs. Rhymer's, now here. The family went off in all directions. They're not talking to me."

"I'm sure Amy would talk to you if she'd talk to me. After all, she hardly knows me. It looked as if Stef trusted you yesterday."

Fred sighed. "Yeah. But the grown-ups don't trust me because of Lani." He sighed.

"It's clear to anyone who looks that you're an honorable man." I said.

Fred turned his head to look at me with sudden surprise. "Why do you say that?"

"It seemed obvious to me."

"Well, it is true but no one ever said it before."

I had a sudden thought. "Is it generally known that the Rhymers are friends of Mrs. Madrone?"

He shrugged. "I guess. Why?"

"Because maybe somebody thinks Mrs. Madrone will pay a million dollars to get Admiral Rhymer back."

Fred snorted. "Yeah. Right."

"Amy asked me."

Fred's face softened. "Amy is a sweet girl, but she's even more naive than you are." He shook his head. "I agree with the Israelis on hostages. Don't pay ransoms. Go get them back. But who would do that for the admiral?"

I shrugged. I didn't know the answer to that question. 'Most everyone I'd spoken to wanted him gone.

"Look," Fred said, "I've got to do something about this. You want to talk here or back in town?"

"Back in town. There's a courtyard with tables and chairs where I'm staying. You want to follow me?"

"Okay. But you drive too slow, I'll meet you there." So he knew where I was staying.

"If you know a quicker way, I'll follow you."

"Yeah, do that."

I glanced back into the store before getting into the car, but if Helen was watching, she was not visible. I followed Fred Luna's Trooper back into San Diego. He didn't speed but it was a very direct route.

(14)

Less than an hour later Fred and I bought soft drinks
from the vending machine in an alcove off the lobby
at my hotel. We went to sit at a white-painted wrought-
iron table, one of several clustered in the tile courtyard
that circled the fountain. A lone businessman tapped at
a laptop computer over on the other side of the fountain
but the rest of the tables were deserted. Nonetheless, I
was sure the hotel staff was keeping a watchful eye on
us.

"The police found drugs in the admiral's bourbon."
Fred said without preamble.

"The police told you that?"

He shook his head and smiled. "No. But the cops like
talking to Lani. A girl like her, you know they'd make
a special effort to interview her as often as possible.
One of them told her what they found in the bourbon."

I shrugged. "What kind of drugs?"

"Seconal—strong sleeping pills. Okay, I have put
drugs in the admiral's liquor before—but nothing that
strong. Still, they'll find my fingerprints on some of the
bottles."

"But they didn't arrest you?"

He shook his head grimly. "They didn't *find* me. I
should never have told Stewart about it. That was my
mistake. He would not have thought of it on his own, and
he was too stupid to do it right. You see, I talked to a
medic I know. He told me how to get some real mild

sleeping pills at the *pharmacia* in TJ. I got so I could figure when he'd pass out by how much I put in. Usually he
wouldn't get in trouble if he passed out a couple hours after he started drinking. Stewart must have got lazy."

"Do you think Stewart Meade might have been involved in the kidnapping?"

"If he was, somebody double-crossed him. My guess
is, Meade was just sloppy. He's dead now, we can't ask
him."

"We don't know the admiral drank that drugged
bourbon," I pointed out. "Amy and I heard a message
from him that must have been recorded sometime
around noon. The morning after Stewart was killed. So
he was definitely alive, awake and talking at that point."

"Okay."

"And Colleen has refused to pay ransom till the kidnappers prove the admiral is alive."

"*What?*" I felt a perverse satisfaction in surprising
such an unflappable man. "Where the *hell* does she get
off speaking for the family?"

"The kidnappers called her at work." I told him about
the call to Amy's office and the sign on the van and the
fax to Ivor's office. "They seem to be rotating the phone
calls among family members to keep from getting the
call traced."

"Well, that's so smart it's stupid, you know why?"

"Why?"

"Because the cops are going to assume it's someone
who knew the family well enough to know everyone's
work phone number."

"Either that or it's someone who plans ahead and
does a lot of research."

"That goes without saying."

"But what you say means it's not too likely the admiral killed Stewart."

"The *admiral!* Kill Stewart? Why would he do that? Stewart was going to make him rich."

"Maybe the deal fell through."

"There are other deals. The admiral may do things on the spur of the moment but he is not a bad man and he's not crazy enough to kill a business partner, even if he got pushed into a corner."

"What about the admiral's kids?"

"What about them?"

"When I was at Amy's earlier today there was a suggestion that maybe someone might have kidnapped the admiral to dry him out."

"Amy said that?"

"I think Brad was talking about it."

"Yeah, Brad."

"You don't think Brad might have done something like that himself?"

Fred shook his head. "Little Brad? He wouldn't have the *huevos*."

"More or less what his father said at that party."

"The subject came up at this party, huh?" Grim amusement traced a smile on Fred's lips. "Some party."

"Well, the admiral was attempting to shoot his video camera up Brad's girlfriend's skirt."

Fred laughed. "What did the old man say?"

"Brad wasn't man enough to protect his girlfriend, something like that."

Fred nodded sagely. "Yeah. Well, it's true. Brad is always trying to get something he ain't qualified to get. He'd like to be an officer but he ain't got the guts to go through basic. He washed out of the ROTC. Now he wants the nice spacemen to come and make everything all right. The kid is a couple cans short of a six-pack. Still, maybe he's better off than Dwight. If Dwight doesn't put down that Bible, and soon, he can kiss his career good-bye."

"It looked like that Bible was about all that was holding him together."

"A man's got a right to his religion, but it's not getting his job done for him. Ask Colleen if she likes wearing the pants in the family. Dwight just gave up."

"There is another suspect, you know."

"Who—me?"

"Well, you said the admiral was heading for Thailand. You might need the cash."

"I have a pension and I can find other work for a few months."

"But what about Lani?"

"They were working on a business deal in Thailand. That's all." But Fred looked sick at heart for a moment. I felt sorry for him. It looked as if pride were wrestling with anger. Or had he already heard that the admiral might be planning to drop Lani? Had he taken steps to ensure both their financial security?

Fred fished out his cigarettes and glanced at me sideways. He threw the pack on the wrought-iron table, but didn't touch it. "Lani is my sister's girl. My sister went off to Hawaii with a Filipino-Chinese guy. He was connected with some gamblers in Honolulu, too fast and flashy for his own good. He wasn't around long. He never married my sister but his family in Hilo took Lani in and my sister stayed in the islands too. She was kind of wild. She died five years ago and my wife and I got Lani. She was fourteen then and wilder than my sister ever thought about being. But Lani really liked the admiral and she made sure he noticed her. He told me he wanted to make an honest woman out of her. I don't know."

He retrieved the pack of cigarettes, pulled one out of the pack and lit it. "I hate to say it about my own niece . . ." He looked away and inhaled about an inch worth of tobacco in the first gulp.

"Are you sure you're not being a little harsh on her? She did look like a tease, but . . ."

He blew out smoke. "Yeah, well, maybe I know more about her than you." There was a pause, and he said, "Do you know that guy? He's staring at you."

I looked around for the first time since we'd been talking. I wasn't sure which balcony went with my room but it must be the one where Mulligan was sitting in a lounge chair, feet up, beer in one hand. Raoul was perched on his lap, his round fuzzy head stretched forward to allow his chin to be properly scratched. Mulligan raised the beer can to me.

I must have stared thunderstruck because Fred half rose from his chair. "You should look around you a little more. He's been watching us for half an hour."

"This is my day for stalkers," I said a little more brusquely than I had intended to.

"I don't want to get you in trouble with your man. I'd better go."

"Sorry to get upset, but they shouldn't have let anyone into my room."

"Okay." Fred sat down and smiled without showing any teeth. He raised his cola to Mulligan, but I could practically feel the surge of nervous energy. "So someone thinks this guy is your boyfriend. What do you think? You want him in your room? You need some help to evict him?" He leaned back in the chair, but looked ready to spring up at any instant.

"Thank you, Fred, but that's not necessary," I said, genuinely touched, because although he was nearly a foot shorter than Mulligan, I had the feeling it was a sincere offer on Fred's part, even if it would get him into trouble. "I don't want him hurt," I added. "But I'm going to kill whoever let him in." The surprise was wearing off and my usual mixed feelings regarding Mulligan had started to surface.

"I think you don't mean that literally," Fred said.

I nodded. "You're right. I just like to make my own decisions."

"Sure." Fred studied me carefully. "Are you certain this guy won't give you a hard time? I could go up with you." But he did not look anxious to do so. Given that he was already dodging the police and San Diego was alive with reports of police stopping cars and demanding proof of citizenship with no other probable cause than Latin looks. Fred must often wish he had his Navy uniform back.

"It's okay. He's not dangerous. He's just . . ."

"Your boyfriend."

"Not exactly, well, he could be."

"Ahh, he will be, then. Your face tells me that. I'll leave you to it. But if he treats you badly, let me know." He touched my shoulder and left.

I sat at the table for a few moments before I got up and started toward the room, half-sick with dread and desire. But there was only one thing to do. I did stop at the desk and left Ambrose a tart note about giving out my room key without my permission.

(15)

I let myself into the room just as Mulligan was closing the terrace door with Raoul watching complacently from a secure perch on his shoulder. He was a large man, tall and square built. By no stretch of the imagination could he be called handsome. He had a face like a blond bulldog and dark brown eyes that I wanted to look into forever. For some reason he had electrified every nerve in my body since the first moment I saw him, shedding tears for the death of Nina, his lover, who had also been my best friend. I wasn't sure if by both of us loving Nina we had too much in common or not enough.

"Hi," he said, "I was going to wait for you downstairs but I ran into Ambrose and he told the desk to let me in to wait for you. It seemed easier."

"I wish I'd had some warning."

"Sorry." Mulligan scratched Raoul's ears. "I could have waited down in the lobby but I've been missing this critter." He ran his huge hands over Raoul, who stared into his face adoringly, putting a paw up to his lips as if to stop him from talking.

"Excuse me." I headed for the bathroom. I hesitated before going back out to Mulligan and looked at my reflection in the mirror. Seeing Helen waiting on Magda hand and foot reminded me of how I had globe-trotted around after my ex-husband Griff solving practical problems while he took pictures. It seemed so easy to give in to this overwhelming physical attraction but I didn't want to be trapped.

When I came out of the bathroom Mulligan had settled down with Raoul on the sofa in the living room of the suite. "I've never seen a place where you lived before."

I didn't say anything for a moment. I didn't have to look around to realize that within forty-eight hours I had managed to spread a fine layer of stacks of papers, books, and magazines over most of the flat surfaces.

I shrugged. "I work best this way. When I'm researching something, I like to have the papers at hand." I stopped. "I guess it looks pretty cluttered to you. I seem to recall your apartment was surgically clean."

"Well, I didn't do any actual surgery there," Mulligan said with a smile.

I opened up the fridge. I noticed that he had contributed a six-pack of beer and a bottle of Chablis.

"When I traveled with my ex-husband," I said, pulling out some ice cubes and a liter of cola, "we carried everything in two backpacks. His was mostly photographic equipment. Mine was everything else. I never bought souvenirs anywhere we went unless I was prepared to ship them home. But when I have some time and can spread out—" I shrugged.

"You spread out."

"Yeah." I looked at him, a little surprised.

"I wasn't attacking you for it. I think it's cute."

I let out a breath, surprised to find I'd been holding it in. "Oh, sure, now you think it's cute. Give it six weeks and you'll be demanding separate toothpaste tubes."

He laughed. I was startled. I had known him for about two months and never heard him laugh out loud.

We had met in such a dark time that there was a lot more crying than laughing.

He ran his hand over his longish pale hair. "I guess the shock of losing Nina nearly drove me insane." He shook his head. "I don't know if I'm coming out of it or just waking up. I just know I wanted, I needed, to see you."

I poured myself a tall glass of cola and gulped down some immediately. Unaccountably, I was still thirsty.

"You want anything from here?"

"No. Just come and sit down over here." He patted the sofa.

I went and sat next to Mulligan, reached across him to pet Raoul.

"So you backpack too," he said.

"Only when I have no choice."

"How about camping out?"

"I try not to make a habit of it." I put the cola down on the table not far from where he'd put his beer.

"But you went all over the world with your ex-husband? Nina had a book of Griffin Fuller's pictures of the Himalayas."

"Yeah. The roof of the world. That was a few years ago, I was in my twenties then."

He smiled a little sadly. "Nina was older than me and she sometimes made me feel like a green kid. Now you're making me feel old." For several seconds neither of us said anything. He put his hand out and touched my face. "I missed you."

"I missed you too."

"Tell me about this guy you were talking to, down in the courtyard?"

"Fred Luna. He's the admiral's driver." I explained

a little more of what was happening. Mulligan listened and asked relevant questions.

As I finished explaining the situation with the admiral's kidnapping, Raoul hopped off the sofa and padded over to leap onto the top of the television where he stretched out with his front paws crossed, his head resting on them, eyes half-closed.

Mulligan leaned forward. "Why is the cat doing better with you than I am?"

"Because the cat needs somebody right now or he won't survive. You can use a can opener. Actually for all I know you can cook better than I can and you don't need fresh kitty litter every day."

I went over to pet Raoul, who shot his claws out in pleasure and rolled over so I could scratch his stomach. I felt awkward looking at Mulligan. "Things have been so crazy since we met. I just wonder if deep down, you really want someone more like Nina. And I can't just step into Nina's place."

"I'm not asking you to do that. I'd be lying if I said I wasn't hurting."

I turned to go back to the sofa. Raoul extended a front paw as if to pull my hand back, then stretched instead and lay back. I sat on the sofa next to Mulligan. I couldn't help it, I took his hand, which made it irresistible when he pulled me closer. I had to protest. "Look, I'm not very rooted, even before I took this job, and traveling is part of the job."

"And you've gone and taken on a cat?" He brushed my hair back out of my eyes and ran his hand along the side of my cheek. I've always been a sucker for that gesture. "Don't you know cats are more conservative than any person? As much as missing Nina, Raoul is probably pining because he wants his old room back and his garden and his turf." He let go. The next step would have been a kiss. But we weren't done talking.

"Well, I'm not letting you take the cat back."

"I could stay for a few days. I've got a few vacation days at work. I brought my laptop so I can keep in touch there. At least there'll be one familiar thing in the poor cat's life."

I stopped what I had been about to say and looked up at him. He had a faint smile on his face that I hadn't seen before. We had met in such a tragic moment and I had been so stunned by the electricity between us that I had not taken the measure of his wit. "You're saying that I should sleep with you for the cat's sake." I started to laugh.

Mulligan let me go and went to the mini-refrigerator in the kitchenette for another beer. "Who said I'd sleep with you? I can sleep on the sofa in the front room here."

"Yeah, right, and we can leave a roast chicken on the table overnight and Raoul won't touch it."

Raoul lifted his head up to stare at me for a moment. He knew his name and I suspected he might also know the word "chicken."

Mulligan opened the beer and came to sit on the sofa across from Raoul's television perch. "If you'd like, I'll get a room somewhere else," he said. "There are other hotel rooms, even on Coronado Island."

"No—now that you're here . . ." I could hardly bear it if he left the room now. I sighed because I didn't know what to say. I suspected at this point he could read my mind because my thought processes weren't very complicated.

"Look at yourself for a minute, Jo. Have you ever thought that you might be running away from what's happening between us? You were about to sleep with that guy Fred what's-his-name who was just here."

"What! Just because I invited him to talk in the courtyard?"

"Well, you two were putting your heads together down there. From here it looked pretty cozy."

"Damn it, he said the same thing about you."

"Huh?"

"Fred Luna just now said the look on my face told him I was going to sleep with you."

"You talked to *him* about sleeping with me?"

"No. Of course not. I was irritated that Ambrose let you in without letting me know and Fred asked if you were my boyfriend—oh, never mind!"

Mulligan took a sip of beer. Now he seemed amused. He didn't say anything.

"He's a married man. Believe me, I do not sleep with married men. I suffered too much when I was married and I discovered my husband cheated on me."

"Okay, so maybe I'm way off base." Mulligan looked at the coffee table and leaned down to put his beer on top of a file folder. He appeared to have grasped that I wasn't the sort of girl who would rush to find a coaster. "I didn't mean to say you had no control over the situation."

"Yeah, well. It sounded like it." I looked at the floor a little mollified. "Believe me, I wouldn't have slept with him. True, there was some chemistry. But not like it is with you—"

I broke off because I had found my way to stand so close to him that the power surge arcing between us should have dimmed lights all around the greater San Diego Metropolitan area.

"Let me see that look on your face that's so clear to

everyone else in the world," he said, running his fingers down the side of my face. Then he pulled me into his arms and our lips met in a kiss that set off seismic shocks down to my toes. All I could do was cling to him until he broke away and led me by the hand through the alcove toward the bedroom.

16

After tripping on discarded clothing and fetching up against the wall for a long, timeless time, we eventually made it to the bed. In the silence between waves of sensation I heard the faint thump of a feline presence on the bedside table and Raoul's loud purring. The next objective thought I had was sometime later, when the sheet managed to get twisted into such a knot that one of us, or both of us, it was hard to tell at that point, kicked it totally off the bed. It was a warm night and neither of us seemed to miss it.

I was a little shocked to find out how well I did sleep, once we had worked each other into total exhaustion, and I awoke to find Raoul curled up on a blanket that wound up on the bedside table, I wasn't quite sure how.

Mulligan was snoring boyishly. There were a couple of pages in the Kama Sutra that I felt I'd never totally understood before. "Thank you for coming down here," I said softly. I wasn't sure I was up to saying it to him yet when he was awake.

I drifted off to sleep again and awoke. It was still dark. A muffled sound in the next room had awakened me. There was something frightening about the sound. I froze motionless and listened again. I registered that I was alone in bed and suddenly terrified. I looked around the room. No one. But I heard the sound again. I found my robe hanging on the bathroom door and slipped it on as I went into the front room cautiously.

The sound again. Mulligan had pulled on a shirt and shorts. He was sitting cross-legged on the sofa sobbing, his bulk towering over Raoul, who crouched about a foot away regarding him solemnly. I went to him and put my arms around him. He laid his head on my chest and cried. I stood for a while with one arm around his neck, stroking his hair with the other hand. Finally I needed to sit down. I moved around to sit beside him, exhausted, not touching.

"I miss her so much," he said. "I didn't know it would hit me this way. I'm sorry. I just can't stand it."

"Don't blame yourself. It seemed like it would comfort us." I sighed. "It did, for a while."

"Jo, it's not your fault. I shouldn't have come here. I wanted you. I wanted to make everything better and you were so wonderful, you are wonderful." He looked down at me with tear-starred eyelashes and I kissed his cheek and stroked his hair. I could not think of a word to say.

"Now I just want Nina back and it seems like everything I do takes her farther away." He started to sob again. I went to get a roll of paper towels from the kitchenette. I couldn't for the life of me remember where a box of tissues might be. I tore off a couple of paper towels and gave them to him. He wiped his face.

"What can we do?" I asked, tearing off a towel for myself as well and running it over my own face. I was almost surprised to find that I wasn't crying at all. I felt as if I should be, but I wasn't. I had a wild hysterical thought that maybe this was a whole new era for me, instead of men making me cry, I would make them cry—and feel just as rotten, or possibly more so. I put the roll of paper towels on the table in front of the sofa.

"I have to sort this out. I feel like I lost Nina all over again. It's not your fault, Jo." The fact that he said it made me wonder if it was.

"Don't beat yourself up, Thor," I said, surprised to find myself using his first name, which he didn't tell to everyone. He didn't seem to notice.

I breathed another shaky sigh, trying to think. "First of all, neither of us would have done this if Nina was alive. We just got thrown together by the way she was killed."

"I don't know why," he said, taking a deep breath, "but it feels wrong."

"I didn't say it was right." I looked at the ceiling as if some guidance was written up there. "I don't know if it's wrong exactly either. It felt astonishingly great when it was happening."

He laughed and hugged me briefly. But he let go after a moment. I wondered if my very touch hurt him now. I shook my head in disbelief. How had we got past the feels-wonderful part so fast?

Mulligan tore off another paper towel and mopped his tear-swollen face and runny nose. "I've got to get out of here. It's almost dawn, I'm going out for a walk." He went into the bedroom and came out hurriedly dressed, putting on a jacket against the predawn chill.

"Wait," I said, as he started to open the door. "It's not like we betrayed her. You can't cheat on someone who's dead."

"Are you sure about that?"

"No," I said to the door. The door that had just closed behind him.

I sat on the sofa, blindly petting Raoul. What hurt the most was that it bothered Mulligan so much more than it bothered me.

I couldn't face the bed again, so I took a long hot shower, got dressed, and made some coffee. Mulligan came back while I was drinking the coffee and looking out the terrace window to the courtyard.

"I'm going to take a shower too," he said, observing my still-damp hair. "Would you like to go to breakfast?"

"Sure." While he showered, I called Amy. She was getting ready to go to Stewart Meade's funeral. "Could you come?" she asked. "I'm not asking for a ride, well, I do need a ride, but I could use some moral support too. Ivor's not going. He wants to go to work, even though he doesn't have classes. If you drove me, he could have the van."

"I'd be glad to drive you."

I hung up and Mulligan came in, wearing a terrycloth robe and toweling his hair. "Who was that?"

"Amy Russo, the admiral's daughter. I'm driving her to the funeral."

"Oh." I didn't ask if he wanted to go. He didn't. I didn't either, but I wanted to talk to Amy.

I felt a deep desire to embrace him, but from the way he was keeping his distance, that didn't look like a very promising course of action. Instead I put on a navy blue shift that I figured would do for Meade's funeral. It was Southern California, where shorts and sandals are appropriate everywhere—with the exception of Mrs. Madrone's circles, and Stewart Meade's funeral counted as one of those circles. I also put on the lightweight linen jacket I had worn the other evening to the Feathers' place. It was comfortable now but I expected to take it off as the day wore on.

Walking through the lobby, Mulligan and I encountered Ambrose who was leaning against the front desk reading my tart note about not letting just anyone into my room. He greeted us gravely, and said, "Objection duly noted and filed, Jo. Morning, Mulligan."

"What's a good place for breakfast?" Mulligan asked.

After his initial sarcasm at seeing us together following my protest, Ambrose immediately took in our mood and thoughtfully directed us to a place on Orange Avenue.

"Have a nice day," he said. Raising his eyebrows a micro-millimeter above usual, he went on about his own day without further comment in either words or body language, a remarkable display of delicacy from Ambrose, who could get as much ironic mileage out of a simple tilt of his head as most people could with caustic comments.

Mulligan and I walked through the brilliance of the morning, so different from the Puget Sound gray sky and green water. Here the water and sky reflected the same hot turquoise and the sun was already heating up the morning. "It is different here, isn't it?" I ventured. "Have you ever lived in this part of the world?"

"No. I've always been in the Northwest, except for a few years back East in college." I was too depressed to ask him where he went to college. Somehow we had traveled from intimacy into a bad first date.

The café Ambrose recommended turned out to be an old-fashioned place with jukeboxes at each table that were silent at this hour. We seemed to have come after most of the breakfast rush because the only other customers were a young man wearing a tuxedo jacket, white shirt, and tie over neatly pressed blue jeans, and his date, who wore a short silk party dress and high heels, although her face was scrubbed clean of makeup. Another morning-after couple. After we had ordered, a man in his 30s came in wearing running shorts and a T-shirt that read *"The Only Easy Day . . . Was Yesterday!"* The logo it framed showed an eagle wearing scuba gear and gripping an assault rifle.

I nudged Mulligan. "If that guy isn't a Navy SEAL, he's a serious wannabe," I whispered.

Mulligan managed a smile.

The breakfast was good and I perked up enough to ask Mulligan where he had walked. He said he'd gone along the marina, then over to the beach and watched the sun come up. "There's a ferry you can take to San Diego. If we were vacationing that would be something to do."

"Yeah." My heart rose a little at the prospect. I risked putting my hand on his and he held it for a moment, and then unexpectedly raised it to his lips and kissed the knuckles. The couple at the other table came out of their own morning glaze to stare but the guy in the *Yesterday* T-shirt never looked up from wolfing down a post-workout stack of pancakes.

"Come on, I'll walk you to your car," Mulligan said.

As we reached the parking lot at the hotel, I decided to show off Mrs. Madrone's Lexus. "Listen to this," I said. "The remote control is hooked into the alarm so it makes the most amazing sound." I whipped out the remote as we headed for the Lexus.

I pressed the button and a deafening explosion shattered the car's windows and rocked it on its tires. I jumped back against Mulligan who was already pulling me away from the hot slap of air and spatter of glass.

18

Come on! The gas tank could go!" Mulligan pulled me by the arm and I stumbled after him toward the hotel, still clutching the key chain with the small remote control on it. We headed for the front desk and met a stream of people rushing out to see what had caused the explosion.

"It's a car bomb. Call the police," Mulligan told Ambrose, who had materialized with amazing speed.

"The desk clerk is doing that," Ambrose said. "Is anyone hurt?"

"No one was near enough," I said, and we went into the lobby. I headed for the nearest chair, shaken to the core by the thought that I had been about to sit in the very seat that had exploded up through the roof of the car.

I sat and breathed deeply for a few minutes. Then I realized I needed to let Amy know she would have to get a ride elsewhere. There was a funeral about to start for Stewart Meade. I called her on my cell phone and when she answered I found I was so upset I was stammering. Once I managed to make myself understood, she gasped. "My God, Jo. You could have been in that car!"

"Believe me, Amy, that thought has occurred to me."

"Stewart dead. Dad kidnapped, now this. I wonder if it's all connected somehow."

"Have you heard from the kidnappers again?"

"Yes. They faxed Colleen a Polaroid picture of Dad holding today's *L.A. Times*. The police said it must have been taken after the first edition came out. Dad looked strained but okay. Actually . . ." She gave a little trill of hysterical laughter. "The way Dad is holding the paper, he's giving the finger to the camera."

"It sounds like they haven't broken his spirit." I was too shaken to laugh but it did sound like the admiral.

"Colleen also told them half a million dollars was unlikely and they should come up with a more reasonable demand because even raising a hundred thousand cash among the three of us would be hard. She's pushing to get more time. What did Mrs. Madrone say?"

"She said she'd talk to her advisors." A policeman was standing in the doorway of the office where I had gone to take the phone call. "I need to talk to this policeman now. I'm sorry I won't be able to drive you to the funeral, Amy. I'd still like to talk. Can we get together tonight?"

"It depends on where I get the ride. I'll call you later."

I made sure she had the cell phone number.

Mulligan and I were introduced to Inspector Walsh of the bomb squad, one of those red-haired men who start out with no lips and age as if they were turning to stone. Prying words out of him would never be easy but you could see he was a good listener. He had a concentration about him. It might have come from taking apart bombs, but you did get the feeling he was paying attention. Walsh took the remote from me and after putting it in a bag and noting the contents on a form, he handed it off to another officer with a few murmured instructions. Then he sat down and listened to what

Mulligan and I had to say. He asked us to stick around a little longer.

Mulligan and I sat in the lobby and watched as armored bomb squad members began picking up fragments from the roped-off part of the parking lot. There wasn't much to say, but we both understood what might have happened. Ambrose hustled past talking to one of Mrs. Madrone's security people. For a while, Mulligan and I just leaned against each other without the awkwardness that had arisen between us in the last few hours. For the moment, it was enough to be alive and unscathed. The physical contact brought comfort. We watched the police and the hotel staff go about their work. There weren't too many guests around because hardly any nonstaff members were lingering to look at the burned-out car and the bustling police. The staff went about their business without more than brief looks at the ruin in the parking lot and Mulligan and me sitting shell-shocked in the lobby. We probably could have gone up to the room, but neither of us suggested it.

One of the desk clerks said something to the manager about a couple of homeless veterans who had cut through the parking lot.

I looked up to ask how he could tell they were veterans but the manager beat me to it.

"I'm just guessing that they were veterans," the clerk said. "It seems like most everyone in this town is. These were disabled homeless guys in camouflage jackets with bottles of wine in bags."

"They were disabled—how could you tell they were homeless?" Mulligan asked

Both the clerk and the manager looked at him. "Wheelchair, crutches, shopping carts."

"You don't have to be a veteran to shop at the Army/

Navy surplus store," the manager said. "And we have to throw them out of the parking lot if they drink there, no matter what they're wearing."

Inspector Walsh came over just then and asked to talk to me alone. I followed him into the small meeting room the hotel had provided for the police.

"Are you sure you didn't see anything under the car when you approached it before it blew?" He asked again. Variations on this had been his favorite question in our first interview.

I shook my head. "Why?"

Walsh paused, then relented. "Looks like the device was attached on the driver's side to the undercarriage of the car."

"It never occurred to me to look under the car."

"Now that you've see the demonstration, maybe you will. Did you get the idea that you might easily have been in that car when it exploded?"

"Yes." My tone must have conveyed just how frequently I had been asked this question in the past few hours.

He smiled slightly. I realized that it was because he was happy to demonstrate where amateurs could be fooled. "Judging by the blast pattern, it was probably a shaped charge attached to the underside of the car by a magnetic plate right under the driver's side. These bombs are usually radio activated to blow up the driver's seat. But for some reason the frequency was set to the remote that deactivated your car alarm. That's not hard to find—most car alarms use the same frequency. Someone could have been killed by this bomb even if they weren't in the driver's seat. If you'd been closer, you could have been injured. But if you think about it you'd be pretty unlikely to be sitting in the car when you deactivated the alarm."

"Yes. That's true. That's what the remote is for."

"The other way to set off a bomb like this would be to use a different frequency and sit around waiting for you to get in the car, then push a button to set it off once you were settled. But they didn't do that."

A chill ran up my spine. It was hard to think, I felt as though I should be running and hiding. "So you're saying it's possible that the person who set the bomb was trying to scare me or warn me off somehow, and didn't aim to kill me."

"Well, it could have been a random bombing. Or else someone was watching you and knew what car you were driving. Have you noticed anyone following you lately?"

"Well, it's hard to keep track, there are so many." I tossed my head in a weak attempt at humor.

Walsh either didn't get the joke or he had already used up his smile of the day, it might even have been his smile of the week. "Who was the Hispanic man you spoke to yesterday in the courtyard of your hotel?"

Obviously, someone had been keeping track of my comings and goings. I told them who Fred Luna was, although I suspected they already knew. "Some of the hotel staff observed that Mr. Luna left when he saw your boyfriend, Mr. Mulligan. Do you think you might have antagonized Mr. Luna? Did anything happen that might have made him lose face?"

"Well, since I just met him a few days ago and it's the second time I've spoken to him, I doubt it." I could hear irritation creeping into my voice.

He leaned back and put his hands on the table. The hair on the back of them was still red. "Mr. Luna is a

highly decorated veteran, but he also has been arrested
several times for violent behavior, specifically when he
feels he's being challenged unfairly on account of his
race. You didn't reject him, uh, personally, did you?

"No," I said.

"Well, he does have a hot temper. Have you ever
heard of PTSD?"

"Uh—"

"Post-traumatic stress disorder."

"Okay, I have heard of that."

"I have not personally seen Mr. Luna's records but
official sources tell me he's been diagnosed with that.
I'd watch out for him, if I were you."

I nodded, but Walsh was starting to seriously piss me
off. After recent events, maybe I had a touch of PTSD
myself—of course, in my case it was more likely to be
PMS.

"My friends over in Homicide are a little jealous
since they've been wanting to talk to Mr. Luna and here
he is talking to you but not to us."

I could see why Fred wasn't eager to talk to the police. "He seemed very concerned about Admiral Rhymer."

"Let us know if he gets in touch again."

The interview was shorter than it might have been.
Walsh exchanged a few more words with Mulligan and
glanced back at me before he left. I got the feeling I
had been paroled into Mulligan's keeping. My cell
phone rang. It was Amy.

"Are you still stuck talking to the police?" she asked.

"No. I'm free. Where are you?"

"I'm at Martha Meade's house. Ivor dropped me at
the funeral and I came back here with Martha in the
limo afterward. Ivor went to pick up Stef. She's at

Ivor's mother's house in Laguna Beach. He said he could pick me up here later but I hate to leave Martha alone. The thing is . . ." She lowered her voice.

"Amy, I can't hear you, what did you say?"

"It's Brad," she hissed, a little louder this time. "He wasn't at the funeral. I thought he went back home but he's not answering his phone. If I could leave Martha I'd like to go check on him."

"Okay, Amy, maybe I can help." I turned to Mulligan. "I have to go to where Amy is."

"I'll drive you," he said. His face was unreadable.

"Thank you," I said, intensely relieved that he wasn't going to disappear on me just yet. I had half expected him to be on his way to the airport now. But the bomb had changed things. I just wasn't sure how. Into the receiver I said, "It looks like I have a driver. We'll be over as soon as we can." I got the directions from Amy.

Neither of us said much as we walked to the fringes of the parking lot where he had parked his rental car, a Thunderbird. I found myself stopping a healthy distance from it. Mulligan went up and examined it from all angles, squatting down to give the underside a very close look. He got up and shrugged and motioned for me to stay back while he put the key in the door and opened it. No explosion. I took a deep breath. Mulligan was now examining the interior of the car. He popped the hood and examined the engine. I came up to stand with him. "What are we looking for?" He gave an eloquent sigh, which I decided to ignore. "So I can do it on my own if I have to."

"That makes sense. New wires. Metal plates or cases that don't belong here. If something was wired to the ignition it would be over here. Nothing. Whoever put the bomb in your Lexus didn't go under the hood, though. Like Walsh said, he probably stopped to tie his shoe and slapped it up under the car and then kept walking. The bomb squad guys said it was a magnetic plate. There was no reason for anyone to have singled out my car unless they noticed we were together. But it never hurts to be careful."

Amy's directions took us to an exclusive neighborhood above a canyon where the iron gates guarded invisible houses behind stands of carefully nurtured trees.

"Why did the kidnappers take the admiral?" I said as we parked outside the wrought-iron gates. "They should have grabbed Meade."

"Maybe they meant to do that," Mulligan said. "In the heat of the moment things can get screwy. Maybe Meade made too much noise and they shut him up permanently."

"It did look as if he got knocked into the bathroom by accident. That inhaler next to his body was really weird. And there was that acrid smell I noticed. The police said they'd check on that too. But why not take Meade's body and pretend he was still alive? If she lives in this neighborhood, it looks like his wife could come up with a better ransom than the admiral's family."

Mulligan looked at me with amusement. "Maybe they didn't know he was dead, or he wasn't dead but he looked injured and they didn't want to deal with it. You can be a cold-blooded little thing sometimes."

Now I was amused. "You're the first person ever to call me a little thing. Now, cold-blooded, maybe that's been said before, though I can't recall it at the moment."

He smiled. "No offense meant."

"None taken." I couldn't help but smile back.

We walked up the drive. A Rolls-Royce and a flower delivery van were the only cars parked inside the gate, close to the front of the house, which had two wings, meeting at a little portico of a porch with white pillars and an ornate lantern framing the front door. The door opened before Mulligan or I could touch the bell.

The flower delivery man came out the door. He looked upset. I couldn't recall ever having seen a worried flower delivery person. He got in his delivery van and took off so fast he burned rubber.

19

Amy answered the doorbell and surprised me by hugging me as if we were long lost relatives. I patted her shoulderblades, wondering if Lance had been right about Amy having few friends. I introduced Mulligan, but before Amy could greet him, a hoarse female voice cried out from inside the house, "Who the hell is that?"

"Please come in, maybe you can help me. I've tried everything. You'd think I'd be better at this. . . ." she muttered, so low I could just barely catch the words.

Martha Meade was in her fifties with an artful blond streak through her auburn hair. She was so full breasted that she must have once had the snake-charming effect on the male population that Lani Luna had. I didn't doubt that she could still get picked up easily in the right bar in San Diego. The plunging neckline on the lavender blouse she wore with her black silk skirt would have aided in this endeavor.

She sat on the sofa with her feet propped up on a coffee table, displaying very high-heeled pumps dyed the exact shade of lavender as the blouse. As we entered, she was weaving back and forth in the chair, trying to put a lit cigarette in a holder.

Mulligan moved forward and crouched by her chair. He took the cigarette and holder from her, put them together, then handed them back to her, flinching only a little when she breathed smoke into his face and blinked purple-ringed eyes at him. "Who the hell are *you?*" she said in wonderment, nearly dropping her cigarette. She managed to hold on to it, though, and took a puff.

Mulligan moved out of range, correctly suspecting that a cloud of smoke would soon envelop him if he did not. "I'm a friend. You've had a rough day, Mrs. Meade, don't you think you need to rest?"

"Hell, no, it's a party for Stew. In his honor—you know, 'cause he's dead." She reached out for the tumbler conveniently located next to her feet on the coffee table and took a hearty swallow. "To Stew." She nearly fell off the sofa in the process but I had to give her points for being able to reach down to her toes. She was still pretty limber. She returned to staring at Mulligan and then she raised her gaze to me. "Who the hell are you?"

Amy moved in to explain. "These are my friends, Martha, they've come to pay their respects."

"The john is down the hall." She laughed at her own joke. "That's what Stew used to say when he wanted to use the john—pay his respects. He was so polite. And such a rat. A dead rat." She began to weep. Amy sat beside her and patted her shoulder and was totally ignored. A moment later Martha took another sip of liquor and examined us thoughtfully. "Who the hell are you?

Mulligan, Amy, and I moved a little away in the living room, where a table of food had been set up and glasses and ashtrays testified to the recent presence of other mourners.

"Doesn't it make you long for the days when the family doctor would give the grieving widow a shot and she'd be out for a few days?" I said ruefully.

"Actually, it makes me long for the days when the widow threw herself on the funeral pyre along with the husband's body," Amy said, startling me a little with her intensity. "Okay, I'm sorry. She's my dad's friend's widow. What can I do with her? I can't take her in. Ivor wouldn't even let Brad stay with us, and he's family. She's got no relatives that anyone can find and all her friends left as soon as they could. She's smoking like a chimney and there's a medicine cabinet full of prescription drugs upstairs. She's so drunk she could kill herself without knowing what the hell she was doing."

"Presuming she sobered up enough to walk."

"Well, she's been drinking like that for hours." Amy seemed distraught.

"She's right," Mulligan said thoughtfully, "sometimes drunk people are like sleepwalkers. They can cover an amazing amount of ground. She could also pass out at any moment with cigarette in hand and torch the place."

"Still, you can't baby-sit her forever," I said, pacing up and down a little. After all the sitting around this morning, I was feeling a little antsy.

"I hate this! It reminds me of Dad," Amy said with a sudden unaccustomed vehemence. It was so unusual that I realized how much anger she was pushing down and remembered how much I wanted to talk to her privately. This was not the time.

I put my hands in the pockets of the linen blazer and came up with a business card, and an inspiration. "Okay," I said, "let's call Lance and Ondine."

"Why?" Amy seemed puzzled. "No one is dying."

"No, but Meade is dead. They work with bereaved families, so Martha qualifies. More to the point, they are your friends and you need someone to sell you here."

"Okay," Amy said meekly. The phone was across the

room but it had a long cord and she took it into the
hall. I wondered if I was setting her up for another disappointment, and what the hell we'd do with Martha if
the Feathers said, "No." I could have called Ambrose,
but I was feeling a little awkward about asking Mrs.
Madrone for any favors.

But after a moment I heard her giving directions and
she came back into the room looking more surprised
than I was. "They were home. They're both coming."
She sat down and started to cry very quietly. I sat next
to her.

Mulligan went across the room and looked at some
golf trophies in a glass-fronted mahogany credenza.
Martha blinked at us, puffed on her cigarette, and recited her Who-the-hell-are-you mantra whenever she
happened to notice she had company.

It was a long half hour and I had memorized the
inscriptions on the golf trophies myself by the time Ondine and Lance rang the doorbell. I went to answer it
and tersely filled them in as they came down the hall.
They were a little surprised to see Mulligan, but Amy,
having recovered her composure, hugged both of them
and led them over to Martha, who looked up and amazingly said nothing.

Lance alighted beside her, his long limbs and knot
of pale hair making him look like an egret, folding
down long legs. Martha made eye contact with Lance
and remained miraculously silent.

"Ondine, I bet you'll find some coffee in the
kitchen," Lance said gently. "I think that's what's called
for at the moment."

Ondine paused in front of Martha and examined her
solemnly. "Your aura is very depleted. I think we can
clean it up, though." As if in afterthought she snared

the tumbler and bottle of whiskey from the coffee table
and proceeded out to the kitchen. As she passed me, she
gestured me to follow.

Once in the kitchen she put the whiskey on the
counter and turned back to me. "You'd better get Amy
out of here. She should just go home. This is not a time
for her to be taking care of other people." She turned
around to look for something to boil water in. I had my
orders and I was dismissed.

Back in the front room, Lance turned from where he
had taken Martha's hand, and added, "Martha needs to
talk and Ondine and I can listen. You're too close to
this, Amy. Call later. We'll still be here, if you want us
to, Martha. You do want us to stay for a while don't
you, Martha?"

Martha nodded, totally enthralled and either not noticing or not caring that her liquor had vanished. She
said in wondering tones, "You came! I thought you'd
never get here."

The smile Lance turned on us was more than a little
smug but I forgave him and thanked him sincerely. Mulligan and I took Amy out to the car.

20

"Did you ever hear the actual cause of death for Stewart Meade?" I asked Amy as Mulligan drove.

"One of the homicide detectives said it was a heart attack but his asthma was a contributing factor."

I thought of that acrid, stinging air in the cottage—whatever it was, it probably wasn't good for asthmatics. We reached Brad's apartment complex, which was a collection of pink and brown stucco boxes curving around a serpentine maze of parking areas. There were several battered-looking palm trees and some bushes with shiny leaves that had been unclipped long enough to lap around the buildings as if they might take over.

Amy led us through the maze of two-story units, past a swimming pool and back to the farthest row of apartments, crouched uncomfortably close to a freeway overpass. Amy knocked on the door of the end unit.

As she was about to knock again, the door opened a crack and a small face peered out. "Oh, hi." It was Amber, the young woman who had been targeted by the admiral at the party and showed up looking for her purse the next morning with Brad.

"I'm Brad's sister, Amy. Is he here?" Amy asked.

"Brad's not here, but you can come in. I remember you from the party." She opened the door and moved back to let us in. Her eyes settled on me and she smiled faintly.

"Amber, isn't it?" I asked, earning more looks from

Mulligan and Amy. "Well, Brad kept calling her that."

"You're the one who threw a drink on Brad's father."

Mulligan looked back at me in surprise. I'd forgotten to tell him about that. I shrugged. Things had been hectic. "I'm sorry to have missed this party," he said.

"Don't be," Amber said leading us into the room. She lazily stretched with the thoroughness of a cat who has just risen. Her T-shirt, which had just skimmed the tops of her thighs rose up to the point where it was possible to tell that she wore flowered bikini underwear and that she was a natural blond. The apartment was small, but sparsely furnished. An unmade sofa bed took up most of the floor space. A computer sat on a typing table in a far corner with a cheap printer next to it on a milk crate. A continuous roll of paper fed through the printer from a stack housed in the open side of the crate. The used sheets accordion-folded into a stack behind the printer. The pile was now slightly higher than the printer itself. A four-drawer, pinkish gray file cabinet sat next to the computer. The place of honor was given to a huge telescope, which was mounted facing the back window, although all that it could observe through that was the bushes that obscured the freeway overpass.

The only other furnishings in the studio apartment were a television on a chest of drawers at the foot of the sofa bed, and two metal, plastic-seated kitchen chairs pushed up to a built-in counter that separated the galley kitchen from the rest of the place. Posters papered the walls with scarcely an inch of space between them, star charts covered the ceilings. I would have guessed Brad would have science fiction posters. But these were NASA Ames Research Center photos of deep space, the Pleiades, Earthrise as seen from space and closer Landsat shots of the greater San Diego area from several miles up. The ones too far to read or un-labeled looked like galactic clusters or nebulae taken from large observatories.

"I called but no one answered the phone," Amy said accusingly.

"Has Brad been back since yesterday?" I asked Amber.

She sat on one of the chairs. "He ran in like he expected the police to be right on his tail. He took his camera but not the 'scope."

"Where did he go?" Amy asked, a little harshly. She stood wavering over Amber as if to fall on her and choke some information out of her. The funeral and several hours with Martha seemed to have exhausted the last of her self-control.

Mulligan saw it and pulled out the other kitchen chair for Amy. He tapped her on the shoulder and Amy took a deep breath and moved back to sit a safe distance on the chair at the other end of the counter from Amber. Mulligan leaned on the breakfast bar between the two women while I perched on the arm of the sofa bed a few feet away.

Amber regarded us all placidly without saying anything. I refrained from asking if she had forgotten the question. After a few more seconds, I asked, "Who is it you think Brad is going to meet?"

"I think he's going to meet *Them* and he wouldn't take me," she said a little petulantly.

"Them—who?" I asked, throwing grammar to the winds.

"Who or what?" Amber pushed out her lip, still sulking a little. "You'll just think I'm crazy, so what's the point?"

"It might help us find Brad," I said. "Who did he go to meet?"

"They're aliens." She whispered, as if afraid of the word. "They could have taken Brad's father."

I couldn't help but ask, "Illegal aliens? Kidnap a U.S. Navy admiral? Don't they have enough trouble dodging the INS?" No one laughed—the curse of an overactive sense of humor. Some jokes are not going to work. You have to be an incurable risk taker to keep trying.

Amber was certainly not amused. "No. Not that kind of aliens. They're not from this world."

Mulligan asked gently, "Have you ever seen them?"

"No," she said a little wistfully, "but whoever They are They're paying Brad in hundred-dollar bills."

"How often does that happen?" I was curious. Aliens with cash. That was a new concept.

"Every few weeks."

I looked at Mulligan. Hundred-dollar bills are popular among various illegal communities including drug dealers, gunrunners and spies. "Does he take something with him to sell to them?"

"No. He has all his information in the files here."

I looked at the file cabinet next to the computer and wondered if it was locked.

"I think they're buying his silence," Amber concluded.

"What makes you think that?" I asked.

"Some guy called and talked to Brad about the military takeover of the U.S. government," she said with a matter-of-fact tone. "I don't know much more than that. He said it started before we were born."

Mulligan coughed, which might have masked a chuckle.

"Actually, some people said there was a faction in

the military that wanted a takeover during the Watergate crisis. In 1973," Amy broke in authoritatively.

We all turned and stared at her. She shrugged. "I was an American history major. Our dad was at the Pentagon around that time. I thought maybe he might talk to me if I studied up on history he was a part of." She shrugged again. "Of course, he ignored me. Mom liked it. She was hoping I'd become a teacher because she thought I'd never be able to get married. Anyway, there were rumors of some military officers planning a takeover back then, I could cite you several books. . . ."

I was curious. "So did you ever talk to your father about it?"

Amy shook her head wearily. "He walks away whenever I try to talk to him about serious things. I did learn one thing, though. I finally got that to him I was just a broodmare to give him grandsons. You don't have conversations with your livestock." Her face was tense and pale under the fading sunburn.

"Don't you see? It's not over," Amber said seriously. We all turned back to look at her. "They may have been working through the military. They might have kidnapped Brad's father. They're the ones who were behind the military plot to take over the government. Like she said." Amber nodded toward Amy.

Mulligan patted me on the shoulder. "I think I've got it, Jo. The same aliens who might be trying to take over the government might have kidnapped the admiral."

"Yes. That's it." Amber said.

"Actually, I kind of like the idea of the admiral being abducted by space aliens," I said grudgingly, warming to the thought.

Amy began to laugh almost hysterically. We all turned to look at her. I confess I can seldom resist mak-

ing a joke, but this was not the reaction I was after. I
went to get her a glass of water. I found a clean jelly
glass in the dish drainer next to the sink and ran the tap
for a minute, then brought her half a glassful.

"Take a deep breath, Amy," I said, putting the glass
in front of her. "What is it?"

"Oh." She breathed and took a sip of water. Then
another deep breath. "I don't really want anything bad
to happen to my father. I hope and pray that he's okay.
But when I was growing up, he was away so much.
Every time he was gone, I would try so hard to win his
approval. But like Brad said, his motto was 'Good
enough is not good enough.' Nothing I ever did even
came close. Finally, I just wished he would stay gone.
Kidnapped by space aliens would have been good. Now
it's almost as if my childhood fantasy came true. It's
horrible. He'll only treat me like dirt again—but I want
him back." Her voice wavered, on the verge of tears.

Amber tapped me on the shoulder. It was easy to
ignore her in her own living room. "I know you think
I'm crazy. But Brad was meeting with a reporter from
the *Interrogator*. The man's name was Jerry Buck."

"The *Weekly Interrogator*? The supermarket tabloid?"

"Yes," she said with a triumphant smile as if that
proved a major point. "You just try proving that their
stories are false."

It was time to go. "Amber, you said you haven't seen
these aliens. Has Brad actually met them?"

"No. Brad came close, but never when I was with
him. He's on their track, though."

"Have you or the police or anyone looked at his
files?" I asked Amber, as Mulligan stood by the door,
clearly ready to go. I wanted a crack at that file cabinet.

Amber looked at me, wide-eyed. "You mean, his X-files?"

"Or his A-through-W files, whatever he's got. They might give us some idea where to find him. Is it locked?"

Amber just looked at me. No one said anything. I pulled open the top drawer. It slid open easily. The files in the top drawer were labeled Top Secret.

I didn't realize Amy had come to look over my shoulder till I heard her gasp. "Could those be the files from Dad's safe?"

I shook my head. "Unlikely, though anything is possible. These probably aren't really classified. Someone has just written Top Secret on top with a felt-tip pen. Anyone can do that." I put the folder on top of the cabinet though. The rest of the drawer space was taken up by printouts filed by date of what looked like some kind of Internet news-group collection of postings on UFO matters. I glanced at the stack behind the computer and saw they were similar. "Okay. Thanks. Are you ready to go, Amy?"

She nodded.

"If Brad calls or shows up, tell him we need to talk to him." I left a card with my cell phone and the 800 number. As we left, I casually took the files from the top of the file cabinet.

"I hope he comes back," Amber said softly. I turned back to look at her, surprised by her plaintive tone. She had no interest whatsoever in the files. She was resting her chin on her bent knee. Unlike Leilani Luna, there was nothing deliberately provocative about the pose. Amber seemed to be totally unaware of the effect her attire might have on anyone watching. "Brad used to take me to the desert to look at the skies," she said. "He showed me Saturn and all its rings through the telescope. It looked just like it does in cartoons."

As I closed the door I looked back at Amber sitting, staring forlornly at the table, her knees tucked up to her chin and her arms wrapped around them. No one said anything by way of farewell. We walked to the car and I looked at the freeway looming over the apartment complex. "It must be love to live in a place like that with someone," I said. I wasn't really expecting a response and I didn't get one.

Amy seemed to have surrendered to fatigue. She hardly spoke except to direct Mulligan to her house with only an occasional sniffle to remind us that she had been nearly hysterical.

"Do you think Brad believes invaders from outer space are plotting to take over the government?" I asked.

"Well." She sniffed again. "I think he wants attention. If he's got a *Weekly Interrogator* reporter listening to him, that's big-time. That could be where he's getting the money. I've heard they pay for stories."

"We might be able to track down this reporter," I said thoughtfully. "If he is a real reporter."

We dropped Amy off and got directions to the university where Stef would be playing in a chess tournament starting on Friday night.

Mulligan and I found a burrito place on the drive back to the hotel. Somehow with all the excitement we had never got round to lunch and it had been nearly ten hours since we ate breakfast. I was impressed that Mulligan had two burritos. One with a hearty helping of guacamole and sour cream left me happily full. We got to the hotel.

I didn't know what Mulligan's inclination was for the

rest of the evening. An anxious feeling that had nothing to do with the burrito started to build in the pit of my stomach as we entered the hotel room. But once we were inside all I could do was stand and stare. A gentle breeze was ruffling the curtains that framed the sliding door to the deck. The door was wide open and Raoul was nowhere in sight.

(21)

We spent the next hour searching first the hotel room and the small terrace, then every bush, alcove, and ledge in the hotel's inner courtyard. The hotel staff was sympathetic, particularly since I worked for the owner, Mrs. Madrone. But there was no sign of the cat. Mulligan and I searched the outside hotel grounds and then the exterior parking lot where the bomb-damaged area was still closed off, although the area was now deserted, with the hotel security guards keeping a watchful eye. I spent some time in each place standing very still near places where I thought he might have hidden, and talking very softly. I didn't want to scare him with a loud "Kitty, kitty." A few people on the street gave us odd looks, but we saw not a whisker's trace of Raoul. Mulligan was totally silent during this exercise.

At last we went back to the room. We both sat on the sofa and looked at the glass-topped coffee table in front of it.

"Wine?" Mulligan went to the fridge.

"Okay."

He brought out the bottle of white wine he had brought with him. "What a day," he said, handing me a glass and sitting down next to me. He put the bottle on the table.

"It's all the traffic that bothers me," I said, taking the glass and downing most of it. "God, I'm thirsty. Must be the chips and salsa."

"Jo, remember that Raoul is not a stupid cat. He's used to Nina's backyard, he has some street smarts. Maybe he just doesn't feel like coming in yet. He's probably hiding in a bush down in the courtyard."

"That's what Nina told me. Once or twice when I stayed with her, Raoul would be out late and she said that a so-called lost cat is usually very near to you but he hasn't decided to make his presence known, whether he's scared or just not interested in making contact."

"Yeah. That sounds like Nina," Mulligan said, but he smiled reminiscently.

I wanted to lay my head on his chest but I was afraid to touch him. "I feel so awful. He was Nina's cat. If he's out there and hurt or gone for good . . ." I didn't have to finish the sentence—I cursed myself for starting it.

"Don't worry. Nina was probably right about cats. She was usually right."

There was no answer to that one. We sat in silence for what seemed forever. I didn't think I was going to finish the glass of wine and I realized that I was going to have to sleep soon and I didn't know what to say to Mulligan. If it could have been like the night before, I wanted him in bed with me, but not if we were going to huddle on opposite edges, pained rather than comforted by each other's touch.

I took a deep breath to ask what next, when a blood-curdling scream assaulted our ears. I bolted up and nearly ran into Mulligan, who was already on his feet. The sound faded. Then another, louder, anguished wail came again. It came from the courtyard below. Crowding out onto the deck, Mulligan and I could see them. Next to a trickling fountain, two cats faced off, the light from the lanterns painting their shadows huge on the

brick pathways and tile walls. Tails fluffed up and ears
mashed back. One was Mrs. Madrone's Siamese,
Prince. The other . . .

"Oh, my God, it's Raoul!" I yelled. Mulligan followed me to the door. We took the stairs rather than
wait for an elevator.

As we emerged from the stairwell into the lobby we
saw the night clerk, who wore a bow tie with his striped
shirt, even at this hour. He was hovering around the
door that opened from the glassed-in lounge area onto
the courtyard.

An elevator opened and Ambrose came out wrapped
in a sumptuous silk robe. He was pulling on a pair of
elbow-length leather gauntlets and carrying a thin
leather lead. "Good evening," he said dryly. "Prince's."
Indicating the leash with an expert flip. "He travels with
more luggage than I do."

"Mrs. Madrone said he was leash trained." I remembered as the three of us went single file through the
door.

"Ha!" Ambrose remarked. "The leash clips onto his
little harness for insurance. The motorcycle gloves are
so he won't claw me to ribbons or get away when he
turns into a pretzel. The damn cat is double jointed."
The cat screams were much louder bouncing off the
walls of the courtyard. The manager was wringing his
hands as we pushed past him. When he saw Ambrose
the look of mingled gratitude and admiration on his face
was so clear that for a moment I thought he would kiss
him, or perhaps use that excuse to kiss him.

Prince yodeled with a high-pitched scream that was
eerily like that of a shrieking infant. He appeared to be
advancing on Raoul, who was crouched with all of his
long gray hair puffed up to a formidable maximum ef-

fect, and growling like an outboard motor.

Ambrose strode into the area while they were still a few feet apart, adjusting his gloves with the precision of a surgeon or a matador. I felt underequipped, but watched him snatch the snarling Siamese up in both gloved hands by harness and the scruff of his neck.

Mulligan approached Raoul from one side and I took advantage of the cat's hesitation to grip the scruff of his neck, haul him up, and wrap my arm around him. He immediately sank all the claws on all four feet through my clothes and into my flesh. Miraculously, he did not bite me. Mulligan took over the scruff of his neck so that I could put both arms around Raoul, clutching him tightly like a porcupine pillow. After a heartrending moment of suspense, he held still, clinging to me, but not trying to rip his way to freedom. Raoul kept up a guttural, vicious growling, without stopping. Up ahead in Ambrose's firm grip, Prince was bucking and twisting and snarling to get at Raoul.

Over the background music of feline obscenities, I called out, "Let's take separate elevators going up, okay, Ambrose?"

"If you say so."

Lupe met us at the elevator with huge towels. I watched Ambrose deftly fold one around Prince into an improvised straitjacket. "You've got this down to a science."

"After the first five or ten times, that happens."

Lupe came over and offered us a towel, murmuring soothingly something about *pobrecito* to Raoul, who flattened his ears and spat at all of us. Mulligan helped maneuver Raoul into the towel, keeping a steady grip on his neck while I slowly disengaged his claws from my flesh. We wrapped him up, looking even more like a wet owl, for the trip back to the room. Mulligan held him close against his chest and we both talked gently to him. He blinked irritably, but stopped growling the minute the elevator doors closed and he could no longer see Prince. Once inside the room, Mulligan set the bundle on the floor and I raced to close the terrace door. Raoul rolled out of the towel onto his feet and made an immediate beeline for the terrace. I slid the door closed an instant before he got there. All three of us took a deep breath.

The phone rang. It was Ambrose. "You all squared away? Terrace door closed?"

"Yes. How about you and Prince?"

He cleared his throat. "Safe and sound. Since I've got you on the line, do you think Mulligan could spare you between seven and eight o'clock tomorrow morning?"

"I'm sure that will be okay."

I hung up the phone and looked at Raoul, who was hunkered down just inside the sliding door, nose twitching, patient and lethal, his round orange eyes bent on escape and combat. I knelt down beside him for a moment but he shot me a baleful glare and hissed in eloquent frustration. He hadn't forgiven us for removing him from the field of battle, and he was still preoccupied with finding his way back out to reengage the foe.

I looked at Mulligan and we both smiled. We each had another glass of wine and sat in the front room talking companionably about our recent adventure until the wine overtook the adrenaline.

"I should sleep on the sofa here," Mulligan said at last.

"I'll get you a blanket and pillow," I said.

22

The alarm woke me the next morning to a quiet hotel room. The blanket was folded on top of the pillow on the sofa and Raoul was sitting on it as if guarding it. He seemed to have forgiven me for breaking up his brawl the night before, but watched with only mild interest as I heated water for half a cup of coffee. An empty bowl with milk droplets around the edge and another bowl with a few pellets of dry cat food testified to an ample kitty breakfast. A note from Mulligan told me he would be back in a few hours.

When I sat next to Raoul on the sofa, he curled up into the kind of total relaxed cat nap that I envy so much. After half an hour of looking at Brad's folder, I put the files in my briefcase and went to meet Ambrose.

I wasn't surprised that Ambrose knew a café with outside tables and a glimpse of the sprawling old Victorian Hotel del Coronado. Several of the more modern buildings made gestures in imitation of the red-brown gables but without its witches' cap turrets and air of old-fashioned beachfront elegance. Such was the power of Southern California that I couldn't see the hotel without thinking about the movie *Some Like It Hot* being filmed there. When we were seated in the mild early morning sunshine, I consumed a blueberry muffin and café latte, Ambrose raisin scones and hot tea. When the dishes had been put aside and the beverages safely sidelined, Ambrose brought out a folder from his briefcase and I traded him for the stack of folders from Brad's file cabinet.

He finished his first and waited, politely gazing at the old hotel and the yacht harbor across from it until I had skimmed the ones he gave me. I took out a notebook to write down a few things. Asking Ambrose for the same information twice was risky.

"I've been looking into the Russo family a little more closely, as you can see from the folder there," Ambrose said.

"It's sad." Ivor Russo, for all his professorial status, was not doing well in the academic jungle. He had lost two part-time teaching jobs over the past few years due to faculty cuts, and his most recent job was shaky. Amy's job at the Feather Heart Project brought in a small amount but not enough to stave off the family cash-flow crisis. The previous summer, when Ivor hadn't found summer school teaching work, the Russos' second car had been repossessed.

I closed the file. "Reading bad credit reports on people I've started to like is not my idea of how to start the day."

"Then you won't want to see the reports I'm getting from the rest of the family. When Admiral Rhymer was at the Pentagon his influence helped Dwight both directly and indirectly. But since the admiral's retirement, the navy has passed Dwight over once for promotion. You know how that works?"

"Pass him over a second time and they bounce him out automatically. The admiral must have been upset with him."

"The rumor about Dwight is that his staff feels sorry for him. He should have left a long time ago, but according to a certain member of his staff he's an example of the Peter Principle in action—poor lad, promoted above his level of competence." Ambrose shook his head and I wondered if this gossip came from a gay mafia that the navy would like to pretend does not exist. "Poor Dwight comes in every morning early. Not to work but to sit and read his Bible and pray. My informant seems to feel that he would be better off spending that time job hunting. The navy wants him out. It's just a matter of time."

"He did look pretty tense. He seemed capable enough, so far as I could tell. All I can say is, I liked his wife."

"Colleen." Ambrose checked his file. "The realtor who got the ransom call at work and told them the family wasn't paying?"

"I can relate to her sense of humor."

"Whether she's a joker or a hard bargainer, she might have just managed to get her father-in-law killed."

"Brad and Amy were suggesting that Dwight and Colleen might have kidnapped him just to dry him out. They were kidding—I think. But it can't be fun for a religious man having a one-man Tailhook Convention in your guest cottage."

"What was he doing in their guest cottage anyway?"

"His house burned down and he's rebuilding it."

Now Ambrose took out a fountain pen and made a note in a small leather notebook. "Interesting. Tell me more."

"All I heard is that his house in San Marcos burned down and they're not finished rebuilding. I imagine it must have burned during the last fire season."

"Last fire season. Hmm. Do you think the fire has anything to do with the kidnapping?"

"Well, it got him into the cottage on Dwight and Colleen's property, within easy reach."

Ambrose tapped his folders. "All his kids need money. Any one or two of them might have done it. However, I must say that young Brad—" He pushed the file back toward me across the table and I took it, swapping him for Brad's manila folders. "No doubt he wrote Secret all over the folders so no one would find out what an idiot he is."

"Why not just lock the file cabinet?"

Ambrose snorted. "Maybe he screwed that up too—lost the key or never had one. If he did kidnap his father, Stewart Meade's death might be just another screwup. I still haven't found out what he does for a living."

"Amber said he gets paid in hundred-dollar bills."

Ambrose noted that without comment.

"Did you hear anything about what Meade died of? Amy said they told her it was a heart attack, but his asthma may have contributed." I wondered how far Ambrose's connections went. "There was this odd acrid smell in the room. It made my eyes water."

Ambrose nodded. "Tear gas." He thumbed through his notes. "They found residue."

"You couldn't have seen the police report."

"Of course not. The police report hasn't even been filed yet. I have a few connections, though." Ambrose smiled at his own efficiency. "The tear gas would probably account for how they overcame those two men."

"Admiral Rhymer was probably passed out." I told him about the drugs in the liquor.

"Hmm, I didn't hear about that," Ambrose said with a frown, never happy when his information was incomplete. "That may be a flaw in my source. But it would mean that they would only have had to deal with Meade.

Maybe they didn't know he was asthmatic. They put the inhaler next to him but it was too late."

"Wow." I didn't know what to make of the information.

Ambrose nodded and read from the last page of his own notes. "Who's this Jerry Buck person from Brad's files?"

"A reporter for the *Weekly Interrogator*. As you can see, Brad's records of his calls from this Buck person are sketchy. Brad's girlfriend, Amber, said that Buck seems to be looking into evidence of a possible attempt at taking over the U.S. government in 1973, during the Watergate crisis. Not a *Weekly Interrogator* kind of story."

Ambrose tapped the file again. "What's Brad got to do with that?"

"The only connection I can get is that his father was on the fast track at the Pentagon those days."

Ambrose raised his copper-colored eyebrows, but made no comment.

"We discussed all this at his apartment with his girl-friend, so it might have lost something in translation."

Ambrose said nothing but waited for more details. "Amber suggested that aliens kidnapped the admiral."

"Illegal aliens? Aren't they seriously overworked just making a living?"

I looked at Ambrose strangely. "I said the same thing. We must be starting to think alike, Ambrose."

"I'll take that as a compliment if you will."

"Fair enough." We both smiled. Ambrose's warm side was much closer to the surface than I'd realized during the first several months I'd known him. "Amber thinks extraterrestrials might have taken the admiral." I told him what Amy had said after she stopped laughing.

"Well, she may have got her wish—the old man may not be coming back. What if she's not as shy and retiring as she looks? If she and Ivor kidnapped him and get their hands on a million dollars, they'll be able to stay away from all their relatives for a long time. You finished with those?"

I glanced through the Russo files and made a last few notes before handing them back.

"Anything more on Lance and Ondine Feather?"

"Only that they were military brats like everyone else in this town. Ondine lived here until Lance got out of the navy, then she went back East to take care of Lance."

"To take care of him? Was he sick?"

"In a manner of speaking. Lance and Martha Meade have something in common. They were both in attendance at the Blue Ridge Institute in 1996."

"Huh?"

"The Blue Ridge Institute is a sort of East Coast Betty Ford Center in Virginia. Lots of Washington-based substance abusers wind up there."

"You're kidding," I said, knowing he wasn't. "Martha did seem to know Lance. She was dead drunk when he showed up, she greeted him like a long-lost boy-friend."

"Maybe not so long lost."

"Except that it was my idea to call Lance."

"What made you decide to do that?"

"He gave me his card when I visited them, told me to call if I needed anything."

"Well, if they were in league with Martha Meade, they couldn't have counted on you calling them, but Lance did make it easy for you."

"How did you find out all this stuff, Ambrose?" I

stared at him in mingled admiration and dread. "Aren't those clinic records supposed to be confidential?"

"That's the theory. But when an institution is interested in getting a charitable grant that will make a substantial difference in their operations, they can be remarkably forthcoming to the right sort of tactful inquiry."

"Remind me never to try to hide anything from you."

"You can always try," Ambrose said, leaning back and crossing his extraordinarily long legs.

"What about Lance and Ondine's irregular dealings in Arizona? Have you found anything there?"

"No hard evidence. They seem to have spent some quality time with some reasonably wealthy sick people who then died and left them generous bequests. The relatives who would have otherwise gotten the money kicked. But in each case the sums involved weren't worth the lawyer's fees to sue. So if the Feathers are crooked they aren't greedy."

"Or they haven't been lucky enough to meet the right sick people for their purposes." I hated to give up the Feathers as suspects, but they did seem like long shots.

"In all fairness, I have to say I haven't been able to dig up any proof that they've ever helped their clients into the next world."

"So kidnapping and murder would be a new pattern for them?"

"So far as we know." We sat watching the ocean for a little while, then Ambrose put all his papers away. "Did you know that Mrs. Madrone is giving the kidnappers the million? Or part of it, her hostage negotiators got them to settle for less," Ambrose said mournfully.

"Really?" I was surprised.

He nodded.

"When?"

"She's done it already. Now they're waiting for the kidnappers to set a time and place." He looked at me as if suspecting I might know more than I was saying.

"Why would she do this for the Rhymers?"

"Well, she doesn't confide in me. Of course, there's her friendship with Sally Rhymer. But above and beyond that, I get the impression there was something back in their youth that makes her care more than most people whether Ronald Rhymer lives or dies."

"Yuck. Sorry. Do you really think she likes that man? I couldn't stand him. The idea of him having anything to do with Mrs. Madrone makes me cringe."

Ambrose laughed. "Maybe he was more attractive as a young man."

"Sorry. Mrs. Madrone has such penetrating insight and Admiral Ronald Rhymer . . ." I was lost for words.

Ambrose persisted. "If you'd seen him when he was Commander Rhymer back in the sixties you might not have felt that way. He was a navy pilot in Vietnam. The right stuff, and all that."

"Right, right. Macho forever. Big brass balls."

Ambrose doubled over in a sudden fit of laughter that continued until his face grew redder than his hair. I sat back and watched a little mystified, because it hadn't seemed that funny to me. I hoped it wasn't like Amy's hysterical outburst.

Eventually he removed a sparkling white handkerchief from his pocket and mopped his face with it. "Don't say that to Mrs. Madrone," he said a little breathlessly.

"Geez, I'd never do that. Give me some credit."

"No. Of course you wouldn't." He rubbed his eyes

and took a deep breath. "I think this place is getting to me—San Diego, Coronado, navy SEALS, fighter pilots. The testosterone level is way too high. Honestly, I'm a great fan of that substance in the properly measured doses."

He lowered his voice even though there was no one in earshot, this was more top secret than all the potentially classified matters we'd been skating around. "Alicia Perrin was a lively young woman in the late fifties and early sixties. She didn't marry Paul Madrone till 1964. Ron and Sally Rhymer married in '61. I'm not going to speculate about anything, but the Rhymer family means a lot to Mrs. Madrone."

Something he said gave me a terrible twinge of fear. "Ambrose. I don't like to even think this but we have to consider it."

"So now you're going to make me consider it? All right. Go ahead."

"If something happened between Ron Rhymer and Mrs.—well, Alicia Perrin, back then? Do you think Sally Rhymer could have found out about it and be blackmailing her old friend, even if it's just emotionally?"

Ambrose fastened his briefcase and made ready to go. "My first duty will always be to protect Mrs. Madrone. I'll keep my eyes open." Ambrose was always security conscious. Another thing we had in common was growing up with fathers in the intelligence community—which had guaranteed growing up as civilian outsiders on military bases and living around secret information without being privy to any of it.

"Do you think you'll be able to find out when they hand over the ransom?" I asked.

"Jo, you must not go anywhere near that family.

They're all going to be very closely watched."

"Just curious."

"Well, I don't have extra time to go bailing you out of jail just now. Stay out of the way."

I nodded and Ambrose took the check. "Watch out for those power-mad space aliens. I'll let you know if I find that Jerry Buck, boy reporter."

23

When I reached the room I found Mulligan sitting on the terrace with a glass of orange juice on the wrought-iron table in front of him and Raoul lounging contentedly in his lap.

"Did you get breakfast?" I asked, a little reluctantly, since the generous muffin and double latte had filled me up.

"Yeah. You get something?"

"Yes."

I sat on the chair next to him and Raoul seized the moment of distraction to squirm away and head for the balcony railing. I sprang up to retrieve him and sat down with a firm grip on his thick neck ruff.

"I'm worried that he might get away to start another fight with Prince," I explained. "Would you mind if we went inside or at least put him inside?"

Mulligan led the way back in and closed the terrace door. I put Raoul down and he settled into a crouch with his eyes on the slice of space between the sliding door and the frame.

Mulligan sat on the sofa and I sat beside him. He put his arm around me, but I was so much expecting bad news that I just looked at him.

"I have to go," he said. "This is just too much for both of us. I think I've been trying to hide from the pain of losing Nina. I need to go back to Seattle."

"Okay." I didn't know what else to say.

"The thing is, I hate to leave you in the middle of all this."

"It's almost over," I said, though I wasn't sure that was true. After the roller coaster we had been on lately, I realized I expected him to say something much worse than that—though I wasn't quite sure what. I was almost relieved. "I do understand. You need to sort things out. I should too. I'll probably take some time off when this assignment is over."

"Josie. There's another thing."

My heart contracted again. "What?"

"It's Raoul. I want to take him back to Seattle. I think we owe it to Nina to take better care of him than you can here."

I looked over at Raoul who seemed to feel my eyes and glanced back at me before returning to staring at the terrace door.

I thought about it. "It's just a few more days."

Mulligan looked at the rug rather than meet my eyes. "But then where are you going? Raoul is the king in the backyard of the building. That's his turf. If you'd open up Nina's old apartment, he could stay in there."

I sighed, feeling horribly selfish, but I just couldn't agree. "I know what you mean. I will be there in a few days, we'll figure out something. I just don't know what. I don't want to put him in there alone."

"Well, it's your decision. I could stay in Nina's apartment with the cat. I realize that you inherited the place and the logical thing would be for you to move into Nina's apartment, but until you do—"

"You're saying you don't mind staying there?"

"I'd stay there temporarily, or I'd rent it myself if you wanted me there."

I looked at him totally confused. "Wouldn't it bother you that she was killed there?"

"I also have good memories of Nina there. Look, Jo, I'm not trying to tell you what to do. But you're the one who told me cats need someone every day. Nina loved that cat, she would have wanted him taken care of properly."

"I agree with you, but I can't let go of the cat, or the apartment just now."

"I'd be happy to have him stay in my place till you get back to Seattle. That way he could go out in the backyard. He can't enjoy being cooped up here, waiting for you to come back from a day of running around."

"You live in the basement with no windows. I don't see where being stuck in your apartment waiting for you to come home would be much different. Look, it's only another week or so, I kind of need him."

"Okay. But if anything happens to him . . ." Mulligan stood up. "I've got to pack."

I followed him into the bedroom, sat on the corner of the bed and watched in silence while Mulligan put his clothes into a duffel bag. Raoul followed us in and leaped up and settled beside me, purring when I started to massage the back of his neck. I felt like crying. Mulligan didn't seem angry or tortured the way he had been in the depth of that first night. But we were disagreeing and it gave me a sinking feeling. I felt as if there should have been one of those instructional public address system announcements, "This will conclude the intimacy portion of your relationship. You may now return to fighting about the cat." I knew I was being selfish, and the cat would probably have preferred Mulligan's plan. But I couldn't part from him. It was bad enough losing Mulligan.

Mulligan zipped up the duffel bag, put it on the floor, and sat next to me on the bed. He took my hand and held it. "Let's try to get through this without hurting each other, okay?" he said.

"Sure." I barely trusted myself to speak.

He leaned over and kissed me briefly on the lips, gave Raoul one last pat, and then he was gone.

Raoul and I were alone again. After Mulligan left he went to crouch by the sliding door. There were too many unsorted feelings stacked up inside for me to begin to process them, so I pulled out my laptop computer and attacked the reports.

The first concerned whether to renew the grant to Magda. It seemed an easy decision until I started to think about how Helen had given up everything, including the job I was enjoying so much, just to be with Magda. Sacrificing for love was a touchy subject. I kept the report down to a factual description of Magda's art and the impact the grant had had on it. Helen's report had been glowing. I had to add that I found Magda's statues compelling.

Something about the arrangement nagged at me and I had to put the report aside, unfinished.

The preliminary report on Amy's situation made me wonder how she was doing. I didn't seriously suspect her of kidnapping her father and certainly not of killing Steward Meade, but I couldn't help worrying about her. I put that report aside and dialed her number.

She answered on the first ring, breathless. I asked how she was.

"Good. I can't talk, we're expecting an important call."

"Just one question about Stef's tournament tomorrow

night, do you have the number of whoever is in charge?"

"I'm looking it up. I should warn you, if you don't play, those tournaments can go on longer than you would ever imagine possible." She gave me the number of Ernesto Garcia, the tournament director, a retired businessman originally from Cuba. Then she said, "I've got to keep the line clear."

"Don't take any unnecessary chances," I said. But she had already hung up. I called Ernesto Garcia, who assured me that spectators were welcome as long as they respected the need for quiet, and described the site in some detail, including directions.

I hung up and sat a moment, thinking about the previous day with Amy. That reminded me that I had last left Lance and Ondine Feather in charge of Martha Meade.

Ondine answered when I dialed Martha Meade's number. I started out with a half-hearted apology. "I didn't mean to rope you and Lance into a marathon widow-sitting operation."

"It's okay, Jo." Ondine sounded as placid as ever. "Martha needs some help now and she has no one. Lance and I forwarded the phones over here. How's Amy?"

"I just talked to her and she sounded okay, but pretty busy." It didn't seem prudent to mention the ransom money situation, but I listened carefully for any sign that Ondine might know about it. "I take it Amy didn't call."

"No." Ondine didn't sound troubled or worried.

"I hope this isn't destroying your schedule, Ondine. I mean, you must have other clients."

"Don't worry about it. Lance is doing his usual er-

rands and speaking engagements. I'm just staying here
with Martha instead of staying home. If any calls come
in who need hand-holding like Amy was doing, we'll
just refer them elsewhere."

"So how is Martha doing?"

"Much better."

But not well enough to answer her own phone. I
asked if I could drop by later and Ondine agreed cheerfully. But, much as I wanted to avoid it, I kept having
this urge to drive by Amy's house and see if she was
going off to deliver ransom money. There was no ra-
tional reason why I should, but I told myself I had to
go out for dinner anyway, promised to bring back some
seafood for Raoul, then stopped at the doorway, realizing that with the Lexus destroyed, I didn't have a car
to drive. I consulted the Yellow Pages and an hour later
I was driving a white Subaru. The time for fitting in
with upscale cars was past. I turned into a mall looking
for a seafood restaurant and found a plus-sized clothing
store instead. That gave me the excuse I'd been looking
for to buy some lightweight cotton shorts and even a
cotton gauze skirt and blouse in the pale pastels that
everyone seemed to favor here. I was in a more cheerful
mood when I left the mall.

That mood evaporated when I cruised near the intersection a block from where Amy and Ivor Russo lived
and I was pulled over by a San Diego police car. I half
expected to be given some official excuse and turned
back, but the officer leaned in the window and asked if
I was Josephine Fuller. He seemed to know the answer
to that question already. So either someone was following me unobtrusively or they already knew my new
rental car. He politely asked if I would follow him, and
he got into his patrol car and led the way to the gates

of the navy base. He showed me where to park and drove off. A moment later a stocky figure got out of a Mercedes parked a few cars away.

I recognized him even before he removed his hat and motioned me out of the car. He was the bald African American who had been making himself a sandwich at the admiral's party. He had seemed wordlessly, efficiently sympathetic so I was inclined to give him the benefit of the doubt. I got out of the Subaru and walked over to where he stood beside his Mercedes.

"I'm Admiral Coffin, Ms. Fuller."

"We weren't introduced but I remember you from the party at Dwight and Colleen's."

He smiled. "Yes. I am frequently a standout at such gatherings. I believe I've met your father."

"That's always a memorable experience."

Coffin chuckled, opened the door and motioned me into the Mercedes. I got in and he joined me in the back seat. The driver started the engine and we entered the naval base.

My father's self-confessed specialty had been walking into a room full of military brass and scientists and convincing them in short order that he was the smartest man in the room. I'd never been privileged to see this but I had no trouble believing it. I was even part of his tactics during my grammar school years, when I played a good game of poker, and it used to amuse my father to invite me to the occasional poker game. I must have looked a bit like Stefanie Russo: young, fat, and solemn. I don't know if my father's goal was to disorient the military officers, but I always seemed to end up taking their money.

The primary lesson I took away from my childhood, since the feminine wiles have never worked at all for me, was to play the hand I was dealt. If Admiral Coffin wanted to intimidate me he was going to have to work much harder than a flag rank and a staff car.

"Why did you have the local police stop me?"

"Aside from the fact that you were getting near an area you had been warned away from?"

"Aside from that." I wonder if he was talking about official warnings or the explosion and threatening note.

"I wanted to hear in your own words exactly what papers you saw in Ron Rhymer's Security Cabinet."

"It was empty except for a single piece of paper—cover sheet that said Top Secret. The sheet had a paper clip on it, but nothing was clipped to it."

"No folder or transcript or envelope or any other materials such as a cassette tape or a computer diskette?"

"So far as I could tell it was empty. I would imagine you have examined the cover sheet for tiny microfilm dots. If there was any Top Secret material visible to the naked eye, it was removed before Amy and I got there."

"The problem is, he wasn't working on anything sensitive for the military or any known civilian group."

"What about Stewart Meade's company? He was doing something with them that had a Thai connection. He said that for everyone to hear at the party."

"Yes." For a moment Coffin fell silent. I glanced out and watched the paved world of the base glide past behind the tinted-glass windows. "You've been talking to the Rhymer family and friends. Any idea what Ron might have had in that safe?"

"You must know what you're looking for. Does it go back to the seventies?"

He gave me a look sharp enough to cut raw meat. "What have you seen?"

"I haven't seen anything. Amy just mentioned that

she was researching the Watergate years when there were rumors of a possible military coup. Because her father was at the Pentagon then, she thought it might bring them closer together. It didn't."

Admiral Coffin gestured impatiently. "What else?"

I shrugged. "Nothing. Except that Brad seems to think it might have some possible extraterrestrial connection."

After a moment of shocked silence the car was filled with Admiral Coffin's loud and sincere laughter.

24

After he recovered his composure, the admiral informed the driver that he was ready to go back to the gate. "Thank you for your time, Ms. Fuller," he said, with an echo of laughter still in his voice. "It's been most illuminating." Judging by how quickly we reached the gate we hadn't gotten very far onto the base.

Standing next to my rental car watching the Mercedes head back onto the base, I felt unexpectedly very irritated. I hadn't even sought out the interview. What did they want?

Contrary to the theory that someone had planted the bomb in the Lexus because I was a threat, Coffin seemed to think I didn't have any of the answers. He was right but his hilarious reaction had put my teeth on edge enough that I felt like driving around a little rather than going back to the hotel for more paperwork. It was only midafternoon. I wasn't about to go back near Amy and Ivor Russo's home, with its rings of police security and possible ransom action.

I drove up the coast aimlessly for a while, meditating Southern California style at seventy miles per hour. Eventually, I found myself heading inland, back toward the Anza Borrego Desert and the little town of Summit.

Helen Hayworth was behind the counter, sketching listlessly on a pad. She watched me approach without enthusiasm. "You haven't forgotten anything, have you?" she said by way of greeting. "Because I don't remember finding anything."

"No, I just wanted to see some of the art again."

Her face softened. "Sorry I was a little harsh with you. I saw you drive off with that man. I don't distrust all men, but that one looked a little scary."

"I understand." Fred Luna did look as though he knew a few dozen ways to kill and maim. I could see why that might make someone nervous. I had my reasons to trust him, and Helen had her own reasons not to. I looked around the shop for what I had skimmed past last time. There it was. On an easel by the door to the back room—so far back that it was almost touching the curtain that divided the storefront from the room behind it. It was an unobtrusive oil painting of the street in front of the store. But it had a certain nagging draw, once you shifted your attention away from the massive metal sculptures. "That painting back there got under my skin," I said, coming closer to examine it. "Are there more oils?"

"Oh." Helen blushed and pushed her silvery gray hair back. "That's one of mine." She went to the painting and stood in front of it like a mother pushing a naughty toddler behind her.

"Do you have more?"

Helen was silent for a moment. "A few in the storage closet in the back room. She gestured with her shoulder toward the curtained doorway.

"Could I see them?"

"Oh. All right." She seemed about to say more. Her eyes darted around as if Magda might come back in and catch her in a betrayal. "Come back here, it's quiet and I'll hear if someone comes in the store." There didn't seem to be much danger of that kind of interruption. I

followed her through the curtain into a tiny back store-
room with stacked display stands, a desk with office
supplies and ledgers piled on it. A door on one wall was
half-open revealing a cramped toilet and sink. On the
opposite wall another door was closed. Helen opened it
to reveal a storage closet almost entirely taken over by
cardboard boxes with a moving-company logo on them.
Opening the closet door had significantly reduced the
amount of space in the back room, so I stood with my
back pushing into the curtain and let Helen bring things
out.

"I keep some of my stuff here." She spoke so softly
that I had to strain to make out the words. But the blush
was gone. She took out a wooden box of painting supplies and laid them on the desk, then reached in behind
the boxes and brought out several small canvases
wrapped in brown paper that had been standing against
the back wall of the closet behind the storage boxes.

I backed out of the doorway to let her through as she
carried them into the store. "The light's better out here,"
she said as if to herself.

Not to mention the fact that the back room had been
suffocatingly small, I thought.

"I used to paint all day out here when we first got
the store," Helen said, unwrapping the paintings, which
were mostly ten by sixteen inches. She propped them
up against some of the smaller statues on the counter.

"Wow." I stood back and examined them. They were
mostly scenes from the small desert town. Here and
there a wind-polished resident would appear, sitting on
a porch or changing a tire at the gas station. One picture
showed an elderly woman seen through the front window of the café next to the faded striped pole of a closed
barber shop. The old woman was staring at the empty

counter in front of her. Something about her neon pink
sweater made me know it was homemade and not
washed as often as it should be. "Why did you stop?"
I didn't have to ask *if* she had stopped, it was obvious
from the dust on the paint box.

"Oh, I stopped when I had to take that 7-Eleven job
last winter. It really wore me out. When we were able
to open the store again, I could have started, but . . . I
don't know, I admire the way Magda perseveres no matter what happens, but I get discouraged, I guess." Now
she was staring at the glass counter under the pictures.
She took a deep breath and started to wrap them up
again.

"Wait. What will you take for the one with the old
lady in the pink sweater?"

"Oh." Helen clearly hadn't thought about selling her
paintings. "I don't know. A hundred dollars."

"Can I write you a check?"

"Sure." Instead of smiling she looked shocked. But
she wrapped up the painting for me. As I handed her
the check, the shop door creaked as Magda came in.

"Well, well. What have we here?"

I turned to face her, noting that Helen was taking
down and wrapping up her paintings hastily, as if hiding
a guilty secret. "I saw that one painting in the corner
and it impressed me, so I asked if there were more. I
liked this one, so I bought it." I pointed to the painting.

Somehow Magda's attitude made me worry for its
safety. She glanced over at the painting in the corner
and came to look at the one Helen was holding. As
Helen handed me the wrapped painting, Magda reached
out and patted the back of the canvas through the brown
paper. "Her work is pretty, isn't it? Like Helen, herself.
She doesn't know how not to be."

I nodded politely and finished noting the check in my register.

Magda went behind the counter to where Helen was putting away the wrapping materials. She put an arm around her and nuzzled her ear. Helen placed her arm around Magda's shoulder and smiled cheerfully. Magda maintained eye contact with me and raised her head for a moment. "You can go now, unless you feel like buying something else."

I could see why Helen rather than Magda handled the customer relations. I left with the painting under my arm. I hadn't found any connection between the two women and the admiral's disappearance, but now I knew what to put in my follow-up report for Mrs. Madrone.

I drove back toward San Diego. It wasn't yet 5:00 P.M. but the rush hour traffic was fierce already. I got off the freeway and pulled into a shopping center parking lot to think and look at my map. Then I got out my notebook and cell phone. Ambrose, with his usual terrifying thoroughness, had included Colleen Rhymer's work number at the real estate agency.

I called and found her in. After a moment she remembered me.

Just to see how she would react, I described my chat with Admiral Coffin.

"I used to be thrilled when the big brass took an interest in Dwight's career," she said with a weariness I could hear even over the phone. "But right at the moment, we'd like to fade back into the woodwork. Brad's crazy ideas are no help at all."

"If it's any consolation, Brad's theories didn't worry Admiral Coffin. In fact they probably gave him a much-needed laugh."

There was a slight pause and I could hear the tension in Colleen's voice. "Let's see, one of the most powerful men in the U.S. military, who happens to be my husband's boss, is laughing at my crazy brother-in-law. No. Not much of a consolation, thank you very much."

"At the very least you don't have Admiral Rhymer hanging around your house, that can't be something you and your husband miss."

"You're right. That part would be refreshing if we could only be let alone to enjoy it. It's nice and quiet in between the aircraft taking off, and at least I know my dear father-in-law won't be all over me like an octopus every time I turn my back."

"I'm surprised you and Dwight didn't just give him his walking papers and tell him to get a hotel room with his little girlfriend."

"I would have done it in a heartbeat, except that the old letch really has been a positive force in Dwight's career. Even when Dwight leaves the navy he'll want to stay in good with the admiral's buddies."

"That does sound very practical. I won't keep you from your work any longer. I called to get an address, and directions from you."

She seemed to be totally mystified at why I would want it, but she gave me the address and directions on how to get there. Half an hour later I was staring at the half-reconstructed ruins of what had been Admiral Rhymer's home in San Marcos.

I had expected to find the whole neighborhood burned out. I vaguely remembered hearing that there had been destructive forest fires reaching into the San Diego suburbs during the previous year's fire season. But Admiral Rhymer's house was the only one in the area that showed signs of fire damage. The landscaping appeared to have been flattened, while every other house on the block had trees and lawns intact and unscarred. The Rhymer chimney was black with soot, the house boarded up with plywood, and a building contractor's sign affixed to the front.

I got out of the car and walked up the driveway. It was just past five and there were no workers on the site, and no neighbors visible on the street. An Isuzu Trooper pulled up. I recognized it a moment before Fred Luna got out. He joined me in the driveway and we stood a moment contemplating the construction site.

"Are you following me? Because the police are very anxious to talk to you."

"Tell me something I don't know."

"My car was bombed."

"Oh, that nice Lexus. Poor baby."

"The police think the bomb is similar to the kind of shaped charge the SEALs use. Mrs. Rhymer said you were in munitions."

"No." He sighed. "I was in the infantry in Vietnam and in ordnance in the navy. It was nice of her to remember that I know how to blow things up. Why would anyone want to bomb a harmless girl like yourself?"

"Aside from the theory that anyone who uses a bomb like that is crazy? It might have been aimed at Mrs. Madrone. It is her car. But if they knew I was driving it, maybe someone might want to scare me into leaving town or at least staying inside my hotel room for the foreseeable future."

"I can see how well it's worked. You stick your nose in some fancy places. Admiral Coffin is a high-level aide to the Secretary of the Navy."

"So you have been following me!"

"Only till you took the turnoff on Seventy-eight. I figured you'd be coming back the same way pretty soon. I was right."

A neighbor drove past slowly and gave us a long appraising stare. "Fred, I don't think either of us belongs in this neighborhood right now. Unless you want to spend the night in a jail cell, we'd better talk quick and part company."

"Okay, tough girl, what did Admiral Coffin want to know about?"

"He seemed worried about the contents of Admiral Rhymer's security cabinet. There was a Top Secret cover sheet with nothing attached to it and the drawers were all empty."

Fred whistled. "Okay."

"But Coffin said Rhymer wasn't currently working on anything Top Secret. He got a little rattled when I mentioned that Brad was looking into something in the 1970s in Washington, but of course he wouldn't say what."

Fred shook his head. "Admiral Coffin went out of his way to help Admiral Rhymer. But that's what happens when you serve together in a war zone. When someone earns your trust like that, it sticks."

"You're an idealist, Fred."

"Think so? Is that all?"

"Well, I came over here to see about the house. I expected to find the whole neighborhood rebuilding. Wasn't this part of the canyon that burned last October?"

"No. That was further north. This house burned a couple months ago."

"In the spring? Not even fire season. Was it arson?"

"Maybe. Probably."

"They couldn't tell?"

"Fire inspectors found a can of gasoline tipped over on the garage floor next to the water heater. The place went up less than half an hour later. No mess, no fuss, no evidence. Didn't even need a match."

"You're sure it wasn't an accident?"

"We did have a spare gas can. But I sure as hell did not leave a can of gasoline next to the hot water heater and I know Lani didn't. She wouldn't touch anything in the garage anyway—she doesn't even pump her own gas at the self-serve stations."

"What about Admiral Rhymer, maybe when he was drunk?"

Fred shrugged. "Maybe. Except that someone stole the admiral's garage door opener out of his car the day it happened. Didn't steal the car. Didn't steal anything else. We didn't even realize it was missing till everyone got back home that night and the house was already gone. Someone could have opened the garage door, tipped the gas, closed the door and left. The place was halfway destroyed before the neighbors saw the smoke and called the fire department."

"Was anyone hurt?"

"No. They were lucky. The admiral went up to a golf weekend and Lani drove him. I had the day off."

"That garage door opener reminds me of the bomb that got Mrs. Madrone's Lexus. It was detonated by the remote control door opener. The bomb squad guy said garage door openers are very popular to remote-start bombs. If the person who burned the admiral's house was trying to send a message, it might have been the same person. But what was the message?"

"Let me take a wild guess here—he was pissed off?"

"He or she," I said. Fred shrugged. I continued to speculate. "Could Admiral Rhymer and I have gotten the same bomb thrower angry?"

"Well, whoever it was, watch yourself. Check your car for unusual things on the undercarriage." He leaned down and looked at the underside of the car, balancing on the bumper with one hand to do so. When he looked up, he shrugged. "Never hurts to check."

Another neighbor's car cruised by slowly on its way to a driveway down the block. There were not a lot of Latino faces in this neighborhood and the neighbors of a possible arson fire site were bound to be particularly nervous. I asked Fred for the date and time of the fire and wrote it in my notebook. I might need to check someone's alibi for that now. Fred and I parted company.

26

I called Martha Meade's house and Lance Feather answered and told me to come on over. I noted he didn't consult her before inviting me. Of course, the last time I'd seen her, she hadn't had a lot to say.

Ondine cooed a cheerful greeting when she saw me at the door and led me back to the dining room. I noticed she was wearing a robin's egg blue warm-up outfit. Someone must have gone back for more clothes.

Lance was also looking fresh, his feathery white-blond hair tidily trimmed.

Sitting next to Lance was a red-haired woman in a purple paisley silk robe. The hair with its blonde streak identified Martha Meade immediately, but without her makeup and the flush of alcohol, it was hard to recognize her. She raised deeply ringed eyes to me without recognition or interest.

I mumbled a few words of condolence. Martha looked at me as if from a great distance. "Lance tells me I met you after the funeral," she said in a husky voice. "I'm afraid I don't remember much after the funeral. Please sit down. Dear?" She looked at Ondine as if she had run out of words.

Ondine came over and briefly massaged her shoulders. "Would you like some more broth? Or maybe I could rustle up some tea. I'm going to make tea for Jo, I know she likes it."

I sketched a smile, feeling almost as wan as Martha

at the memory of the last tea Ondine had rustled up.

Martha sighed and shut her eyes. Ondine must have taken that for a yes because she went on into the kitchen. "You've both been such sweethearts to help me out," she said, opening her eyes as she tilted her head toward Lance. Lance reached out and squeezed her hand.

I sat on one of the oak chairs and looked around the room. It was elegantly furnished and every polished surface gleamed. A glass-fronted cabinet of gold-rimmed china faced us. In the center of the table, an arrangement of tulips and tiger lilies stood in a vase and spilled a few petals onto the polished wood surface. Either Martha had regular, intense cleaning fits, or she hired some very scrupulous help. The last few days of disorganization weren't enough to seriously undermine this orderliness. Even the cut-crystal ashtray holding Martha's cigarette was polished clean.

On the table in front of Martha and Lance were stacks of business papers, ledgers, and bankbooks. Lance saw where I was looking and patted the ledger in front of him. "Martha's going over Stewart's business affairs and I'm helping her make sense of them."

Martha beamed at him. "Lance is such a sweetheart. I don't know if I'm a wealthy widow or one of those old ladies eating cat food out of a supermarket dumpster.

"You won't have to go near a dumpster, Martha," Lance said, leaning his head close to hers. "It looks like your husband left you with a healthy cushion."

This was followed by a stifled yelp and such a throaty laugh from Martha that I had to keep my eyes from widening when I realized Lance had just pinched her under the table.

"I'm sure that's very helpful," I said, covering my surprise with a question. "Don't you have an accountant to do all that?

Lance and Martha gave me a pitying look as if I didn't have a clue of how grown-ups did things. I was getting that look a lot in San Diego and it was starting to irritate me. "Stewart did all that himself," Martha said. "He was *so* secretive. I tell you I had to break into his desk to get at his books. He kept the key on his person and the police haven't released his effects yet. He was like a sweet little ol' parasite."

"Huh?"

"My big bug, I used to call him."

"That's, uh, an unusual nickname," I murmured. "May I ask why you called him that?"

Martha nodded. "Stewie's specialty was helping people. He would get involved in every single deal a client had going, just chew his way in like a big ol' termite. Then all of a sudden the man couldn't do anything without Stewie's say-so. Stewie would own the man."

Termite-infested homes don't have a rosy future. I wondered if killing ol' Stewie was someone's method of fumigating for termites—death by tear gas would have a certain poetic justice in that context. I asked, "Did your late husband have one of those safes for secret documents, like the admiral?"

She nodded. "He did. But the authorities came and took it almost as soon as the police arrived to give me the news."

Whatever Admiral Coffin was interested in must not have been in Meade's safe. "How long had your husband and Ron Rhymer been working together?"

"Stew and Ron had worked on projects together in the navy, so once Stewie moved into the private sector, he got several contracts through Ron—well, I mean, he still had to bid, but he knew how to bid. When Ron retired he kept on working with Stewie, but he wasn't in charge anymore. I think that bothered him."

"Did you know the Rhymers in Washington in the seventies?"

She examined her purple nail polish, which was starting to chip. "We traveled in different circles. Ron was a hotshot war hero, which is how he got to the Pentagon so early. Stewie had to fight his way up, every step of the way. Ron would come to our house to unwind. Maybe because we had no kids and the boys could let their hair down."

Ondine brought a tray with four bone china cups on saucers, three dangled strings with tags from a generic brand of orange Pekoe tea on the label. The fourth cup steaming but with no string or label. Ondine took it and noticed my glance. She smiled and showed me. "I put lemon in hot water with honey," she said. "I can't take regular tea and I haven't been out to buy any herbal."

So Ondine at least had been baby-sitting Martha around the clock.

Lance helped Martha to tea as if she were a clumsy small child. I got up and fetched mine so that I could claim a little of the sugar and milk in it. Ondine settled in on Martha's other side facing me. Instead of sitting across the table again, I went round to pull out the chair at the end of the table next to Lance. If he pinched her again I wanted to see where."

"So you say you didn't know Admiral Rhymer's family?"

"Sally didn't approve of Stewie or me, but we were Ron's business associates so we got invited to the major parties and one or two smaller couples' gatherings. She didn't want us near their kids but they were all packed off to boarding schools by then anyway. Heck, I'm not sure I'd recognize the kids on sight. The girl kept gaining and losing weight so much—who knows what *she* looks like now?" Martha cast me a sly look to see if she could unsheathe her claws without getting swatted. I looked back at her, wondering which tactic would squeeze more information out of her.

"I take it Sally Rhymer didn't confide in you directly when her marriage broke up."

Martha smiled and shook her head. "Stewie told me." The predatory redhead the alcohol had unleashed surfaced for a moment in her eyes.

"Things started to go bad for them about the time the admiral's first driver was crippled in that traffic accident."

"Excuse me for interrupting, Martha, but wasn't the admiral's first driver killed in a hit-and-run?"

"Oh, no, no, no. It was a hit-and-run but he wasn't killed. Douglas was hit while he was walking along the Pacific Coast Highway. He'd been spending the night off base at one of those motels down there—he had quarters on the base so he might have had a woman there, he never said. But Douglas Dufrane was a handsome enough fella. They never found the driver or the car. He lay there until another driver stopped and called for help. Doug never saw the car that hit him. He survived but he never walked again. So sad. He was so athletic."

"Someone said he was in the SEALs."

"Yes. He was a navy SEAL in Vietnam. Really and truly. A lot of those who claim that are just liars, but not Doug. It was terrible that he came through the war in one piece just to be paralyzed in a traffic accident.

After he recovered, he worked some for my husband's company. He was very good at customizing weapons."

I must have blinked in surprise. "Your husband made weapons?"

"Weapons components, darling, what kind of thing do you think the navy buys?"

"This is the business that they were talking about moving to Thailand?"

"Oh, they're always moving to find cheaper labor. At first it was here, then part of the operation moved to Texas. I would have thought Mexico would be next but maybe Thailand was even cheaper. I can't say I was too interested as long as the money came in." She sighed.

"But the admiral's ex-driver was on your husband's payroll."

"Not on the payroll. I think it was on a project-by-project basis. In fact, I just saw his name this morning on some checks Stew wrote."

"Could you recall the amounts of the checks?"

"Let me look." She pulled a set of half-lensed reading glasses out of a pocket somewhere in the printed silk caftan and opened one of the ledgers, running a lacquered fingernail down the column. "Here it is. In January a check to Douglas Dufrane for five thousand three hundred and twenty-seven dollars. He must have been working on a project this year. At least up till January. That's the only check for this year and it's June already. Last year there are several checks. So he's not living in financial straits on his disability check."

I looked at her for a moment. "Do you think it was an accident, the admiral's driver getting run down?"

She smiled. "Like I said, Douglas was handsome enough. If he had a hotel room with a woman and no one went looking for him when he was missing, I'd guess he picked up someone else's wife. The husband could have found out about it, maybe followed them."

"That's a pretty detailed speculation. Was there some gossip about it?"

"Let's just say that Douglas was driving the admiral's car when he stayed at the motel. Ron was out of town but he got back early and when he didn't get any answer calling home or calling Doug, he called my husband from some bar downtown. Stewie later told me Ron Rhymer's wife, driver, and car were missing. By that time Douglas was in the hospital, they found the car at the motel."

"Where was Sally Rhymer all this time?"

"Good question." Martha smiled beatifically. "She said she was visiting a friend out of town. The friend confirmed it. No one ever proved differently." A sudden coldness ran down my spine—could the friend have been Mrs. Madrone?

"Okay. So Admiral Rhymer got a new driver, Fred Luna. Did the Rhymers break up after that?"

"Not right away. But Ron started to get really wild. I wouldn't have put up with him and I'm famous for my tolerance."

"Did he bother you? I've heard he was so hands-on, he even groped his daughter-in-law."

"That little brunette? I bet he did, and I'll bet it drove his Jesus-freak son up the wall. He was getting worse and worse since he retired. He used to steal a kiss in the kitchen now and then, but this stuff just wasn't fun anymore. Freddy was the only one who could manage him."

With a little help from the pharmaceutical industry, I thought, but I didn't mention Fred's methods. "How long has the admiral been going out with Fred's niece?"

"Oh, that was after Ron and Sally broke up. I feel sorry for Fred Luna. It must kill him to have his niece shacking up with his employer. He's so straight and conservative deep down inside. Still, he can be a real fun little guy when you get him drunk."

"When you called Dwight and Colleen's house the other morning you seemed to think Ron Rhymer would have furnished your husband with prostitutes."

"That has been a problem in the past." Her hand knotted into fists for an instant and white-hot anger flared briefly under a cynical mask. "I was worried when I heard that he and Stewie would be alone together. It turned out I was right to worry."

"I don't mean to tire you out. But before I go, just one last thing I wondered. Did your husband or Admiral Rhymer get any unusual demands for money recently?"

"Well, of course, Ron was rebuilding that house and he had a pretty little girlfriend, so he had been bugging Stew about something that had to do with money. Like I said, once Stew got his little suckers into someone, he was in charge, so all he had to do was tell Ron no. Whatever it was Ron wanted money for. I heard Stewart tell him more than once, 'The genie's out of the bottle on that one, Ron. Live with it.' " Martha sighed. Her voice sounded exhausted.

I thanked her earnestly. "I'll go now. It's so good that you and Lance knew each other before."

"What!" Martha seemed more shocked than the question warranted. I had expected her to simply deny it. Everyone at the table froze and stared at me. Even Lance seemed at a loss for words. "What makes you think that?" Martha asked in a choked voice.

"You seemed to know Lance when he came in the other day."

Everyone appeared to relax, so I had to add, "I wondered if you had met at the Blue Ridge Institute in '96?"

No one was prepared to meet my eyes but Lance stood abruptly. "Let me see you to the door," he said in a grim tone of voice.

Martha pointedly looked away from me, as stiff as a wax figurine, despite Ondine, who patted her purple paisley clad shoulder. Her face crumpled and she began to sob.

I followed Lance to the door. "You are aware that you're bullying a grieving widow and you've probably undone about a day and a half of healing work we've done here," he said in a low, hard voice as he opened the door. "Why did you even bother to call us if you just wanted to hurt her?"

"I called you because she didn't have anyone else to turn to, but it was fortuitous that you gave me your card. You still haven't told me if you two were in touch here in San Diego before her husband died."

He closed the door in my face.

27

I decided to go back to the room and Raoul. I stopped at a grocery store first and bought some red snapper to ensure an enthusiastic welcome.

When Raoul and I were happily sated on fish, he began his postmeal grooming ritual and I cleared off the table, opened my laptop computer, and finished the report updating the information on the grant to Magda. It was made easier by the fact that Helen was not named by more than initials as the person who wrote the first report.

When I finished printing it, I called Ambrose. He wasn't in. I was so worried I'd change my mind that I made a special trip to the lobby to drop off the envelope with my report in it.

The desk clerk handed me a sealed message from Ambrose. It simply said, "Jerry Buck, *National Interrogator*," and included a telephone number. I took the paper upstairs and then remembered that I wanted to ask Ambrose what he could find out about the admiral's business with Stewart Meade. I left him another message, imagining him rolling his eyes at my inefficiency.

I decided to leave the reporter for the next day.

I called Mulligan. The machine answered. He must be back in Seattle by now. I didn't yet know him well enough to know if he turned off the bell on his phone if he wanted to sleep. I couldn't bear to miss messages myself, but not everyone shares my attitude. I called the building manager, Maxine, trying to convince myself that I was just keeping in touch rather than checking up on Mulligan.

"Mulligan got back this afternoon," Maxine said, "but I assume you know that."

"I called but I just got his answering machine."

"I think he went in to work. So when are you coming back to sort out Nina's apartment? The one underneath it will be ready to rent soon too. If you're going to be stuck down there for a while, we could go ahead without you."

"Gosh, Maxine," I said, pressing my suddenly cold hands to my face, as the shock of Nina's death washed over me once again. "Maybe you and I can go through it when I get back next week."

"Okay, it's your decision." I heard an ear-splitting shriek in the background and Maxine turned from the receiver to scold Groucho, the big green macaw whose screeches penetrated every apartment in the building and most of the block.

"You know, Maxine, every time he screeches and you talk to him, it makes him screech more because he just got your attention."

"Yeah, but sometimes I just have to screech back."

I laughed. I suspected Maxine secretly enjoyed terrorizing everyone with her attack bird. He was even more aggressive when he could put his beak in your face. I didn't mention the car bomb. I was pretty sure Mulligan wouldn't mention it either. I asked how her daughter and the other tenants were doing. She was glad to give me a recap of the week's gossip. It was oddly comforting to hear about her daughter Hope's boyfriend and the ins and outs of his legal problems, and Maxine's feud with the neighbor across the street who sneaked his dog onto the lawn.

I felt melodramatic and maudlin for doing so, but after I hung up, I picked up the laptop and typed a few paragraphs by way of last requests. Not exactly a last will and testament, but an explanation that Mulligan should take care of Raoul and that they could drag my boxes of earthly possessions out of Nina's basement storage and divide them up when they parceled out Nina's stuff. If I had pressed that remote button when I was standing very close to the Lexus, I might have joined my friend in death not a month after we scattered her ashes over Puget Sound. Some of what Amy was doing started to make a little sense. When someone close to you dies, your own death seems not only plausible but somehow closer than you could have guessed.

I crawled into bed expecting to toss and turn, but to my surprise I fell asleep before I had the time to even turn, let alone toss. I woke up with Raoul companionably curled up against my hip.

I decided eight-thirty would be a fine time to call the *National Interrogator* reporter. Jerry Buck's voice on his machine was brisk and briefly advised leaving a detailed message.

Raoul watched me get dressed with a cynical eye. I was about to abandon him again. "You'd only be watching Mulligan get dressed if I let him take you back," I said. Raoul appeared unimpressed, but allowed me to scratch under his chin. I asked him what the trick was for making his mind go blank. It seemed like a very useful thing to know. The phone rang and it was Jerry Buck calling back.

"I understand that Brad Rhymer spoke with you. He seems to have disappeared," I said.

"Along with his dad, huh? Think there's a connection?"

"Do you?"

"How well do you know Brad?"

"I met him a few times and several of his family members as well. I'd like to get together to trade information."

"A phrase usually used by those who have nothing to trade. What the hell, I'd be willing to let you buy me breakfast. I know a good restaurant in Seaport Village."

I arranged to meet Buck in the tourist jungle part of San Diego in front of a restaurant with a big plate-glass window. The first breakfast rush had subsided but it was still early enough that there wasn't much traffic. Buck had to be the short, thin man who was waiting on the sidewalk, surveying the menu that was posted on the restaurant door. He had light auburn hair and a face tanned to almost the same shade. He wore a red nylon windbreaker over matching red nylon shorts, displaying thickets of auburn hair on every appendage.

From a distance, he reminded me of a boyfriend I'd had in college who had made a point of shattering every negative stereotype about short men. I remembered that it was an exercise I enjoyed a great deal at the time since I had some stereotypes of my own to demolish. We had even derived a certain perverse pleasure from walking hand-in-hand, seeing people's reactions to the Amazon and the jockey, and knowing that we would probably enjoy ourselves more in the next few hours than some of those people staring at us would all year.

Before I could summon up a sigh for the simpler passions of youth, Jerry Buck destroyed the comparison for me by the way he looked me up and down and dismissed me instantly and thoroughly. His disdain was so visible that he seemed to be steeling himself to not walk away. He did take note of my outfit—the linen jacket and stylishly cut gauze blouse and shorts must have convinced him that I would be capable of paying the check. After a moment of uncertainty he opted to tolerate me for the sake of possible information and, of course, the free breakfast. I wondered how he got other people to confide in him, because he gave off a furtive quality that made every hair on my body stand up in protest. If I hadn't needed to ask him about Brad, I would have turned on my heel and left perhaps before he did, if only in honor of the memory of my college sweetheart.

We went inside and sat down. It was chilly enough in the air-conditioned restaurant that he kept his windbreaker on. Buck kept warm by jiggling his legs nervously, a habit he didn't appear to be aware of. He ordered a steak, eggs, and hash browns with toast and coffee. I wasn't sure I wanted any of their coffee, so I took a pot of tea and an order of toast.

"So, what do you want to talk about?" he said, sitting back and looking at my purse.

For a moment I thought he was going to try a purse snatching, then I realized. "I don't have a tape recorder in my purse, if that's what you're thinking."

"Well, I do. In my pocket, to be exact," he said, raising a tiny recorder half out of the pocket of his jacket so I could see it.

"I'm looking for Brad Rhymer."

"Something to do with his dad being kidnapped?" Jerry Buck's grocery check-out tabloid only came out weekly, but if he got hard information on a kidnapping he might be angling to sell a story to a more legitimate newspaper.

"Why? Does your paper think Brad sold him to the space aliens?"

Buck's lip lifted, sketching a sneering version of a smile. His toast and coffee arrived and he filled his mouth.

"Why would you even bother to meet with Brad? He must have had some evidence that interested you or the *Interrogator*?"

Buck took a slug of coffee and paused a moment, buttering his toast. "He had a tape. From the time period he described, I thought it might have something to do with the possible coup back in '73." For a moment his eyes actually lit up. "That would be a story, huh? That could be a book."

While visions of Woodward and Bernstein danced in his head, I asked, "What was on the tape?"

Buck spread some jam on his toast before answering. "Brad seemed to think it was a UFO abduction but it was pretty clearly a flight-deck recording of a bombing mission. From all the talk about SAMs and so forth, it did sound like the Vietnam era. The pilot was shot down yelling something about Wild Weasels not working. Sounded like a straight equipment glitch."

I watched him eat a little more and pushed my own toast away. He wasn't a messy eater. I just didn't like him and it made me a little sick to be around him. "If it wasn't important, why did Brad take it from his dad?"

"Don't know. Don't care," Buck said. His breakfast arrived and he cut into his steak and chased it down with some egg and hash browns before continuing. "Probably because Admiral Rhymer saved the tape and hid it for so long."

"Having listened to the tape, why do you think the admiral saved it so long?"

"People get screwy about souvenirs. Some people collect matchboxes, there's no accounting for taste."

"Obviously you can't see any way to fit UFOs into the information on the tape."

"UFOs are infinitely flexible. They can fill in any blanks you want them to." Buck put his elbows on the table and warmed his hands on his coffee cup. He almost met my eyes and then put down the cup, picked up his fork and went back to breakfast again. "Brad wasn't the first person I've heard of putting a UFO spin on a war story. The Vietnam War was bad news when it happened. Now it's not even old news. Even if he'd had photos and an actual story angle, it wasn't anything our rag could use. I did offer to get the audio enhanced for free, to see if there was more on the tape than it originally sounded like. But he wouldn't trust me with it. He wanted to sell it. He decided to try to peddle it somewhere else." Buck shrugged and turned his attention back to his plate.

"So you weren't paying him in hundred-dollar bills."

"Yeah, right." Buck snorted at the thought. "We weren't paying anything," he said without missing a bite of breakfast.

"And you say the tape sounded like a bombing mission that went wrong over Vietnam?"

"Yup. Fortunes of war, baby. Fortunes of war."

"So he took the tape with him and went—where?"

"Try Area Fifty-one. He's probably up there with his UFO buddies trying to convince them that the aliens were shooting down jets in Vietnam."

"Thanks for your time in talking to me."

"Too bad it's wasted. You got nothing to give me, right?"

"On the contrary." I got up, opened my purse, and dropped a twenty-dollar bill on the table.

"You're not going to tip?" he asked, glancing at the twenty.

"I'll let you pay the tip, if you happen to feel like a grown-up." I left before my internal attack dog could slip its collar and attempt to rip the seams off his surly manner. The stress of the past few weeks had taken its toll, or he wouldn't have been able to force me so easily, so far over the edge by simply showing contempt. I've seen a bit of contempt in my time and usually I can mirror it right back without breaking a sweat. This time it was Jerry Buck who was unruffled. As I walked past the window I noticed he was starting in on the plate of toast I'd left.

I went for a stroll down by the harbor to clear my head and warm up after the frigid air conditioning. The waves were that Southern California azure that is so breathtaking. The faint veil of haze was already burning off. I wondered if I could train Raoul to walk on a leash, and if so, whether he would like to walk down along the waterfront. Somehow I doubted it. He was a tall-grass kind of character. I headed for my car and drove back across the high-arching bridge to Coronado Island.

I parked and got as far as the sidewalk outside the hotel when someone called out, "It's you!"

28

I turned to see Helen Hayworth. She came sprinting over to me and held out her hand. For a disoriented moment I didn't recognize her away from that quiet shop in the small desert town. She seemed thrilled to see me. She carried a shoulder-strap briefcase and was carefully made up and dressed in a businesslike pantsuit.

"How wonderful to run into you here. I've got an interview in there." She indicated Mrs. Madrone's building. "It's not for an hour—I'm early. Look, are you free for coffee? There's something I want to tell you."

I realized that my appetite was back and a latte and pastry would be just the thing. "Why not? There's a café down here." Thanks to Ambrose I now knew a few nice places nearby.

I was curious what Helen planned to do in the hotel. She knew Mrs. Madrone and her staff. Perhaps she was visiting. As we walked a few blocks to the café, Helen kept up a running inventory of how the neighborhood had changed since she had last been here.

I didn't have to wonder whether Ambrose had ever taken her to the café. "Oh, my! This place is new. It is so wonderful to get back to civilization." Helen wasn't asking questions. She was talking so urgently that she scarcely paused for breath. We bought coffees. She picked out a chocolate croissant and I took a key lime tart. We sat down, but she was so energized that she looked ready to leap out of the seat.

"I am so glad to run into you. I don't even remember your name, but I have it written down from your check because I wanted to write and thank you."

"There's no need to thank me. It's a wonderful painting. I liked it, so I bought it."

"Yes. And when you did, you made me realize what I need to do. I decided that night."

"Decided what?"

"To leave that town and the shop. It was killing me. Remember how I told you I used to work for Mrs. Madrone. I'm going to get my old job back."

I concentrated on not choking on my latte. "Really?" I asked in a carefully even tone of voice. I felt as transparent as the window we sat next to.

Helen nodded, beaming happily. She was so pleased with her own prospects that she didn't seem to notice any reaction on my part. "It's something I need to do," she explained. "Finances have been so bad, in another few weeks we would have had to close down again anyway. I'd be looking for the only kind of work there is around there—making beds at the motel or standing behind a convenience-store counter all night."

I tried to conceal my dismay while she earnestly explained this. All I could think of was that I'd managed to get Mrs. Madrone's Lexus bombed and her beloved Siamese into a fight. She might or might not blame me for the nearly million-dollar ransom she had just paid—but CEOs have been fired for less. Mrs. Madrone might be eager to replace me at this point.

"What about your art?"

"I won't have as much time to paint as I did at the store. But I think it will be good for me to be closer to the galleries and the art scene here. You can't imagine what it's like on a limited income in a little isolated town like that." She looked me up and down. "You're a student and you can't know what it's like." She was assessing my wardrobe. She didn't seem to find it out of line for a student. She must have thought I was one of those perpetual students with rich parents.

I didn't ask What about Magda? But even as Helen chatted about how San Diego got flashier every year, Magda was as present as if she were sitting at the table scowling at not having her own cup.

I wasn't about to tell Helen the truth but I didn't feel like spinning more involved fiction about my graduate school project. Helen asked how it was going and I vaguely said it was coming along. We finished our coffee and pastries and Helen looked at her watch and found it was near enough to the interview to go on up. We went back out onto Orange Street again and back toward the hotel.

Magda's dusty and battered Toyota truck was parked behind Helen's old Chevy Cavalier in front of Mrs. Madrone's building. Helen fell silent. As we approached the entrance, Magda climbed out of the truck, and slammed the door. She joined us on the sidewalk. "I saw your car. I waited," she said to Helen, then she turned to rivet me with a fierce gaze. "So," she said. "You."

"Actually, we just ran into each other," Helen piped up with a conciliatory flutter. "Quite a coincidence."

"Yes. Quite." Magda turned away from me to look at Helen. The hesitation in her manner made it clear how hurt she was. She would have preferred to be angry at me.

Helen appeared to be amused by Magda's appearance but otherwise totally unmoved.

"You say you need space. You say you want to get

better work. What kind of work is this?" Magda indicated me with a jut of her chin but she continued to stare at Helen. I noticed that Magda's eyes were bloodshot, and while she wasn't covered with dust, her blue jeans were faded and she looked as if she hadn't slept in some time. I started to edge away from them on the sidewalk. A few people walked past and glanced cautiously at the three of us. But Helen and Magda ignored them, locked into their own drama.

The sparkle in Helen's mood was dimming every second.

"Maybe you got her phone number while she was in the store?"

Helen, from her new height, spoke at last. "No, baby. It wasn't like that. I needed to get away to think about my future. I ran into Jo by accident and we just had coffee and talked. Come on." She put her hand on Magda's elbow, which at first prompted a furious scowl and then a kind of relieved relaxation. "We'll walk down to the water and talk. Good-bye, Jo."

" 'Bye."

Magda managed to shoot me one last glare before she turned her attention to Helen, who was speaking in a soothing tone as they walked. I went around the block to maintain the fiction of my nonconnection with Mrs. Madrone, and beat a hasty retreat into the hotel through the back entrance.

The manager was at the desk when I came in. He called my name and held out a wrapped bouquet, the blooms of a dozen red roses peeking out of the top. "These came for you. They didn't come from one of our usual florists so we had the security guard check them out for explosives."

He looked at me earnestly. I realized he wasn't joking

and glanced at the door to the street. That was a new
security guard next to the door. This one looked big and
tough and carried a side arm.

"Thank you." I took the flowers, hesitated a moment,
then went up in the elevator. The flowers might be from
Mulligan, but he would be in Seattle by now. Calling
from another city I would assume he would have been
likely to use a major florist the hotel would be familiar
with.

I greeted Raoul, who came up and wound himself
around my legs. I opened the small sealed envelope.
Block letters filled the card inside.

> STAY AWAY FROM THE RHYMERS.
> DON'T TALK TO POLICE
> OR
> YOU'LL LOSE MORE THAN A CAR.

I dropped it on the glass table as if it were suddenly
red hot. Gingerly, I picked up the bouquet and peeled
the cellophane and waxed paper off its stems. I started
to tremble when I saw the cat's flea collar wrapped
around the base of the stems, secured with a rubber
band.

29

I threw the bouquet down on the table and scooped up Raoul, who protested as I did so. He let me hold him for a polite second and squirmed free. A moment later he did that cat levitation thing, leaping up on the table with the incredible ease that seemed so contradictory to his bulk. Raoul sniffed the stems of the roses and the paper with the diligence of a forensic cat. Suddenly, I wondered if there might be some toxic substance on the flowers. But as I started up to remove the bouquet, Raoul's velvety gray nose had arrived at the flea collar. He blinked in distaste and turned away. He hopped off the table and strolled over to settle down alertly near the terrace door, which had become a favorite observation area.

The cat collar wrapped around the bouquet showed no signs of having been worn. Raoul probably would have examined it more closely if it had cat scent on it. It was an ordinary plastic flea collar. I left the bouquet and its wrapping paper on the table. I wanted to throw them out, but I wondered if I could learn something from them first. I wasn't sure what to do.

I went down to lobby. The manager was still there. I leaned over the desk. "The flowers you just gave me, when did they arrive?"

"A few hours ago."

"Tell me about the delivery person who brought them?"

"As I said, I wasn't familiar with the floral company but he did wear a coverall with a name on the pocket, I don't remember the name. Isn't the name of the florist on the roses?"

"No," I said, "there isn't any company name at all, which you should know. You said you checked the flowers carefully because it wasn't your normal florist."

"Yes." And because it was for you, who brought this bomb to our parking lot, his eyes continued, although he wasn't about to say that out loud. I worked for Mrs. Madrone.

"So what else do you remember about the person who delivered them?"

"A young Latino fella. He did keep looking over at the security guard, but then that's not uncommon. It's the uniforms."

He saw my puzzled look and explained further. "The new security company has uniforms very similar to the border patrol guards." He gave a nasty chuckle. "It spooks the illegals. That man might have been illegal. It wasn't the Latino man you were talking with in the courtyard the other day," he concluded with a barely concealed edge to his voice.

I just looked at him. After several seconds his smile died and I could almost see the gears turning in his mind as he tried to calculate whether he had gone too far, just how well I knew Ambrose, and whether he had just offended someone who could put in a bad word with Mrs. Madrone. I left him to contemplate the wrath of Ambrose and how an unfavorable reference from Mrs. Madrone might put a permanent pall on the higher forms of employment in the Western Hemisphere.

I went back up in the elevator almost as thoughtful as the manager. Raoul was still pointed toward the terrace door, but his alert posture had subsided into a nap. Although he twitched his ears when I came in, he didn't look up.

I called Ambrose. "There's something you should see."

Five minutes later he was looking down at the bouquet and the note that had come with them. Raoul roused himself to come over and rub against Ambrose's leg and thoroughly inspect his shoes—probably for traces of Prince's scent. Ambrose sat on the sofa and pulled the cat onto his lap and petted him while we talked. Raoul settled down happily under his touch.

"You want to put him in a cat carrier and leave now?" he asked over Raoul's fervent purring. "You could. Mrs. Madrone would understand."

"I'm tempted to do that." I sat down on the chair next to the sofa. "I can't see that I'm doing much good here now. I ran into Helen Hayworth coming in. Do you know her?"

"Yes." Ambrose raised his eyebrows. "She's in with Mrs. Madrone right now. Helen taught art at Amy's high school and she's known Sally Rhymer forever. Did she mention when you interviewed her out in the desert that she wanted her old job back?"

"No. I'd have put it in the report if she'd said that."

"Of course you would. You're not the devious type."

"Well, I didn't tell her I was working for Mrs. Madrone."

"I stand corrected, Jo. I've never asked how you do your job and as long as you don't break any laws, I don't want to know." We both sat still and listened to Raoul purr. "Are you finished with the Rhymers, do you think?"

"Except for the chess tournament tonight at the university. Have you talked to Mrs. Madrone about that?"

Ambrose nodded.

"I thought I'd go there, just say hi and good-bye. It's a public event, as I explained earlier—not near any of the family's homes or anything."

"All right," he agreed reluctantly. "But this afternoon maybe you should stick around here. I'll see about another security guard for you and make sure they're watching out for catnappers as well."

"More trouble and expense for Mrs. Madrone."

"Don't be a drama queen. You didn't kidnap Rhymer, and believe me, if you've let us know about a possible threat that could extend to Prince, you've helped us all. Whoever kidnapped the admiral might not be too choosy about which cat they grabbed."

He gave Raoul a final pat and deposited him on the sofa as he got up to go. Raoul promptly climbed down and followed Ambrose to the door. "I wonder how they knew to threaten your cat," he said as he went out. I suspected the staff was in for a grilling.

Stuck inside with only paperwork to distract me, thoughts of Mulligan came on with a vengeance. I would be a useless wreck in short order. The blind eye of the television stared at me, but I left it off, knowing it would not be able to hold my attention at a time like this.

I turned on the radio instead, cruising the dial looking for music that spoke to me. When people ask what kind of music I like, I say all kinds. I'm embarrassed to admit the truth, which is that I turn to music for a certain kind of exorcism and I never quite know what kind of music will do it, until I need to use it. Music, like sex or dancing, takes my words away and I have no armor. That afternoon I wanted the words in my head gone.

Sex would have been nice but none was on tap so I turned on the music, surfed the dial, and cried at sentimental songs. I danced when the music had an infectious beat and cried more under Raoul's occasional gaze. I pushed back the memories of Mulligan over the last few days. The taste of him, the smell of him, and his touch. The unreachable place he had retreated to. The music rolled every hurt my heart had known since puberty into one long, present-tense blue reel of tears.

Finally, I stopped. I was finished. Not done but tired enough to have to stop. I snapped off the radio, sat and stared at the wall, unable to think of one thing I wanted to do. The words were gone for the moment and thoughts of Mulligan were banished. I took a shower, brewed a cup of tea, and sat staring blankly at the band of sky visible through the glass terrace door. My hair was nearly dry and Raoul had curled up into a motionless ball of total relaxation. Then I had an idea.

After looking up a few numbers I called the naval base and asked to be connected to Admiral Coffin's office. I left a message—no real expectation of speaking to the man right off the bat. He called back a few moments later.

"Ms. Fuller."

"Admiral Coffin. I was just calling because I'd heard an extraordinary thing about a tape that might have been in Admiral Rhymer's possession."

"Tell me what you've heard." He wasn't laughing now. I could tell he was interested, and wary.

"I still haven't got hold of the tape, but I spoke to someone who had heard it. He said it was a flight-deck recording of a Vietnam-era bombing mission. The pilot was shot down but just before he was, he said something about Wild Weasel being compromised."

There was silence at the other end of the line. "You heard this tape?"

"No. I'm afraid this is secondhand. Brad Rhymer had it and I can give you the name and number of someone whom Brad Rhymer played it for."

"Please, if you would be so kind."

Saying "please" so nicely made up for the way he had laughed at me at our last meeting. I was smiling as I gave him Jerry Buck's name and phone number. When I mentioned Buck's place of employment, Coffin went so far as to curse under his breath, which made my day. He instantly recovered himself enough to thank me in an even tone of voice.

I hung up the phone with the closest feeling to pleasure I'd had since Mulligan left.

30

The chess tournament started at seven o'clock. I'd arranged to meet Ivor at his office at the university at six-thirty. For once there were no stern ladies to impress so I just put on a cotton blouse and pants. I still had a few hours to kill. Even if I went in a little earlier. That gave me another idea.

I called Martha Meade's house and got Ondine Feather. For the first time since I'd met her, she sounded sulky and irritable. I asked to speak to Martha, and she said curtly, "Wait." A moment later she came back on the line, and said, "I hope you won't do any more damage. She said she'd talk to you, even though I told her she doesn't have to."

Martha Meade came on the line, whispering a very cautious "Hello." She did seem sober, for which I was intensely grateful.

"Hello, Mrs. Meade, I'm sorry things were so difficult the last time we spoke. But I'm calling because I have a chance to find the people who may have done this terrible thing. I just need one piece of information. You said the admiral's former driver worked for Stewart. Do you have his number?" She called Lance to get her husband's address book and gave me the number. As I wrote it down I realized it wouldn't hurt to ask. "You wouldn't happen to have a copy of any of the admiral's cassette tapes would you?"

Her voice got a little stronger, speaking of entertainment matters. "No, dear, we switched to CDs long ago. I doubt that there's a cassette tape left in the house."

She hung up before I could say another word.

I tried the number she gave me. It rang so many times that I nearly hung up when a man answered. When I asked for Douglas Dufrane he didn't seem suspicious. "My son is out. I don't expect him back till late." Something in his voice gave me the idea that he was not adverse to chatting with a female caller.

"What time tomorrow would be a good time to call?"

"I'm not sure. Sometimes he stays up in our place in San Berdoo, he's got a machine shop set up on the old premises."

"That's a long commute from here."

"Douglas doesn't mind. It's been years since he got that vehicle with the hand controls but he'd still rather be behind the steering wheel than in a wheelchair—no offense if you're in a chair as well."

"No, actually I'm a friend of a woman who is, though." I hoped Mrs. Madrone would forgive me this imposition although she would never know of it.

"Really?" It sounded as if the idea interested him.

"Yes. I'm not sure if I have the right person. Someone had said something about his doing customization on wheelchairs."

"Oh, yes. He's done work on some. You'll have to ask him yourself, though I'm sure he'd like to help."

"Well, I'll try again tomorrow."

"Do you want to leave a number?"

I had to pause. For some reason I really did not want to leave a phone number with this man and I wasn't sure why. But I ended up leaving the 800 number that Ambrose answered for me and said someone there could take a message for Josie. Even leaving that much information gave me the feeling of having made a dangerous mistake. Was it because Douglas had been a navy SEAL and the bomb that destroyed the Lexus had used SEAL expertise?

Yes, Jo, I told myself, *that's a pretty good reason not to leave your number. And why didn't you think of it before you did, hmm?*

I had to keep my mind in motion or I would start to get very nervous indeed. I called Dwight and Colleen's house. Dwight answered. I asked if he had a number for Fred Luna. He said he thought so, sounding both patient and massively put-upon as he gave me the number.

I thanked him a little more warmly than I expected. "Oh, since I've got you on the phone, may I ask you a military question?"

"A military question? Yes, ma'am, I'll try to help you out if I can."

"What is a Wild Weasel?"

He seemed a little startled but answered readily enough. "It is, or was, a radar-equipped, two-person F-4 aircraft. The navy used them with their Intruder series to draw fire, target, and hit antiaircraft installations. The old Wild Weasel F-4s have all been discontinued. I think some of them were sold to other countries. Nowadays they use specially equipped F-16s to draw and suppress enemy fire."

"Obviously the fact that you can tell me that means that the Wild Weasels haven't been classified information for quite some time."

"Yes, ma'am. That's correct. In fact, I have a plastic model of one in the cottage behind my house that I put together several years ago."

"Yes, I believe I saw that. Were those the planes your father flew in Vietnam?"

"He flew F-4s but he was an Intruder pilot, not a Wild Weasel." His voice was infinitely weary but there was a certain affectionate pride there as well.

"Thank you for explaining all that to me."

"No problem. It's the most interesting question anyone's asked me in several days."

"You wouldn't happen to have heard a Vietnam-era flight-deck recording your father had?"

He hesitated and I wondered if someone else, such as Admiral Coffin, had asked him this question. "No, ma'am. My father and I didn't listen to tapes together," he finally replied with a touch of disdain, as if listening to tapes with his father would have been an improper thing to do. I did note that he used the past tense when he referred to his father.

I thanked him and said good-bye. I couldn't think of any way to ask what I really wanted to know, about the ransom payment and his plans for leaving the navy, and whether his father's crude advances to his wife had made him snap and do something he now regretted.

My last call was to Fred Luna's house. A woman answered. "Mrs. Luna?"

"Yes." I could hear Spanish-language television or radio in the background.

"I'm Josephine Fuller. I'm working for Mrs. Madrone and I have a question to ask Lani."

"She's not here right now. You want me to take a message?"

"I wonder if she has a tape the admiral might have copied. It's a pilot talking to a control tower. If she has it, I'd like to borrow it."

"Okay, I'll tell her."

I got to the university at five-thirty, totally uncertain what I would do for the hour till I could talk to Ivor. The Life Sciences Building was quiet after most of the daytime classes were over and the evening classes had not yet begun. I walked along the institutional linoleum halls. One looked like another and I wasn't totally sure whether I was passing the same set of laboratories again or a new row of identical frosted-glass doors. The halls had the time-honored science-building air of formaldehyde and a kind of stressed-rubber smell that must have something to do with gaskets on lab equipment. Bulletin boards lining the halls held tide tables, anatomy diagrams, and Gary Larsen cartoons.

At last I found Ivor's office. It was locked, although the light was on behind the frosted glass. I knocked but there was no answer and no sounds of life coming from inside.

The Life Sciences Department office at the end of this corridor was locked, its window darkened.

A door to one of the darkened laboratories opened and I realized I was alone in that long hallway. It had been several minutes since I'd seen another human being. Worse yet, I was so lost in the maze of closed doors that I had no idea which direction to run.

You're early."

The figure coming out of the darkened lab was Ivor.

I leaned against the nearest wall, realizing my heart was pumping wildly. "You startled me. What were you doing in the dark there?"

"I don't know if you realize that it may not be that safe around here. Parts of the campus are practically deserted during summer session. There's a security guard escort to take women students and faculty to their cars."

I gulped. "I wish you'd mentioned that earlier."

"Sorry. I knew you were coming to the tournament, but somehow I didn't realize that you'd be traveling alone. When Stef and Amy come, I make sure they don't go anywhere unaccompanied. Parts of this campus can be dangerous even in the daytime when there aren't a lot of people around."

"Dangerous how?"

"It's an urban campus. That's one of the reasons I lock my office when I go down the hall." He seemed distracted. "Amy and Stef will be meeting us at the student union. There's time to get a sandwich. Want to come?"

"Sure." I realized that with all the talk about crime on the campus and danger to unaccompanied women, he hadn't answered my question about what he was doing in the darkened laboratory. I asked again.

He looked up from writing a note on a notepad affixed to his office door. "In case someone from the tournament comes looking for me," he said, tapping the
notepad. "In answer to your question, I was napping."

"Why not in your office?"

"I happened to be in the lab using some of the equipment and I got drowsy. I try to sleep when and where
I can, Ms. Fuller. It's been total chaos at home, it's a
relief to come to work sometimes, even when I'm not
teaching classes."

I wasn't totally satisfied with his answer, but I had
no reason not to believe him. "Sorry, but you really
scared me, coming out of nowhere like that."

"Once again, I apologize. I heard something in the
hallway that woke me up and for all I knew, it could
have been a junior criminal trying to break into one of
the offices."

"That's happened?"

"Well, sometimes the scientific trappings give kids
the illusions that we might have drugs here, which we
do not. Or expensive equipment worth stealing, which
we do."

We walked across the lawn in the late afternoon sun.
"It's a beautiful campus."

"Yes. It's a pity I probably won't be working here
anymore. I'll have to go back out on the job market
with a couple of thousand other part-time professors."

We went through the student union to the cafeteria.

"Not too many people here," I said as we walked into
the sparsely populated lounge.

"Normally we'd get all the night students coming in
about now, but there aren't that many night classes in
the summer."

Several groups of younger students gathered at tables in groups, wearing the latest trends in Southern California casual wear, talking loudly. A few more serious-looking, older people arrived in ones and twos, some still dressed for the office while others had the trademark short haircuts and disciplined bearing that gave them a military look even in civilian casual clothing.

Ivor led me to the cafeteria counter. There was no line. He recommended the meatless hamburgers with hearty amounts of lettuce, tomato, and sweet onions and bottled juice drinks.

"The casseroles Zane brought to your house the other day—are you vegetarians?"

"We're hovering on the edge. Zane is always encouraging us to take the plunge and give up the bad stuff." He smiled indulgently. It was clear that even thinking about his playful friend lightened his mood. "His family is vegetarian and pacifist. I don't think Zane has ever tasted meat, coffee, tea—certainly not alcohol or drugs. He's skipped a few grades and he's getting close to finishing a Ph.D. in molecular biology. Both his parents will be playing in the tournament tonight."

"That must be unusual."

"Well, one parent is more usual. The Birches are part of the liberal underground in this town. His dad was a draft resister. After the amnesty his family moved back to the U.S. Dr. Birch got a job at the university here, but it's like a bunch of doves nesting on a rifle range. I've always thought it was a classic case of rebellion that Zane is so fascinated by military things. It must drive his parents crazy, although they never speak of it. They are proud of his chess. He has tremendous strategic ability over the game board, but he's probably destined to be a professor like his dad."

"It is a little odd that Stef would be such close friends with all these adult chess players."

"Zane is good with all the younger players," Ivor said gently. "Maybe because he's young for his age—" Ivor broke off in midsentence and stared at me for several seconds. "If you are suggesting that I would leave my daughter alone with any adult who might not be trustworthy, I resent it. Parents in this day and age can't take any chances with their kids, and I don't."

"Sorry, I didn't mean to suggest that. Does Amy play chess?"

"No," he said immediately. Then he tilted his head and relented. "Well, she's played some, but she doesn't enjoy tournaments. She doesn't have the killer instinct. Just as well for me, I guess." Ivor smiled and shook his head. Then he fell silent as if suddenly thinking of the nongame lethal situation they were caught up in.

We finished the sandwiches in mildly uncomfortable silence. We were sipping the last of the juice when I asked him where he intended to apply for his next teaching job.

"Everyplace where there is a suggestion of an opening. I have to apply everywhere." The tension that had receded into the background instantly shot back up with an almost audible hum.

"There are just too many of us male, white baby boomers with Ph.D.s. I blame the Vietnam War."

"That's an odd theory."

"Not when you think about it. I came from a poor family. I enlisted in the military right out of high school. It was what my father did. It seemed like the honorable thing to do. But when I go back, aside from the antiwar protests, what did I find? Rich kids who were keeping their draft deferments current by getting doctoral degrees they never in a million years would have otherwise attempted. The whole educational draft-deferment policy ended up producing a generation of over-educated, underdisciplined elitist—"

"Uh, excuse me." Dim memories of modern history classes had begun to surface. "Wasn't the draft a lottery?"

"That was toward the end of the war. I wasn't the only person to notice how all the rich kids weren't getting drafted because they had carved out a room in the ivory tower. Now, what exactly is a Ph.D. good for?"

He stared at me. I shrugged.

"A Ph.D. qualifies you to teach college," he said glumly.

I didn't want to set him off again. He was talking a little too loudly and people at other tables glanced at us. They couldn't quite catch the words but the bitter edge to his voice cut across the room.

"Look!" I noticed Amy and Stef entering the cafeteria. Ivor and I waved. When they came to sit with us, I noticed Amy got a bottled apple juice, Stef a carton of milk.

"No dinner?" I asked.

"We heated up one of Zane's casseroles at home," Amy said.

"I get nervous if I eat just before a game starts," Stef said.

"You don't look very nervous."

"That's because right now there's no chess clock ticking and no guy glaring at a chess board in front of me," she said cheerfully.

"You've got a confident kid there," I said to Amy and Ivor.

"That's the best kind," Ivor said. Amy only smiled.

But something must have been communicated by some kind of spousal telegraph because within a few seconds both of them were getting ready to go over to the Humanities Building where the chess tournament was being held. The Russo family was answering no further questions.

Stef was several paces ahead of us on the stairs up to the second floor. The tournament took over a couple of large classrooms. Long tables were lined up with chairs on either side. It took me a few minutes to realize that there were very few women of any age here. Men were unrolling plastic mat chessboards, setting up chess sets and taking clocks out of their small cases. The elevator opened and several more men came out, a few rolling in wheelchairs. A bookseller had set up shop behind a long, folding table at the end of the hall. I went to look at his wares, all chess books, most of them with diagrams, small travel chess sets, and even a few of the Golden Triangle Chess Club shirts like the one I had seen Zane Birch wearing. I didn't see Zane, but I was pretty sure one of the guys in a wheelchair was the gruff Duke, although this was the first time I had seen his companion outside of the shadows of the van. Juan was short and wiry but strong looking. His skin was as dark as mahogany and he glanced around at the tournament with total disinterest, exchanged a few words with Duke, and went to sit in a chair in the hallway and almost immediately began to doze off.

For a few minutes Amy, Stef, and I were the only females in the area, then one or two other women arrived. Stef was still by far the youngest female here, although there were a few males her age.

I asked Stef what the purpose was of the sheets of paper bearing numbers that were taped to the tables at each chess board. She explained that the numbers referred to the ranking of the boards. "See that man putting the notice on the bulletin board out there? He's the tournament director and he's posting the pairings. The highest-rated players start on board one. Two, three, and so on. The top players are paired with lower-ranking players in the first round. It's the Swiss system."

"Okay."

"We have some really good players here," Stef said, naming several people whom I had never heard of. It must have been clear that I was lost because she said, "Well, I've got to go set up my board."

"Good luck."

"Thanks."

I looked around and Ivor was talking to a man and a woman about his own age. Could those be Zane's parents?

Out in the hallway Amy was talking to a disheveled man in blue jeans and a Guatemalan poncho. I came out just as he was embracing her firmly. His long mane of curly black hair was liberally streaked with gray.

"We had great morels up in the Sierras last month. Even this late, they tell me some are still showing up on Vancouver Island. Why don't you take off for a week and come up north? If Ivor's busy you could come with me and Jocasta. Bring Stef, or has she turned into one of those girls who won't get her hands dirty?"

Amy looked more animated than I'd yet seen her. "I wish we could go. But Ivor's teaching summer session and Stef has a couple of summer classes too. Maybe we can get away later."

He shambled off down the hall like a big brown bear in a cotton poncho. Amy turned to me a little wistfully. "I miss the mushroom people."

"What's that?" Ivor asked, coming out of the player's room and closing the door on the ticking of many clocks. "They've started, so we have to be quiet." The man in overalls disappeared around a corner at the far end of the hall and all of a sudden the hallway was deserted except for Ivor, Amy, and me, and Juan dozing in the folding chair outside the tournament room.

"Aren't you playing?" I asked Ivor.

"I am, but my opponent is late. He has the white pieces so he has to move first. All I can do is set up the pieces and wait. If he's an hour late, he'll forfeit the game, but he's pretty highly ranked, he's probably just trying to psych me out."

"I was just talking to Stanley," Amy told her husband. "He was trying to tempt us out on the morel trail. He said they're showing up on the logging trails in the Sierras."

Ivor wrapped an arm around Amy's shoulders. "You'd like to get away, wouldn't you?" he said softly.

"Yes." She sighed. "We could get there by tomorrow dawn. If we didn't have this crisis going on, it would probably do Stef some good to get away too."

For a moment, the Russos seemed lost in their own private world. Ivor came out of it first. He squeezed Amy's shoulder and then dropped his arm and drew back, "Even if we didn't have this whole thing with your father missing, I just can't take time to go off chasing mushrooms with a bunch of mycologists right now." He lowered his voice. "Not till this whole job issue is resolved."

He glanced back at me with some mistrust and summoned up a smile that wasn't very convincing. "If this job disintegrates and another one doesn't show up by fall," he explained for my benefit, "we can go forage for all kinds of wild plants every weekend and during the week, when I'm not looking for another job."

For a moment, I wondered if the Russos' finances were so dire that they had to search for wild nuts and berries. I decided it was more likely a hobby thing they couldn't afford to indulge just now.

Amy nodded to her husband but I watched as a wave of surprise went through her body like a shock wave when the elevator doors at the end of the hall opened. I turned to see Ambrose standing aside, holding the door for Mrs. Madrone, attended by two nurses and Sally Rhymer.

32

Juan sat up and examined the new arrivals with bleary-eyed interest. After a few seconds, he got up and carried the duffel bag into the room where all clocks were ticking.

Ambrose hailed us and I went over to greet Mrs. Madrone and her group. Sally Rhymer and her daughter looked each other over cautiously. "We've come to see Stefanie play. She is playing, isn't she?" Sally asked of no one in particular.

Amy slowly walked over to her mother and stood before her. "Hi, Mom." They exchanged a brief embrace, from which both stepped back awkwardly.

Ivor stepped in and took Sally by the elbow. "Come on, she's in here. She's doing pretty good tonight, she's on board twenty. The first round just started a little while ago, so not much is happening yet, but we'll have to be quiet. She's paired up this round. That means Stef's opponent is higher ranked than she is. I don't want her to think she has to entertain us." He looked at Mrs. Rhymer with a sternness that was only partly in mockery.

"Of course not, dear," Sally Rhymer said meekly.

I glanced over at Amy. Her face was completely still, her eyes narrowed in mistrust.

With Sally Rhymer in tow, Ivor and Amy led the way into the room of ticking clocks. I followed Mrs. Madrone and her attendants. Even with the ticking of a few dozen clocks, the room was full of silence.

Stef had just completed a move and hit the button, stopping her clock and starting her opponent's. Across the table from her, a young man in a UC sweatshirt and jeans scowled at the board. Stef got up and stretched her arms a little. She seemed relaxed and serene, despite the almost palpable concentration that seemed to vibrate off the players like steam off boiling water. Stef looked around to see her grandmother and Mrs. Madrone advancing on the room. She got up and hugged her grandmother, who hugged her back but whispered something to her that must have been an admonition to return to the game.

I was surprised to find that Mrs. Madrone's presence with her nurses, Ambrose, and Sally Rhymer made no stir whatsoever. The group worked its way around the room pausing at certain boards to briefly examine the positioning of the pieces. Ivor whispered loudly enough for me to hear that only the opening moves could be seen so early in the evening.

I had time to look more carefully at the players. There were three players in wheelchairs. The tables had been set up with wide enough aisles to let them wheel around and look at the other games, so of course Mrs. Madrone could do so as well.

Juan now sat with the duffel bag in a chair on the sidelines, near the row of boards where Duke was playing.

Duke had scarcely looked up when the Madrone group entered, but as they approached his board with Mrs. Madrone leading the way, Duke glanced up, blinked at Mrs. Madrone, and then stared at Sally Rhymer. She paused and nodded politely to him. "Douglas."

He nodded curtly, and muttered. I was just barely

close enough to hear him say, "Ma'am. Forgive me for not getting up." He bumped the table as he swiftly wheeled back from it. The chess pieces trembled on the board, causing his African American opponent to steady it with one hand and give him a look of alarm.

Duke rolled out of the room without looking back. Juan grabbed the duffel bag and trotted after him. Mrs. Madrone and company emerged from their circuit of the room in time to see Duke round the corner of the hallway.

Mrs. Madrone asked, "Who is that man?" so softly that I almost didn't hear her.

Sally Rhymer took a moment to answer. "That's Ron's former driver, the one who was injured in the traffic accident. I haven't seen him in ten years."

Stef joined the group in the hallway. They congratulated her on her ranking in the tournament. "We don't want to distract you. Go on and get back to your game," Mrs. Rhymer said. Stef nodded and turned back into the room with its air of deep concentration hovering on the percolating ticking of all those clocks.

Amy walked her mother and Mrs. Madrone back to the elevator. Ambrose looked at his watch. Almost as if on cue, the elevator arrived and Dwight and Colleen got off. They greeted Sally Rhymer and Mrs. Madrone with equal affection. Clearly they weren't familiar with chess tournament etiquette because Ernesto Garcia bustled up to them and very softly told everyone to please be quiet for the players' sake. Some of the players were less polite about it, and several loud shushes came from irate players who had come out to the hall to quiet the group. Ivor came over and introduced the tournament director to the newcomers. I could tell the old man recognized Mrs. Madrone's name, and he bowed over her hand with Old World courtesy that appeared to charm her.

I hung back with Ambrose and the two nurses. "Did Dwight and Colleen mean to come to the tournament?"

"I think they wanted to stop by and thank Mrs. Madrone," he said.

Amy had the same idea. I heard her tell Mrs. Madrone, "We are so grateful to you for helping us try to get my father back alive." She bent to kiss Mrs. Madrone's cheek and it was the first time I remember seeing my employer truly moved. Then the elevator door opened, Amy allowed her mother a brief hug, and Mrs. Madrone and her entourage swept through the doors and out of sight. Dwight and Colleen took a curious circuit of the room where the tournament was going on before they left. Stef was back at her board and concentrating so fiercely that they could not have gotten her attention if they tried.

After the elevator closed on Dwight and Colleen, I turned back to see Amy Russo staring at me. It took a moment to realize that she was furious. She came over and tapped me on the elbow. "I need to talk to you now," she said, her mouth tight with anger. "I don't want to disturb the players. Follow me."

We went along the hallway to the stairwell and out the fire doors. We were alone in the hallway. I could feel Amy's anger and it gave me a sinking sick feeling. I realized I liked her and I wanted her to like me. Right now she hated my guts. Her face was flushed and her pale blue eyes had a dangerous light to them.

She led the way down the stairs to the entryway just inside the glass doors at the front of the building. Another set of glass doors led back into the first-floor classrooms. When classes were in session most students probably wouldn't bother waiting for the elevators in the middle of the building. It was far enough away from the chess tournament here that even if we yelled we wouldn't disturb the players.

Amy did look angry enough to shout, but she kept her voice down, although her words were clipped. "What the hell are you doing bringing my mother to see Stef? I realize you work for Mrs. Madrone, but if I decide my daughter is better off not seeing her grandmother, how is it remotely any of your business?"

"You guessed it yourself, earlier. Mrs. Madrone was considering giving a grant to the Feather Heart Foundation because your mother was worried about you and missing Stef."

"It was your excuse to snoop, in other words."

"You didn't seem to mind my hanging around, or Mrs. Madrone's interference when it was useful to you. Frankly, I told your mother if she took an interest in Stef's chess, it might be a way to see her. Mrs. Madrone actually plays chess—"

"So you took it upon yourself to invite them!"

"Look, they behaved themselves. Stef didn't seem too upset, what's the problem?"

"The problem is that you can't even imagine the damage that woman has done to me." Amy leaned so close for a moment that I backed up a step instinctively. She was so angry that she was literally trembling, on the verge of violence or tears, it was hard to tell which. "Did she happen to tell you I tried to kill myself twice before I was sixteen because of her constant nagging?"

"Amy, I apologize. I didn't want to bother you because of the whole thing with the kidnapping. I didn't mean to interfere. But I do understand some of what you're going through. My parents kept bugging me too when I was a little fat kid. My mother died when I was thirteen—"

"You were lucky." Amy sat down in one of the folding chairs and let out a puff of breath. "I'm sorry. I didn't mean that. Sometimes I wish everyone who was mean to me would die. And when someone is mean to my little girl, I literally could kill them."

"I understand," I said, and I did, although for a split second I couldn't help but wonder whether Stewart Meade had ever teased Stef. I pushed the chair with the writing desk arm out of the way and pulled the other folding chair close and sat near Amy.

"When I was teased at school because of my size I couldn't go to my mother," Amy said. "Because she treated me worse than any of the kids. She told me it was my fault I was fat and I deserved to be teased. Sometimes the diets made me lose weight for a little while. I was always hungry and I tried my best. But no matter how little I ate, I would always stop losing and then start gaining again. Then my mother would blame me for cheating. Once I didn't eat anything at all for three weeks and I gained four pounds. No one believed me." She wiped away a tear and I looked in my purse for tissues. None.

Amy took a deep breath. "My father just vanished; once he saw I wasn't going to be a pretty little doll, he wrote me off like a bad debt. I tried so hard." Her chin quivered and for a moment I thought she would begin to sob. "For as long as I could remember, everyone thought I was not just fat, but deceitful and evil and ugly."

"I know. I have been there," I said, not really expecting her to hear me.

"Ivor saved my life by seeing me as a woman and

loving me as a person. Now my father treats me with minimal respect because I produced a smart grandchild. But my mother only saw me as a problem, a girl who wasn't pretty. I won't let her do that to Stef." She fell silent and wiped her eyes on her sleeve.

"But what does Stef—"

"I won't let them at Stef," she broke in before I could finish. "The damage is done with me, but Stef has a chance. We make sure she knows we think she can do anything she sets her mind to. She has chess and she has friends who don't rip her down. She has a father who spends time with her. I just feel so guilty that . . ." She started to sob.

I looked in my purse again and miraculously, found my travel pack of tissues, and held it out to her. She took a few.

"Amy, I was a fat kid too," I said earnestly. "My parents took me from doctor to doctor and from diet to diet. But when I was fifteen I met a large woman, Nina, who was older and very beautiful and she told me I was okay the way I was and not to let anyone tell me different. I'm telling you that now because it's true."

"It's not only Stef," Amy said softly. "I know I haven't been a good wife to Ivor." Her voice sank to a whisper and she glanced around. "Those faculty wives. I hate that social jungle. It's everything my mother wanted me to be and I never was. Ivor must have thought I'd be good at it, coming from a military family. But those women scare me. They sense how much I've been beaten down. It was okay when Stef was little because they keep their claws sheathed around the kids. But once she got older, I was on my own. I was really looking forward to another baby, but when I lost it, I realized I wanted the baby as a shield to protect me from those bitchy women."

"Do you even have to socialize with them, if you don't like them?" I asked.

"I do. Ivor is about to lose this job. Oh, I don't blame myself totally, the university is cutting back. But people wonder why Ivor can't get tenure anywhere. I couldn't make them give it to him, but I haven't exactly helped, have I?"

"Ivor hasn't said anything like that, has he?" I wondered if Ivor had an abusive side I had not witnessed.

"No." She sniffed and wiped her face with a tissue.

"Amy, you are an intelligent, lovely woman. You and Ivor care about each other and about your daughter. Blaming yourself for things you can't control only makes them worse. I think Stef is stronger than you realize, but she's going to need you to be there for her, telling her she's okay—especially when she becomes a teenager. It's hard work, but for Stef's sake, you have to learn how to not beat up on yourself. Because if you do, she'll learn that from you."

Amy looked at me bleakly. I wasn't sure if she could understand what I was saying, let alone accept it.

"I think she could stand a little bit of contact with your mother," I said. "You might have to set some ground rules to make your mother behave."

"You've met my mother. Does she seem like the sort of person to follow anyone else's rules?"

"Actually, by staying away from her this past year, you've made it easier," I said, risking a pat on her shoulder. "Just tell her clearly that the first comment she makes about your appearance or Stefanie's, or any kind of diet promotion talk, and you will leave. Tell Stefanie she doesn't have to listen to it either. If your mother

says one word that puts you down, tell her she's been
warned. If she says one more word, leave the room."

Amy looked at me carefully for several seconds. "I'll
think about it," she said at last. "Once this mess is over
with Dad, I'll talk to Ivor. What you said might work."

"It really is up to you," I said. "But your mother has
self-control. I'll bet she could swallow her insults if you
make it clear that that's the only way she'll ever see her
granddaughter."

Amy sat for a minute absorbing this. "Jo, I've never
told anyone this, but when I had the miscarriage she
told me it was my fault because I was fat."

For a moment I thought how satisfying it would be
to hit Sally Rhymer. "That's the stupidest thing I've
ever heard of. That's pure prejudice," I said, enraged at
the idea. "I'm so sorry, Amy." I wanted to hug her but
I thought she was probably still angry with me. "I had
no idea she was that cruel. Just forget what I've said.
If your mother can't be trusted to keep a civil tongue
in her head, you shouldn't see her or let Stef see her."

Amy smiled the faintest ghost of a smile and reached
out and clutched my hand for a moment. We both
sighed. "We should get back to the tournament, but I
think I'd better go to the ladies' room first," Amy said
after a moment. I went with her. After she had bathed
her face in cold water, she looked reasonably normal
and we went back in to the chess tournament. I stayed
a few more minutes. Everyone had settled down to seriously staring at chess pieces on boards. The only
sound was the ticking of a couple dozen chess clocks
and the occasional scrape of a chair when someone got
up to wander around and look at other people's games.

Ivor introduced me to Zane Birch's parents. The father was short and thin, and wore a tweed jacket despite

the balmy San Diego evening, while his wife, a little taller but also thin, wore what looked like a handwoven dress with a tangle of amber necklaces and matching bracelets. I hadn't seen Zane, so I asked if their son was attending. I didn't mention that I'd been anticipating some new military costume. They told me Zane had been forced to skip the tournament to complete some grant applications.

I said good night to Amy and Ivor with the thought that I would probably not see them again. I gave Amy one of my cards and asked her to call if she needed to talk.

It wasn't until I was crossing the floor of the dark-ened parking structure that I remembered Ivor's lecture about crime on campus. Like so much of the campus, the place was sparsely populated. I heard an engine coming around the central structure and a battered Toy-ota Corolla pulled up in front of me blocking my way as I hurried toward the rental car.

I stepped between two parked cars and was about to run for the exit when I realized that I was standing next to a green Saab like the one Lance Feather drove. A familiar voice called, "Hey! Stay away from my car!"

Lance and Ondine Feather were walking toward the Saab, one on either side of Martha Meade.

"What are you doing here?" I asked.

Martha drew herself up to an unusually dignified pos-ture. "It's not your business what Lance and I did in rehab back in Virginia," she said. Ondine murmured something to her and shot me a venomous look.

"I just gave a talk on the hospice movement to a medical ethics course," Lance explained, ignoring Mar-tha and Ondine. "Amy set it up and then she didn't come to hear it." He seemed more miffed by Amy's lack of attendance than by my accusations.

"She's at the chess tournament. Her daughter is playing," I said.

"Oh." Lance seemed slightly mollified. He opened the door for Martha to get in the passenger side, while Ondine climbed in back. "Good night."

"Good night." I turned away as Lance started the engine and gunned the Saab out of the building with a squeal of brakes. I went toward my rental car, but before I could open the door, the battered Toyota cruised past again and stopped.

The driver rolled down the window and I saw it was Fred Luna holding out a cassette tape. "My wife said you wanted this." He held out a tape cassette.

"You had a copy?"

"Lani took all the cassettes with her. She said the admiral used to play this one from time to time. He used to keep it in his classified documents safe, she said, but then he started keeping it out with the rest of the tapes. He never said much about it to her, just played it. It got mixed in with hers."

"Have you ever listened to it?"

"No, it's the first I knew it existed. I just got it from Lani about an hour ago. You think that tape will help?"

"Admiral Coffin sure was interested in it."

Fred whistled. "Okay. Are you going to give it to him?"

"Well, I might give him a copy," I said. "But first I'm going to take it to my homegrown expert and find out what this is all about. By the way, how did you know to find me here? Are you following me?"

"Nope. Don't have to. I've got to keep moving. 'Bye."

33

Traffic was light and half an hour later I was knocking on the door to Ambrose's suite, which was on the floor below Mrs. Madrone's penthouse. Fortunately, he was in and agreed to listen to the tape with me and see what could be done about it. I had never seen Ambrose's personal space before. Either he traveled with an assortment of personal possessions or he maintained the suite between visits. The place of honor was given to a large print of an early California mission. I counted four clocks of artistic design.

Ambrose handed me a glass of cola while he powered up a compact, but high-tech, sound system. The tape began with a crackle of static that announced a very bad recording. Then a scratching sound that might have been fabric against fabric, and a voice, very loud, saying:

"Hey, Vincenzo Lorenzo, baby. I saw you two weeks ago in a bar in Patpong."

"So what, Rhymer? You've got some nerve coming in here."

"It was the Blue Orchid on Soi Katoey. So that's where you go."

"So what? You were there too. Get fucked."

"I did."

"That's why you went there, isn't it?"

"They had a barmaid too—a little something for

everyone. Hate to bother you but that tape you've got, play it for me, would you?"

There was a pause and then a resigned sigh.

"It's gonna get lost, listen while you can."

The rest of the tape was fainter, but it was indeed a recording of the last few minutes of a pilot's flight into heavy antiaircraft fire, ending with the frantic exclamation:

"Fucking SAMs are on top of me! Where the fuck is Wild Weasel?"

This was followed by several seconds of static.

"Poor bastard."
"Get out, Rhymer. Show's over."
"Vincenzo, baby, you think Wild Weasel is compromised?"
"Fuck if I know."
"Thanks."
"Don't bother me again."

That was the end of the recording. The rest was static.
I looked at Ambrose. There was an odd light in his eyes. "Do you know who Vincent Lorenzo is?" he asked.
"No."
"Try the Chief of Naval Operations."
"That's like the Joint Chiefs of Staff."
"One of them."
"You think it's a security thing, about the Wild Wea-

sel?" I explained what Dwight Rhymer had told me about the Wild Weasel. "It was classified during the war, although it isn't now."

"I'll look into that. It's clearly a Vietnam-era recording. It was probably a breach of security to mention it on radio where the enemy could hear it—not that the pilot would have lived to answer to any inquiry. But I'd bet the frame is more valuable than the picture. Ron Rhymer must have made the recording with a hidden tape recorder, just to get Lorenzo to confirm it. Do you know what Soi Katoey is?"

"No."

"In the Patpong District in Bangkok, Thailand, it means Homosexual Street."

I left the tape with Ambrose and went down in the elevator thoughtfully.

As I went to put the key in the lock to my room, someone moved in the shadows. I leaped back several steps before I even fully grasped what I saw.

34

The person in the shadows sniffed mournfully and I looked closer.

"Amy! What are you doing here?"

"I had your room number and I came up. I wanted to wait for you. It's important. We need to talk inside, where no one can hear."

There was an urgent tone in her voice. When I opened the door, I noticed that she was half carrying, half dragging a very heavy backpack. I went straight to the refrigerator and brought out the bottle of cold water. She followed me there. I poured a glass and held it out for Amy.

Her face was frantic and she gestured as if to knock it out of my hands. "No! There's no time."

I drank most of the water myself before replying. Somehow during the evening I'd got very thirsty and I was getting very tired by the continual crisis of the last week. "Tell me what happened?"

"They've got Stef!"

"What! The kidnappers? How could they? I just saw Stef at the tournament."

"I don't know how they did it. Tonight at the chess tournament she left the room where they were playing for a minute. I was talking to Ivor, I didn't see where she went. I thought she might have gone to the restroom but she wasn't there. She just disappeared."

"But why? How do you know?"

"I couldn't tell you before what happened with the ransom. The police told me not to tell anyone. But the kidnappers called last night and told me to take the ransom out by Mission Bay. I drove out where they told me and waited for hours. But no one showed up to take it. The police said they would call again, but they never did. Tonight while we were looking for Stef someone came up to tell me there was a call for me on the pay phone in the hall. It was them."

"The kidnappers?"

She nodded. "They said they knew the police had followed me before and if I wanted to see my daughter again I should tell the police nothing and bring the money over here to you."

"Oh, my God."

"It's my daughter's life." Her eyes lighted on the bouquet of flowers with the cat collar around it, and she gasped. "No! I found one of those on the seat of our van when I went home to get the pack with the money. Only it had Stef's watch wrapped around it. Her Minnie Mouse watch." Amy began to cry again and I sat down next to her and hugged her.

As I patted her back, I couldn't help but look over her shoulder to see that the deck door was open and Raoul was nowhere in sight. I couldn't imagine they would be so organized as to kidnap him along with Stefanie Russo. Or had someone taken the trouble to open the door and let him stroll out into the night?

The phone rang. It was my cell phone. "Give Amy the phone," a muffled voice said by way of introduction.

I handed the phone to Amy. "They want to talk to you."

She took the receiver. "I understand," she said. "I go

home. Leave the money here. Don't say anything to the
police or . . ."

She started to cry again and blindly handed me the
receiver. I realized she suspected me of being connected
with the whole thing, even as I became totally certain
that she, for one, wasn't involved in it.

"What?" I asked curtly. Amy stared up at me through
tear-starred eyelashes, alarmed that I might be antago-
nizing them. She was right. I took a deep breath. "What
do you want me to do?" I asked evenly.

"Follow my instructions exactly. Take the backpack
to your car. Cross the bridge back to San Diego. Do not
call the police or notify anyone of what you are doing,
or I'll be forced to kill the little girl."

"Okay," I said. It cost me a great deal not to ask if
he knew what had happened to my cat. But if a child's
life was only useful to them as a bargaining chip I didn't
dare let myself wonder about the fate of a cat.

"How do we know you have Stef and that—" I
glanced at Amy and took a deep breath. "That she's
okay? Could you put her on the line?"

There was a pause and I pulled Amy close to the
receiver. We both heard Stef's voice. "B three."

Then the rough voice came back on the line. He
sounded suddenly angrier than before. "Get going. Tell
Amy to go home. Don't tell anyone and the girl will
live." The line went dead.

"Okay. I'm going." I grabbed my purse and pulled
out my notebook. I scribbled a quick note and folded it
and put it in Amy's hands. "Slide this under the door
to room three-oh-one on your way out."

Amy looked at me forlornly but she nodded. She
seemed a little distracted. She kept murmuring Stef's

words. "B three—it sounds like a chess opening. Ivor will know what it means."

I took the bag from Amy. It felt as stiff and heavy as if it were loaded with concrete blocks. I put it over my shoulders and stood upright with difficulty.

I walked out of the hotel with a desperate desire to call out to someone, but the lobby was nearly deserted. The night clerk was talking on the phone to someone. As I looked at him I began to wonder if there was an accomplice somewhere here in the hotel. Had I sealed Stefanie's death warrant by handing her mother that note?

I went out to the parking lot. The night air was pleasant. The heat had been tempered by a refreshing breeze from the ocean. Even with a new complement of security guards since the bombing, the lot seemed naked and exposed. I had the definite impression that whoever had called was watching me.

As I got in the car and started it, it was hard to make myself breathe properly. The car moved out of the parking lot with the smoothness of a dream. I forced myself to watch the street, the sidewalks. Everything was so unreal I was afraid I would miss something major like a truck in my path. I turned off Orange and onto the approach to the bridge.

My cell phone rang and I flinched so hard that I almost swerved into the car in the next lane.

35

I ignored the angry honking of the motorist whose fender I had nearly clipped. I pulled out the cell phone and concentrated on driving sensibly. What if I were to get into a wreck and the police were to find a backpack with ransom money in it? I answered the phone.

"Are you on the bridge?"

"Yes."

"Take 5 south. Keep going till you get further instructions." He disconnected.

Coronado Island receded into the background and I descended from the swooping height of the bridge to the freeway turnoff. South on 5 would take me into Mexico if I kept going. The cell phone rang after I was heading south for a few minutes.

"Take Highway 15 east and stay on it till I call again," was all he said.

On Highway 15 I drove for several minutes in jumpy silence. I kept driving through Miramar Naval Air Station without going on the base. There was not a lot of traffic at this time of night. I passed the turnoff for San Marcos, where Admiral Rhymer's burned-out house was. I had approached it from the west when I went there earlier in the week. I swept on past.

It was a very Southern California feeling. Driving sixty-five miles an hour into the darkness with only the vaguest idea where I was and even less idea where I was going. Come to think of it, maybe this feeling was not limited to Southern California, there were just better freeways and more hospitable weather here to indulge it.

I didn't want to think about what might have happened, or be happening, to Raoul. If I thought about what might happen to Stefanie Russo, I was afraid I might lose what composure I had. I breathed deeply and concentrated on my driving. The cell phone was silent. The traffic had thinned down to the occasional oncoming car just as the freeway had become a highway.

Driving on through the dark in the silent car I consciously forced myself to think about who might have put this evening's entertainment together.

Seeing Sally Rhymer encountering Duke lent some credence to Martha Meade's story about a jealous husband running him down. It was pretty clear that Douglas or Duke had every reason to hate the admiral. But Duke had been working for Rhymer via Stewart Meade for years, why suddenly decide to take revenge? Did it have something to do with the fact that the payments hadn't been flowing to him this year the way they had in other years? If that was the case, who cut him off and why? Even if Duke had decided to take revenge, I couldn't see how he could have gotten the admiral out of that cottage behind Dwight and Colleen's house. Juan might have helped. I could imagine Juan delivering the flowers, with a few nervous glances at the security guards with their INS-like uniforms. But it seemed like the kidnapping would have needed two able-bodied people.

Martha Meade's testimony about the accident might also be suspect if she had been involved in the kidnapping herself, perhaps with some help from Lance and Ondine. She was certainly benefiting from Stewart's death and she would have known about his asthma. If she had been involved with Lance since their Blue Ridge Institute days, they might have planned it together.

Sally Rhymer was a remote possibility. Maybe Duke was only pretending to be so offended by her presence. Perhaps she had lied about not seeing him for ten years and they had kept in touch all along and were only waiting for the right moment. She might even have evolved the ransom scheme on her own as a way of supplementing her alimony. She was a strong, athletic woman and she and Juan could have moved the admiral. If the admiral were half-conscious I could almost see her half walking, half dragging the admiral on her own. For all I knew, she might have dragged him to bed on many, many drunken occasions during their marriage. Could she have been so eager to see her granddaughter that she kidnapped her as well and was now using her as a pawn? I didn't know, but it was a male voice on the phone, so if Sally Rhymer was involved, she had a male accomplice.

Dwight and Colleen were still strong suspects as far as I was concerned. Dwight's future once he left the navy was unknown. I couldn't see either of them as a murderer, but they could have hung around the chess tournament to kidnap Stef, who would have gone with her aunt and uncle if they had a good reason.

After what had happened to Stef I had stopped suspecting Amy. But Ivor's speech about the killer instinct and all the talk about searching for mushrooms in the mountains made me wonder if he had the admiral, and now his daughter, stashed away in some mountain hideout. Highway 15 was heading toward the mountains all right. Ivor might have faked his daughter's kidnapping but he would have needed help to spirit her out of the tournament without his own absence being noted. Despite the deep vein of anger he had displayed in the cafeteria, he hadn't seemed unbalanced enough to put his little girl on the phone to lie. And that had been Stef's voice, although why she said "B three" was a total mystery to me.

I didn't want to leave Brad out as a suspect, even though I wasn't too impressed with his organizational skills. He seemed to be more adept at fogging up things and avoiding harsh reality than at putting together actual plans for good or evil. Still, the money could be a strong motivation. He might have friends in the UFO conspiracy underground who would help him if he explained it in terms of the admiral's possible connections with the Bermuda Triangle. There was the question of the criminal record he so proudly confessed to, and the mysterious hundred-dollar bills Amber had mentioned. If the tape Brad had tried to sell to the *Interrogator* was the same one I got from Lani, I was even more confused. There might have been a copy in the safe, but there were others floating around as well. If it wasn't that secret, why was Admiral Coffin so interested?

Just to be thorough I included Admiral Coffin and possibly an unknown military motive. Perhaps this Vincent Lorenzo might have commissioned someone to get the incriminating tape back. The Joint Chiefs of Staff would certainly have access to covert operations personnel, but the timing looked all wrong. Why descend on Admiral Rhymer now when they had let the whole matter rest for decades? Did they not know that there was more than one copy of the tape? Also, asking for a million-dollar ransom seemed a little tacky and definitely not the American military way of getting things done. That was milk money for the Pentagon gang.

Holding up individual citizens for ransom was really more of an Internal Revenue thing than an armed forces thing.

Then there was Zane Birch. His fascination with all things military was so strong that I could imagine him daydreaming about a paramilitary fund-raising operation like this one. I just couldn't imagine him doing anything about it. If it wasn't a board game, did he have any idea how to play it? If he had planned such an exercise, I would have expected him to tell everyone about it rather than do it. I also couldn't see him hurting Stef. I remembered watching the two of them chatting on the first night I met them and they had seemed like genuine friends.

I didn't include Fred Luna in my list of suspects because it seemed to me he had more of a stake in keeping the admiral in circulation for Lani's sake, if not for the sake of his job as driver.

I drove past Temecula and Lake Elsinore. The dashboard clock told me I had been driving for over an hour. It was dark. This had been farmland and the suburbs had not totally reached out here.

A sign informed me that there was a women's correctional facility at Norco. Other signs announced that the Pomona Expressway U.S. 60 was up ahead. It was dark but I knew we were headed in the direction of the San Gabriel Mountains. I hoped the goal of this trip wasn't some remote mountain lake.

Approaching Ontario, a sign advised that gas could be purchased near the next exit. I drove off and into the nearest gas station. No sign of life from the cell phone. I filled the car and used the restroom. My face looked pale and tense. I felt as if I had been wakened from a fever dream and still carried the unreality of the fever.

Still no sound from the cell phone. For a moment I thought of dialing *69 to call them back, but I didn't want to antagonize them while they had the little girl. I got back on Highway 15 and started to drive. The minutes ticked away.

When the phone did ring I fumbled for it and nearly dropped it. The voice informed me to get off 15 and take Foothill Boulevard south—when a car flashed its lights at me I should follow it. Then I was listening to the dial tone again.

Foothill Boulevard was really more like an untraveled highway. I remembered from a book I'd read that it was part of the old Interstate Route 66 that led from the Midwest all the way into Los Angeles. Once a thriving cross-country route carrying Dust Bowl refugees and Hollywood-bound dreamers, now the old road was an antique—drained of importance and traffic by freeways and reduced to bearing local traffic and history buffs tracing the ghost thread of the old Route 66. In some places the old road was literally buried under the new freeway, but Foothill was a slice of the old interstate. At this hour, well past midnight, it was nearly deserted with long stretches of empty roadside and the occasional abandoned business caught like a fly in amber at the moment of death. A boarded-up gas station offered gas at twenty-five cents a gallon. Had I even been born when that place had closed?

The car pulled out ahead of me and flashed its headlights three times. I turned my lights off and on in reply. The car drove on a little longer, then slowed, flashed its lights again and pulled into the weed-seamed parking lot of an abandoned tavern. My headlights flashed on a billboard behind it long enough for me to read a faded slogan advertising a long-defunct brand of orange soda.

The car ahead stopped. I stopped, put the car in park, but kept the motor running.

The driver got out and strode back to meet me. He wore dark clothes and a ski mask over his face, but even with his blond braid tied up and his face covered, I would have recognized Zane Birch from his lanky frame. He was carrying a semiautomatic weapon. I had never seen one except in the movies. It was small, held in the crook of his arm like a toy, but it looked efficiently lethal in person.

He gestured to me to roll down the window. "Give me the backpack."

I hauled the heavy pack onto my lap and tried to raise it through the window. "Wait. It's too big. It won't fit. I'll have to open the door," I said, speaking very clearly, because I was beginning to get the sense that this was not a well-planned endeavor and I didn't want to spook him into test firing the weapon. He backed up a little and I slowly eased open the door and handed it out. He appeared to have almost as much trouble as I did hefting the thing.

"Did you know they took Stef, Zane?" I said gently, praying the shock of being identified wouldn't cause him to shoot me without meaning to. "You of all people should not be involved in kidnapping Stefanie."

He made eye contact. "What?"

"Didn't you know they kidnapped Stefanie from the chess tournament tonight?"

"No." His voice faltered as he said, "I never meant to kill him."

"Stewart Meade, you mean?"

"Yeah. The old guy. I saw he was choking and I did what I could."

"I know you did. I'm sure you never meant to hurt him at all."

"I just thought the tear gas would control them, because there were two of them. The gas mask was a good disguise. Duke thought so. He was impressed I thought of it, said I had potential. How could I know Meade had asthma? I put the inhaler in there with him but I guess he couldn't use it." His voice sounded close to cracking.

"Zane. Help me, please." I spoke loudly and slowly. "Duke has Stephanie."

He didn't seem to have heard me. "I was so goddamned weak!" He hit the side of the car with his fist.

I flinched at the sudden violence, and bit my lip, forced myself to concentrate. "What do you mean?"

"I was supposed to carry or drag the old man out, but he was a dead weight, I couldn't move him. I had to go back and Duke said to haul the old man into his wheelchair. Like he was expecting it. He knew I wouldn't be able to do it. Juan had to help me get him into the van."

I tried again to get through to him. "Zane, did you know they took Stephanie?"

"No." He looked at me as if just realizing I was there.

"Where would they keep her? The same place they have the admiral?"

He made a gesture toward his ear as if batting away a persistent insect. He cocked his head, listening to what someone said in an earpiece. He slung the gun over his shoulder and produced a flashlight from his pocket and turned it on the interior of the car. "The cell phone. Give it to me."

I took a deep breath and held back the urge to curse at him instead. His flashlight picked up the cell phone.

I slowly handed it to him through the window.

He threw it on the ground and stamped on it. I stared as his heel ground it into the asphalt.

I could see that he savored the violence of destroying something. "Zane," I said to him, "this is not a game. Help me here. You're a scholar, you don't have to throw your life away like this."

"Wait," he said, holding up a hand and tilting his head sideways again to listen. I was forcibly reminded of the old record company that had the dog listening to "his master's voice" on the gramophone. He lifted his eyes and raised the gun at point-blank range so that I could see the hole the bullets would come out.

"Zane! *No!*" I ducked under the wheel and squeezed along the seat of the car, seeking the floor.

"No," I heard him say very softly to the invisible presence in his earpiece. "No," he said again with more force, "I won't."

I didn't hear the shot but the windshield erupted into a spiderweb of shattered glass.

36

The next thing I heard was a scream from in front of the car. I moved the door open farther to look, and caught a glimpse of Zane on the ground a few feet to the left of my front wheel, one hand still resting on the heavy backpack. The door jerked in my hand from the impact of another shot. The dashboard lights went out.

The motor was still running. I kept down but slid back behind the wheel, jammed the car into gear and gunned it, steering sharp right around where Zane lay with the heavy backpack and his parked car. If there were more shots I didn't hear them. I drove as fast as I could, half looking out the side window to steer and hunching down to look under the spiderweb crack on the windshield. It wouldn't do to plow into a telephone pole and conveniently kill myself and save everyone else the trouble.

Half a mile away I was amazed to find that no one followed me. Indeed, there was no other traffic on that road. I drove in to the small parking lot of a long defunct grocery store, slid the car out of view of the highway, and waited. A few minutes later a van drove past. I recognized it. I wondered if Stefanie was in it. I wanted to follow it, and I wanted to go back to San Diego. Instead I turned back to where I had left Zane. I didn't want to do it but I couldn't help it. I saw the car up ahead when it disappeared in a flash of light followed by the boom of an explosion and flames. That guy sure did like to blow up cars.

I stopped dead in the middle of the road. Then I turned the car around and drove toward San Bernardino. It must have been less than five minutes but it seemed like forever before I found a pay phone in the parking lot of a grubby liquor store that was simply locked up for the night, rather than boarded up forever. The dashboard clock was not working but I figured it must have been well past 2:00 A.M. I called 911 and explained that there had been a bad car wreck on Foothill Boulevard and a man was injured.

I took a deep breath and called the number noted on my pad as Duke's home phone. When the old man answered I apologized profusely for calling so terribly early. Beyond shame, I babbled on about being up with my friend—the one in the chair, she'd had a bad night.

I hoped I hadn't laid it on too thick but he was cordial enough. "Never mind. I was up. I don't sleep so much these days myself. You must care about your friend to be going through this with her. I'm sure my son would like to help if he could but he's not here. Like I said, he might be up in San Berdoo."

"Actually, sir, that's why I called. We're staying near San Bernardino not far from Foothill Boulevard. I was hoping to get the address of that machine shop here so we could drop by today."

He was happy to give me the address and directions. "Now, you try and get some sleep young lady and you and your friend have some breakfast before you go over there. There's a place Duke and me go to that's set up so you can take a wheelchair right in. I don't recall the name of it but it's on the same road as the warehouse, about a half mile down. You can't miss it. I don't at all mind you calling me but you ladies better stay away from that area except early in the morning unless you have a male relative to come along. It's not a nice neighborhood."

After I hung up I put my head against the pay phone. It made me feel sick inside to take advantage of that kind old man. Now I was going to try to put his son in jail. I sighed and called Ambrose and gave him the street address. His voice was halfway between deep concern and irritation. "We were halfway to finding that address, Jo. Stef Russo told us."

"You talked to her?"

"No. You talked to her. She told you. I'll explain later. Sit tight. Mrs. Madrone's security people will be here soon. Don't do anything stupid."

I heard sirens. A fire truck raced past, headed for the fire that had been Zane's car. An ambulance and a police car followed. I started to feel very conspicuous. I got back on Foothill Boulevard and began to follow Duke's father's instructions.

The old man hadn't been exaggerating about needing a bodyguard in that part of town. A small detachment of marines would have been appropriate. The warehouse was at the end of a block that was occupied by a junkyard on one side and a dirt lot with several deserted buildings on the other. Chain-link fence topped with razor wire was the dominant motif in exterior trim.

When I saw the warehouse with the van parked in front of it, I stopped. I noticed there was a ramp built up to the side of the loading dock. I didn't want to actually drive past it. I reminded myself that Stefanie Russo was probably in the van or the warehouse.

There was no sign of Mrs. Madrone's security people. I drove a few blocks and parked on a side street. I wasn't sure what to do next. Getting killed seemed like the next logical step, based on Duke's expertise versus my total ineptitude. I decided that the diner down the road might have another pay phone, or at least some coffee. The lack of sleep was catching up to me. I took a deep breath and then looked up and nearly hit my head on the mirror flinching backward.

A face had materialized outside my car window right at wheelchair height. I looked again and it was gone.

Someone tapped on the glass and a florid face with bristly white hair and a weeks' growth of beard appeared. He had been crouching beside the car. I rolled down the window, which then stuck halfway.

"Jesus! Admiral Rhymer, you scared the hell out of me. Get in the backseat and hunch down. They may be looking for you."

He started to scramble in, and paused with one leg on the sidewalk. "How do you know who I am? You're not with them, are you?"

"I work for Mrs. Madrone. Get in the damn car."

He complied and then looked me over. I turned to look back at him. "How did you recognize me?" he asked.

I started the car and pulled away from the curb. "I threw a drink on you at a party."

"I'm sorry, you'll have to be more specific."

"At your son Dwight's place last week. You were rude and abusive and I threw a drink on you."

"If you can't give me more than that to go on, I'll never remember. Can we talk somewhere else? I don't want to get locked back up in that warehouse when the others get back."

"Unfortunately, they are back, and they've got your granddaughter, Stef."

"Stef."

"They took her to make sure the police weren't involved when they got the ransom. I just gave them the money. Did they let you go?"

"They did not. The skinny kid cuffed me to a loose table leg. I just got out a little while ago. I was going to walk out of here but when I saw you, I thought I could hitch a ride or with a car like that you might have a cell phone. That was before I saw your lovely windshield."

I was heading back toward the last place I had seen a service station, figuring they would have a phone. As we passed the street with the warehouse on it I looked down it just in time to see the van come hurtling into the intersection and plow into my right front bumper with a horrific crunching sound.

It spun us nearly a hundred and eighty degrees. The admiral and I both saw that he was backing up to have another run at the car. With a remarkable display of unity, we scrambled out the driver and passenger doors and began to run along the chain-link fence away from the van, which had backed up and was now swerving around the now-crippled rental car to follow us. Frantically looking for an alley, steps, something neither a van nor a wheelchair could negotiate, I saw a gap between the chain-link fence and the side of the warehouse. I yelled to the admiral and we both ran into the narrow walkway. The van stopped at that point.

I knew Duke wouldn't be jumping out and following us across that garbage-choked dirt alley. But the admiral, who was now in front of me, stopped in a hurry. I nearly ran into him and looked over his shoulder to see that he had almost run into a wicked-looking machete, which Juan was holding out in front of him. Juan looked

as though he knew how to use a machete. He said nothing, but gestured for us to go down some stairs and into
an open door in the side of the building. The door led
to a hallway and the hallway opened onto a walkway
that had been made into a ramp down to the floor of
the warehouse itself.

37

Most of the building was given over to low tables with machinery. It was only because I knew Duke needed the access that I realized everything was easily reachable from a wheelchair. There were several ramps to other levels. At the far end of the building was a table, two chairs, an army cot, and a couple of buckets. A chain had been looped around a beam. It was easy to see that the chain would stretch to the cot and the buckets, perhaps to the chairs, perhaps not.

"This is where I've been staying," the admiral said, in a voice thick with anger. "Of course, until today I was blindfolded so I couldn't really see my surroundings."

Juan motioned us to the area with the chairs and cot. He motioned me to sit. I took one of the chairs. The admiral took the other. Juan produced a couple of very modern-looking plastic handcuffs from a pocket. He held the machete close to my throat while he strapped the handcuff around my wrist and the chair leg. He did the same thing to the admiral. Suddenly, I felt very tired indeed.

We sat in silence for several seconds before a metal door was thrown open and Duke, or Douglas, rolled in. He seemed almost energized. Shooting people, blowing things up, and smashing into cars agreed with him. Or it could have been the ransom money.

The admiral was staring at him as if he had seen a

ghost. "Douglas! How could you? After all I've done for you."

Duke rolled up to within a few feet of the admiral and glared at him. Hearing him talk was like hearing a rusty machine swing into action. Slow and grinding at first. "You mean like putting me in this chair? You sure have done a lot for me, haven't you? Getting Stewart Meade to take me off the payroll just gave me a little incentive to get it done quicker."

"I told you he did that on his own."

"So you should have paid me yourself."

"I had trouble getting the cash together. I told Stewart that it wasn't an option to stop paying you. But he said I couldn't force him to keep paying and you couldn't hurt him, so he didn't care."

"Yeah, well, he's dead now."

"You killed him?"

Obviously the admiral hadn't been kept up to date on the news.

"No. My young friend and recruit Zane overdid it with the tear gas. He wasn't sure he could handle you two old boys and I guess Meade couldn't take the tear gas."

"He has asthma," the admiral said, shaking his head. "He had asthma."

"You don't remember any of the kidnapping?" I asked the admiral.

Both men looked at me as if one of the pieces of furniture had spoken.

"I guess I was unconscious."

"You were dead weight. Zane brought you out of that cottage in my chair here."

"But why, Doug? We could have worked something out. I told you when you arranged that fire that I was going to get it all worked out. If you just could have waited a little. Now you'll be on the run. Why?"

"Once I finally found out that you ran me down out on the Pacific Coast Highway, it was an easy decision to make."

The admiral ran a hand over his face. "I thought you knew that all along."

Duke shrugged. "Other people on the base knew. A couple of people hinted, but I thought they were bull-shitting me. It wasn't till I tried to call Stewart Meade myself and I talked to that crazy drunken wife of his. She said enough to make me realize what had happened.

"Admiral." Duke's face twitched for a moment in genuine emotion. "You knew how much I admired you."

"Enough to screw my wife. Thanks a lot. I went crazy when I saw that you were in that motel room with Sally."

"Why didn't you come in and have it out with me then?"

"No" He looked away. "I was drunk. I was afraid I'd kill you and her and my career."

"You were drunk or maybe afraid I'd beat you up— you knew I could." Something flickered over Duke's face too quickly for me to catch. "You saw that and knew that and then went out to get a drink?"

"So you'd rather I shot you both? Hell, I was drunk but I wasn't crazy. I don't keep guns around when I drink."

"You ran me down when I came out. I never saw you."

The admiral nodded. "I felt like hell when I realized what I'd done. I was the one that called for an ambulance but I couldn't stay around. Once I sobered up I realized whose fault it was. I didn't blame you so much as I blame her. You were fresh meat, boy. She'd just sent our youngest off to school and suddenly she had time on her hands and something to prove. I was just the guy who'd left her alone to raise three kids. I tell you, though, she was a model wife from the moment we got that phone call about your accident. It may have taken you a few years to figure out who did it, but it didn't take Miss Sally two seconds. She didn't want anyone asking any questions about where you had been the night before and neither did I."

"And neither did the navy."

"I assumed you figured it out when I got you the work from Stewart Meade."

Duke stared at Admiral Rhymer for several seconds. "I thought you were helping me out because you were a good guy. I felt lousy because I'd been screwing your wife and now you were helping me. And all along you were only doing it because you were afraid. Maybe if you'd been a man about it and knocked on that motel room door we'd either both be dead or I would still be walking. But you had to take my life. Now I'm going to take yours."

"What about this young woman here? What about my granddaughter? They haven't harmed you."

"Your granddaughter is in the van. She's unconscious and unharmed. I'll drop her off someplace where she'll be found easily." Duke's eyes flickered over me. "Miss, I'm sorry about this. I did try to warn you."

"With a car bomb! That kind of warning could have killed me."

"If you'd gotten any closer to the car, I would have activated it myself from across the street. You did get my message. It was your choice to ignore it. You're just going to have to pay for the consequences of your own stupidity. I'm sorry this has to happen but you chose to get in harm's way."

"What about Juan?" I asked. "Are you going to kill him like you did Zane?" I looked over at Juan, who blinked when he heard his name, but seemed otherwise totally impassive.

"It's no use working on his nerves, miss. First off, he doesn't have any. Second, he has no English, and very little Spanish. He's Indian from a tribe I met in a South American country that I'm not going to name. He's going home and so am I."

He raised his gun and a shot rang out. I flinched back as I was hit with a spatter of blood. But there was no impact, no pain. I looked up, surprised that I was unhurt, that I could see anything. What I saw was Duke, sagging sideways and forward, almost out of the wheelchair with a gaping exit wound in his neck and chest. The blood that had sprayed out far enough to hit me must have been from an artery. Now it was running out onto the floor. Instinctively I reached out toward him, hypnotized by the idea that I could put pressure on that wound and keep him from bleeding to death. The handcuff held me to the chair leg.

Duke's gun slipped to the cement floor with a dull clatter.

Fred Luna walked slowly across the floor of the warehouse. He was carrying an M-16 rifle. I hadn't seen him come in. He kept an eye on Juan. As he came close to him, he spoke to him, slowly but gruffly. *"Ponga la navaja en la mesa."* Juan may have replied but it was too softly for me to hear. *"Hágalo ahorita."* Fred gestured with his rifle. Juan set the machete down on the nearest table. Fred passed the table and picked up the machete and threaded it through his belt. Then he went over to Duke, who was unconscious and scarcely breathing. He went through his pockets gently, wiping the blood off his hands on the back of Duke's shirt when he found what he wanted.

"Jesus, Fred, that's cold."

He turned his sharp brown eyes on me. "You want me to revive him so he can shoot you? You fucking liberals give me a pain." Fred used a bandanna to take the wallet from Duke's pocket and a large wad of cash out of the wallet and handed it to Juan. He spoke to him again, slowly in Spanish.

Juan nodded slowly, pocketing the cash.

Fred finished up with, *"Váyase"* He swung the M-16 in the universal gesture for Get the Hell Out of Here.

Juan turned and walked very quickly out of the building. He did not look back.

"I told him to wire it to his people and then head for home any way he can. He might make it. They don't ask too many questions when you cross the border going south." He shrugged. "It's coming the other way they watch."

"So cut us loose, Fred," the admiral said, a little impatiently.

Fred came over and stood over the admiral where he was cuffed to the now blood-spattered folding chair. He made no move to cut us free.

"First I got to ask you a question, Admiral. Give me the right answer and I cut you free. Wrong answer and I'll just have to leave you and this young woman here on your own."

"Come on, Fred. The air in here is awful, let's go."

He was right about the air. The sudden violence had

been a shock but now I coughed and tasted smoke in the air.

"Okay." Fred stood over the admiral as if he might almost have been enjoying this but his face was grim. "When is the wedding?"

"What?" The admiral was suddenly red-faced with rage.

"You heard me. When are you marrying Lani?"

"I don't have any immediate plans."

"Okay, then. I hate like hell for this young lady to have to die as well as you."

"Wait, Fred!" The admiral was pleading now. "After Sally cheated on me, I swore I'd never get married again. A woman like Lani, she'd never stay with an old man like me."

"So? If she cheats, divorce her. But give her a chance. Put her in some night-school classes. Treat her like you respect her. If you can't do that, you don't deserve to live." He turned to me. "You must be a women's libber. What do you think?"

I took a deep breath and coughed again. That sure did smell like smoke in the air. "I don't know why any woman would want to marry this old goat, but if she wants to, why not? She's going to have to learn a few skills beyond taking off her jacket in mixed company. Other than that she seems like a nice kid."

"We can get free," the admiral said. "I escaped from here once."

"Okay." Fred turned on his heel and headed for the exit. "You might get out in time," he said over his shoulder. "Did I mention that this place is crammed to the rafters with guns and ammo and that crazy bastard in the chair set the building on fire?"

"Set a date, asshole!" I screamed at the admiral.

"July Fourth," he said instantly.

"That's a good date," Fred said, turning back to us with the machete in hand. "Easy to remember," he said, first cutting me loose, then the admiral, with an economical snap of severed plastic. "Now let's get the hell out of here before we get blown sky-high."

We found Brad Rhymer sitting in the back of Fred's Trooper keeping watch over Stef and the backpack. The little girl seemed to be sleeping peacefully. "Is she okay?" I asked.

"She's totally out of it. She didn't even wake up when I looked under her eyelids to make sure one wasn't more dilated. You know a head injury can do that," Brad said, adjusting a jacket he had put over her. "But I found a bottle of chloroform in the van we took her out of, that was probably what put her out."

"Brad! I had no idea you were so resourceful."

"I camp out a lot. It helps to know first-aid. Anyway, she's breathing fine. We'll have to get her to a doctor, but she doesn't seem to be in any immediate trouble."

"Has Brad been with you all the last week?" I asked Fred.

"Off and on," he said, opening the door for me to get in. I got into the back. They had folded the seats down to make a flat surface. Brad was on one side leaning against the back of the driver's seat. I sat on the other side with Stef stretched out between us. The admiral sat up front next to Fred. He hadn't said a word since Fred cut us loose.

As we drove down the chain-link corridor back to the main road, I looked behind me to see smoke pouring out of the building we had just left. I didn't see any sign of Juan or of Duke's van. We made it to the freeway before we heard the explosion off in the distance, the munitions stored in the warehouse.

"How the hell did you happen to walk in like that, Fred?" I asked. "I didn't see you following me."

He didn't turn his head but I guessed he was smiling. "I told you I didn't have to follow you. I put a transmitter on your car when we were at the house in San Marcos. When I was checking your car out for bombs. All I had to do was keep within a half mile or so."

"Did you see Zane Birch's car—the one Duke blew up after he shot Zane?"

"Oh, yeah. We came up on it right after the explosion. The kid wasn't dead—or at least the paramedics were working on him."

I told them I had called Ambrose and Mrs. Madrone's security team would be on the way. Fred handed a cell phone to the admiral and asked me the number. I gave it to him and the admiral punched in the numbers and spoke to Ambrose and then to someone else. "We'll be there," he concluded, and snapped the phone shut.

We drove in silence. Fred was heading for the nearest freeway entrance. Brad handed me a bottle of drinking water and a roll of paper towels. "Here, you've got blood all over you. If anyone gets a look at you, they'll stop us just on the basis of that."

I took the roll without comment, wet a paper towel, and began to scrub off whatever blood I could remove— the majority of it had hit my blouse. As soon as I could change I was going to get rid of that. I wanted to talk to a high-priced lawyer before I said anything myself. Even if Mrs. Madrone decided to replace me with Helen, I was confident she would want me to have legal assistance.

To take my mind off that grim prospect I tapped on the admiral's seat back—I wasn't about to touch his shoulder. "Admiral Rhymer, that tape with Vincent Lorenzo, what was it really about?"

For a moment I thought he wasn't going to speak to me, but at last he said, "You heard that tape?"

"Yes. It's really about seeing Lorenzo going into that gay bar in Patpong, isn't it?"

He turned in his seat to look back at me and then turned away to face the windshield. "It started that way. He threatened to report something I did—I won't say what. I wanted to have a weapon to keep him off. Seeing him go into that bar just fell in my lap. He was a damn fool, everyone knew what that place was. I ended up not needing to use it right then. But I hung on to it. A couple of years later, when Lorenzo began to have some connections at the Pentagon, I played the tape for him and he decided to help my career. I'm not proud of using it, but it gave me an edge for a while. After I retired, there wasn't much Lorenzo could do for me. I had to find another angle. That's the lesson that Douglas never learned. Things change and you have to find new weapons."

I looked at Brad but he said nothing. "Brad, I have to ask. Amber said you kept coming home with hundred-dollar bills. Where did they come from?" I could tell everyone else was listening intently too; they had no idea where Brad got his money. "Is it drugs?" I asked.

Brad snorted in disgust, sounding a lot like his father. "No. It's not drugs. I run a catering truck to construction sites and factories a couple of days a week, okay? The guy who owns the truck pays me in cash."

"Oh," I said. There was a long silence in the vehicle. "But you said you had an arrest record."

"Oh, just for littering. I had to pick up trash for weeks to work it off."

The admiral snorted in disgust and Fred Luna shook his head. "I didn't realize I was traveling with a desperate criminal."

"If anyone is hungry, I have some cookies and candy bars," Brad said, handing a paper bag to me. I took two cookies and handed it to the admiral.

"You're a couple of little housewives back there," the admiral said gruffly, but he took a candy bar. Fred took one also. They kept the bag.

Not long after that, we pulled into a gas station where a private ambulance was waiting. A man and woman in jumpsuits and jackets pushed past Brad and me to get to Stefanie. We scrambled out of their way. Within five minutes, the little girl was in the ambulance and heading for Ontario International. "They'll airlift her to a San Diego hospital from there," a man in a black nylon jacket explained. "Her parents are waiting there."

The man asked if any of the rest of us were wounded. I had enough blood on my clothes to make me look like a casualty but I told him I had come through it without a scratch. "Admiral?" I asked.

He shot me an outraged look that made him look like a recently drenched owl. "Fred? You driving back?"

"I'll drive all of you back." For some reason we all felt strangely reluctant to leave Fred.

"If you look in that cargo net across the seat—here, I'll get it." Fred dug out a plastic rain poncho. "Put this on. It will cover up the blood for now."

The admiral, Brad, and I got back into the vehicle with Fred. We got back on the freeway when Fred's cell phone rang. It was Ambrose. The minute I heard his voice I sat up with a start, realizing I'd left my purse and all my identifying documents in the car. I explained to Ambrose, giving him the directions as best I remembered. Fred interrupted, "Give me the phone, I can tell him exactly where it is."

"Okay, but I need to ask him if they've found my cat."

I hadn't slept all night and found myself dozing off while I waited to get the phone back again. But once I got Ambrose on the line he told me he hadn't heard any news of Raoul. He said he would send someone to get my ID and settle things with the car rental company. "I hate to sound too concerned with material goods, dear. The important thing is that you and Stef and the admiral are all safe and sound. But may I ask if you managed to rescue the ransom as well?"

I had actually forgotten the ransom. "Brad, have you looked in that backpack, because I haven't?"

Brad shook his head. I leaned over the seat and unzipped the backpack. Brad made no move to either stop me or help me. I could see money inside, wrapped in a transparent plastic bag. It was banded in stacks but the denomination I saw was twenty-dollar bills. It looked intact and I wasn't about to count it. "That can't be a million dollars."

I could imagine Ambrose smiling from the way his voice sounded. "Oh, I'm sure after Colleen drove the wedge in, Mrs. Madrone's negotiators managed to get the price down some."

"Well, whatever it is, it's wrapped up in plastic and it hasn't been touched."

Brad shrugged but made no comment. If he was insulted he didn't show it.

Ambrose said, "Reach under the plastic and see if you find anything else."

I slowly pushed my hand between the canvas side of the pack and the plastic, fearing some kind of explosion of red dye. I know banks use that to mark money and I'd heard of it being used in ransoms. I realized when my hand contacted a cloth bag that I was as much afraid of Duke's penchant for using explosives as I was of red dye. After all, I was already dabbed in blood. What could be worse?

"Uh, Ambrose, what if the guy who bombed my car booby-trapped it?"

"Good point. Sorry, I didn't think. Just stop where you are and close it back up again."

"I did feel a kind of soft cloth that felt as if it was full of gravel."

Ambrose sighed. "Good. Thanks. There were supposed to be some loose diamonds in there in addition to the cash. Just get here as soon as you can safely."

I handed the phone back to Fred. We rode in silence for several minutes.

"Admiral, I don't know why, but Mrs. Madrone put up that ransom for you." I left it at that. Maybe it wasn't anybody's business why.

After a minute or so the admiral said, "You should have seen her in 1960. Alicia was blond but not like Sally. Alicia was more like moonlight and magic. Beautiful as an angel and smart as the devil. Too smart to want me. For a little while there, I thought I had a chance. I think she liked the idea of playing with someone who might be dangerous." He shook his head and said no more.

I didn't have the kind of documentation that Ambrose might be able to find, but I thought I could now guess why Alicia Madrone put up ransom money for Ron Rhymer. She might have some feeling left for a man who still saw her as moonlight and magic. But primarily it must be an offering to whatever gods she believed in—the cash version of a prayer in gratitude for a narrow escape.

39

It was fully light and rush hour when we reached San Diego. It seemed as if a century had passed since I drove out of town the night before. Ambrose met us at the entrance to the parking lot and directed us to the service entrance. He shook hands with the admiral and Brad, who was carrying the backpack over his shoulders. A couple of men in black nylon jackets came up. At a nod from Ambrose one of them took the backpack from Brad and beckoned him inside the hotel. The other man came over. Ambrose introduced him as Colonel Abramson.

"Active?" The admiral asked.

"Retired army. Security," the colonel said. I got the feeling they were going to get along fine.

"Colonel Abramson will take you to the hospital to see your granddaughter when you feel well enough. There's a hospitality suite you can use here for a shower, and someone brought you some clothes."

Lani was standing near her uncle, shyly holding a duffel bag. Fred gave her a little shove and she came over. "I brought you some clean clothes, Ronny."

Without looking at anyone else the admiral hugged her and kept his arm around her. "Colonel Abramson, this is my fiancée, Miss Luna."

"Pleased to meet you, ma'am."

I glanced over to see Fred smiling, but when he saw Ambrose approaching he grew solemn. Ambrose said a few words too softly for me to hear, then he handed Fred a business card. Fred nodded.

Wrapped in the unseasonable plastic rain poncho, I turned back toward the hotel. Ambrose surprised me by hugging me, poncho, blood, and all and then escorting me up to my room via a service elevator I hadn't known existed. "Get a shower and some sleep and then call me," he said. "There's someone you need to talk to before you talk to anyone else."

I was pretty sure that was a lawyer, but at the moment I was so happy to be able to take a shower that I didn't think too far ahead. I did reflect that it was a good sign that no one was asking for anything we had on us for evidence. I noticed that Fred drove off with Brad in tow as soon as he had seen the admiral and Lani reunited.

I took a very long shower. Washed my hair twice. Then I lay down and realized there was still no sign of Raoul. I called Ambrose.

"That was quick. Don't you need sleep?"

"Yes, but I just wondered if you had heard any more about my cat."

There was a brief silence, then he said, "I'll be over in a minute, but don't open the door to anyone but me."

It was five minutes later when he knocked on the door and I opened it to find him holding a wild-eyed Raoul, whom he had managed to stuff into a kind of immobilizing kitty straitjacket with handles. "That was good timing. We just found him. Prince kept throwing himself against the sliding glass doors and eventually I went out and looked and this character was skulking around the shrubbery outside." Ambrose put the case on the sofa and unzipped it. Raoul exploded out of the case and dashed into the bedroom. I followed just in time to see his puff of gray tail disappear under the bed.

"Get some rest, Jo. We'll deal with the rest of it later."

I took his advice.

When I woke up it was dark and Raoul had ventured up to the pillow beside me. He saw I was awake and patted me insistently with a paw on the mouth and cheek. I dragged myself out of bed, poured him some dry cat food, and sat on the sofa and watched him eat it.

When he was finished, I got out his brush and he came to sit beside me and allowed me to attack some large knots in his coat. Eventually he signaled that he had had enough by capturing the hand holding the brush between his front paws and extending the claws just enough to make his point. I put the brush down and just petted him, which he allowed. "I'm taking you home, Raoul," I told him. Coincidence or not he began to purr and half closed his eyes in a feline meditative state. "Mulligan was right, you need your own space."

I picked up the phone and dialed Ambrose, who answered on the first ring. "Good," he said, "You're awake."

"How is Stef?" I asked.

"She's going to be fine. She woke up about midafternoon. She told them Duke lured her out to the van and then put a scarf over her mouth. There was chloroform on the scarf. It knocked her out but when she came round and told you the first move to the Nimzovich opening on the phone, Ivor was able to identify Duke. Duke is one of the few players who uses the same opening every game, it's a big joke in the local tournament circles. I guess Amy asked to speak to the girl to be sure she was okay."

"Right." Actually I had asked that.

"When Duke heard Stef give that opening move to her mother, he became totally irate and gave her a bigger dose of chloroform. It could have killed her, the doc said. The second dose put her out for several hours. She's got a big headache now but she'll be fine. I don't think Duke wanted to hurt her, he just didn't want her getting in the way, trying to escape."

"Did he know then that the admiral had escaped?"

"The admiral says probably not. My bet is that Zane wouldn't have told Duke that the admiral escaped till he couldn't avoid it anymore. The kid is under arrest in San Bernardino County Hospital with major gunshot wounds. The car he was driving was stolen and full of guns and ammunition. He would have been hurt a lot worse but he was wearing body armor. Probably bought it from a military surplus catalogue—I don't know if the guy who shot him was aware he was wearing it. He was afraid of Duke."

"And rightly so."

"Oh, yeah, it's likely that Duke was trying to get rid of Zane after he'd outlived his usefulness." Ambrose shook his head in wonderment. "I guess the temptation to play soldier and score a large amount of cash got to Zane."

"It's too bad, he seemed like such an intelligent kid."

"Look at it this way, he'll have lots of time to work on his chess game in prison."

"If they don't execute him. Kidnapping is a capital crime."

"They may not execute him, he was practically brainwashed and he's got a very good lawyer who is probably already drafting his post-trial book."

"Speaking of lawyers, should I be speaking to one?"

"Yes. We have an extremely tough woman lawyer

who will speak with you soon. She's already talked to
Fred Luna."

I laughed. "I wish I could have heard that interview."

"Oh, you'll have your own interview to occupy your
time. Your lawyer is just working out on the punching
bag in the gym till Mrs. Madrone finishes with you."

"Okay." I felt a strong twinge of anxiety.

"I'm not kidding. The woman is a navy veteran and
an accomplished kick boxer. Very useful training for a
lawyer."

"I didn't know there was a gym on the premises."

"Typical of you not to know. Mrs. Madrone is waiting for you, so fix yourself up a little, and move it."

"Okay." I didn't expect to get fired on the spot, but
I was a little surprised to find that Mrs. Madrone met
me nearly at the door of her apartment. Usually she
waited in one of the more comfortable rooms. I followed her in and she motioned me to sit across a small
table with elaborate marquetry designs inlaid along its
sculpted edges. It took me a few moments to recognize
it as an inlaid chess board. There was no chess set on
the squares. Neither of us said anything for a moment.

"Josephine, I feel I know you quite well even though
you've only worked for me a few years, and you've
certainly gotten to know me and my friends more than
I really intended."

I nodded and swallowed, wondering if this was the
prelude to a very gracious layoff. There would probably
be a good severance payment if so.

"I looked at your recommendation for an artistic
grant to Helen Hayworth in preference to Magda Sobel
if there is not enough to fund both. Your reasoning was
that Helen needed the encouragement and her art was
equal to Magda's in your humble opinion."

She stopped and raised her eyebrows at me.

"Well, I'm not an art expert, but I bought one of Helen's paintings. I lent it to Ambrose."

She nodded. "I saw it."

"I bought it myself with my own money and I don't do that unless I really, really like something. Helen had totally stopped painting—" I fell silent because I didn't know what else to say.

"I'm inclined to agree with you. Helen has asked for her old job back. The job you now fill. But I think in her case it would make more sense to fund a women's art project and let Helen run it. Magda could be employed to teach metalworking and sculpture. I think she could be quite inspiring and it would be good for all concerned."

"So you still want me to work for you?" I couldn't help it, I had to ask.

Mrs. Madrone smiled at my artless eagerness. I don't think she had much concept of all I'd been through in the past day and night. "This has been a difficult stretch for you. Don't you think you need a little more time in Seattle? Ambrose tells me there is a gentleman up there that you'd like to see a lot more of."

For a moment I couldn't find the words to answer her. I just nodded. "Yes, that's true," I said at last. "Also, I'm pretty sure Raoul is not cut out to be a traveling cat. I, uh, hope Prince was unharmed."

"He wasn't injured. Even after that operation, you know, tomcats will be tomcats. It's probably just as well to get him home as soon as possible."

"The cat needs to get back to his turf. I guess I'm thinking about setting up a home base too."

"In Seattle?"

"For the moment." I've always envied people who knew where home was. It was important enough to me that I couldn't say the word casually. Evidently, I couldn't say it at all.

Mrs. Madrone looked so exhausted that it nearly made me ache just to talk to her. She sighed deeply. "Call Ambrose when you've recuperated enough to be useful again. Use your own judgment. In answer to your question, yes, I want you to keep working for me."

"Thank you." I wanted to hug her but instead I settled for shaking the pale, cold hand she held out.

I went off to go a few rounds with the kick-boxing lady lawyer. After that I planned to spend some time walking on a white sandy beach, staring at the magical hot sparkle of this stretch of the Pacific. Soon enough it would be time to take my cat and go back to the rocky gray sands of Puget Sound.

Read on for an excerpt from
Lynne Murray's next book

AT LARGE

Available in hardcover from
St. Martin's Minotaur

Of all the women's job skill centers in all the towns in all the Pacific Northwest, he walks into mine. It had been a rocky week already, and it wasn't Friday yet. In fact Thursday morning was moving so slowly that if I hadn't personally witnessed each second tick off on the big black schoolroom clock across from my desk, I would have sworn that time was standing still. It didn't help that no one was buying my best impersonation of a mild-mannered receptionist. As a woman who has never weighed less than two hundred pounds in my adult life, you might not guess that I can be inconspicuous, but if I keep my head down and my mouth shut, I can usually pull it off. Unfortunately the earnest blue silk pantsuit, pearls and expression of well-bred naïveté weren't working.

Something about this job skill center wasn't quite right. I needed to find out what it was for Mrs. Madrone, so that my wealthy employer could decide whether to award the place a grant. Maybe I had asked too many questions.

By the time Ted showed up, I was already on Delores Patton's radar. The center director was an African American woman who commanded respect with an attitude that could clean brass at twenty paces. She knew I wasn't your usual do-gooder. She just hadn't decided how to deal with it. Ted's arrival made up her mind, and managed to get me fired from a volunteer job—not as easy as it sounds.

Teddy Etheridge was the first male who had entered the office in the three weeks I had been volunteering there. The center was located in Bremerton, about an hour's ferry ride southwest of Seattle. I'd stayed in Bremerton during the week answering phones, helping out and nosing around. On the weekends in Seattle I saw my Persian tomcat, Raoul. Thor Mulligan took care of the cat for me during the week.

I had a crush on Mulligan, but he was still grieving over the death of Nina, his lover and my best friend. It had been three months since she died and I was mourning her too. But I was also fighting off a terrific yearning for Mulligan, who had drastically mixed feelings about getting involved with me, or maybe with anyone at this point.

We had tested this theory by spending a night together six weeks earlier. The night itself had been wonderful—right up until an emotional tidal wave of guilt and grief swept over Mulligan and left me untouched.

He had backed away from me after that. We hadn't talked about it much. I felt guilty about how I didn't feel guilty. As for what I could do next—the short answer appeared to be "not much."

For a split second when Teddy walked in the door, I thought he might be a potential employer who had strayed in without an appointment. Not that I'd ever seen an actual employer on the premises. They did call from time to time to get cheap labor. Oops—I mean to support the Women's Job Skill Center.

Then I recognized him. "Teddy!" It was always Ted or Teddy to his friends. Never Theodore, not even on his book covers. He wrote humor books for a living.

When he realized it was me, his bearded face lit up in a huge grin. "Josephine Fuller!"

"Ted Etheridge. The last of the hopeless romantics."

I came around the desk to shake hands with him, and he pulled me into a big hug. An inch or two over six feet tall and square as a teddy bear, Ted was not quite fat because he was so intensely physically active. I pulled back to take a look at him. Now in his late thirties, he would always be boyish, with a shock of red-brown hair that seemed to fall into his eyes no matter how short it was cut.

Our last conversation had lasted over a dozen hours—the night in Kathmandu when both of our marriages died.

Ted had been married to Francesca Benedict Etheridge, a gifted mountain climber. It had looked as if she might attempt an ascent on Mount Everest. That climb fell through, and she ended up ascending my husband—as he then was—leaving Ted to entertain me in the lobby of the Everest Vista Hotel which, incidentally being quite a distance away in Nepal, does not have a view of Mt. Everest.

I had been married to Griffin Fuller, world-renowned as a photographer, and well-known (except to his wife) as a philanderer. Teddy had been playing the part of the supportive husband of a climber, helping Francesca field media coverage, and occupying himself by gathering local color in Nepal. He had a gift for mingling with serious trekkers and climbers, who sometimes mistook him for one of their own. But his appearance was deceptive. Teddy dabbled in climbing and a variety of other sports. But in everything he did, he was always looking for a punch line.

"Josephine, I haven't seen you—well, since that infamous night. Is it still Jo Fuller or did you get divorced?"

"Yes to both questions. My maiden name was O'Toole, so I kept Griff's last name in lieu of alimony. What about you and Francesca?"

He shrugged. "It's in the works."

"Is that anything like 'the check is in the mail'? 'The divorce is in the works'?"

"You can't know what hard work that is," Ted said. "It's backbreaking labor to convince Francesca to let go of anything she once controlled. Speaking of which, she's still with Griff. Did you know that?"

"I made it a point not to know."

That night in the hotel lobby was etched in my memory. Ted and I had met a few days earlier, as both he and Griff had assignments from the same travel magazine. As we waited in the lobby, it became clearer with each hour that our respective spouses, scheduled to arrive at any moment, were both not showing up.

We adjourned to the bar, and began comparing notes. We were able to put together a pretty strong case for the suspicion that my husband and his wife were spending the night together. Ted and I had some quantity of time to reflect on the qualities we both expected in a spouse. Loyalty was high on both our lists but the partners we were with didn't seem to feel the same way.

We got along famously. We managed to laugh quite a lot, considering the situation. The Scotch whiskey might have helped. There was never any possibility that we might have wandered up to one of the rooms together that long dark night for some mutual comfort. True, we did both have that little kink about not cheating.

But, I must also note that, as a large-sized woman,

I've developed extra-sensitive radar for men who see me as a sexual being, versus men who see a surrogate mom. Ted had cried on my shoulder that night in Kathmandu. No problem, we were consenting adults crying on each other's shoulders. Now I got the sinking feeling that he viewed me as a warm, fuzzy shoulder to lay his head on, and indulge in another sympathy session.

I was in no mood. I needed to stop that in its tracks.

"So what brings you here, Ted? Are you planning a sex-change operation, and lining up future employment? I hate to tell you, but the pay cut is the most unkindest cut of all."

Teddy burst out laughing, which seemed to knock him out of what looked like a looming self-pity jag. "*Et tu*, Josephine!" He quipped with his hand over his heart. "You'll have to stand in line today—grab a knife and take a number."

"Ouch!" I chalked him up a point for quick recovery and the edgy image of Teddy as Caesar surrounded by knife-wielding, female assailants.

But there was a gasp from behind me, and I saw the center director, Delores Patton. She was the image of the Black executive woman of today from her copper-colored wool business suit with matching nails, to her short Afro hairstyle and take-charge expression. Delores had already expressed doubts about whether I should be there. My joking with Ted sent the room temperature zooming downward until I could almost hear her opinion crystallize into a solid, frozen, "No."

Ted got in a flash that I had shocked Delores, and that tickled him even more. He was amazingly good-natured for a humorist—a job that usually comes with neurotic baggage. He wrote a syndicated column, *Ted's Wide World of Bumbling*, based on his attempts to try new and daring destinations and modes of transportation, usually with hilarious results. He also wrote a series of books about adventure travel for the clueless, which had bumbled onto the bestseller list. The first one was *Bumbling Through the Jungle*—about a tourist wandering the rainforests of the world. This was succeeded by *Bumbling Around in Boats*—about sailing boats of all sizes. In Nepal, he had been gathering material for *Bumbling Along the Roof of the World*.

Delores blinked as if she recognized Ted's name when I introduced him as a bestselling author. Ted stared at his feet and mumbled, "Aw, shucks." But Delores continued to look grim.

"Sorry, ma'am, I just bumbled into your office by mistake," Ted said, giving Delores his most boyish look. "What a wonderful surprise to find my old friend Josephine. Can you spare her for lunch?" He asked her, as if begging a parent to let their child come out to play.

"You're supposed to ask me, Teddy," I said, although Delores's reaction was interesting.

"I was getting to that, Jo. If this gracious lady can spare you for an hour."

Delores stepped past me, punched the intercom, and called one of the counselors to cover the phones. She muttered that I was free to go now if I wanted. She didn't say anything about not coming back. But it was there if I wanted to hear it.

So I found myself unexpectedly set free from the office, strolling with Teddy into the late morning overcast of August in Bremerton.

"Would you mind if we took the ferry to Port Orchard?" he asked. "There's a mom and pop restaurant here that's good, but I'm not their favorite person these days."

"What? You didn't tip?"

"It's a long story. Let me buy you a good seafood lunch, if you can spare a little more time. It's only a twenty minute ride."

I thought about Delores, no doubt waiting to pounce when I went back to the center, and decided I would wind up that assignment, no matter what she did. "Okay."

We didn't have to wait long for the ferry. It was for foot traffic only, no cars, and it followed the waterfront all the way to Port Orchard. "You seem to know your way around this part of the world," I said.

"It's a long way from Kathmandu."

"At least we're not praying for an avalanche."

Teddy laughed a little grimly. We both watched the onshore world slip by in silence, thinking back to that night.

If we hadn't both been tortured by thoughts of what our spouses were doing together, we would have had a hilarious time. With each hour that they did not show up, the jokes got grimmer and seemed immensely funnier than they could have at any other time. We decided that news of our spouses having been killed in an avalanche might be welcome or unwelcome, depending on the position of the bodies and the amount of clothing they were wearing when discovered.

As the night wore on, Ted would sneak an occasional amazed look at me. The unspoken subtext was, "What a fantastic woman. I'd go to bed with her in a minute if she weighed about a hundred pounds less."

I had a sharp reply ready. Whenever a gentleman decides to share this priceless insight with me—and an amazing number do—I am forced to cut him, and then stand back out of the way so he doesn't bleed on my rather expensive plus-sized outfit. The violence is confined to words but it's surprising how respectful even a self-important male can become when he grasps that should he overstep the bounds of politeness, you can slice out his ego and hand it to him on a platter.

But Ted made me laugh and never ventured an insult—just those occasional cautious glances. Yep, got it right the first time, she's fat. I guess he'd never spent that much time with a large woman.

I gave him the benefit of the doubt because we were crouching on the same ledge in hell, and he was good company in hell. His face today testified that he'd managed to find a return ticket. We got off the ferry and he led the way to the Bay Street Restaurant, which had crisp white tablecloths, warm bread and a comprehensive seafood menu.

Sure enough, he ordered a double Scotch, single malt. Already planning my drive back to Seattle, I decided to stick with coffee, ordered the grilled sole lunch plate and sat back, resigned to listening.

"Okay, Ted, what's this sad story?"

"It's so incredible running into you like this, Jo. Because you really are responsible for my pathetic and heartbroken state."

"This is not about Francesca," I guessed.

"No. I've been lucky in love since Fran and I broke up. At least I thought I was lucky. I came into that center looking for the woman who was the love of my life. She just left me. But if it wasn't for you, I never would have found her to begin with."

"What's her name?"

"Lucille. How can I describe her? She was a goddess."

He was using the past tense. I sighed noiselessly. Lucille was either dead, or her goddess status had been revoked.

"That night in Kathmandu I couldn't help but kick myself for never having noticed you before. But more than anything that night, I hated Francesca. Did you know I left Nepal the next day?"

"No. I was a little preoccupied. Griff and I spent a few days fighting before I left."

"I still hear from Fran. I'm bugging her to sign the divorce papers. But she still hasn't quite accepted the fact that I didn't retire to a monastery after we broke up. But you don't care do you? You've found someone else—I can tell."

I was a little startled by his remark, but I didn't deny it. "Yes, I guess I have, but—it's complicated."

"But you're happy."

I almost said, "I am?" But I didn't want to get into my problems. Neither did he. He wanted to talk about his.

"I was as happy as you, until a couple of months ago."

A chill went down my spine for some reason. "What happened?"

"Her name was Lucille. She was a waitress at a little mom and pop place in Bremerton."

"The one where you're no longer welcome." I raised my eyebrows.

He managed a faint smile. "It's your fault, Jo, that I noticed her the way I did. She was bigger than you— over three hundred pounds, not that I could estimate. She told me that later. She had green eyes and the most amazing hair, like twenty-four-carat gold, with wonderful olive skin that set it off. She had this luminous cheerfulness about her. She just wore a simple white blouse and black skirt, but when she stood next to the table and I looked up, her breasts seemed to go on forever. We chatted a bit, and I guess I just basked in her simple friendliness. When she brought my order, I told her about my book and she seemed thrilled—which got my attention." He smiled.

"So you're telling me she gave signs of sharing your enthusiasm for yourself?"

"Yes, I love that in a woman." This time he came up with his most winning smile but then stared back into the middle distance and conjured up the past. "When she went to get me more coffee, I told myself here was a warm, charming, lovely woman whom I once would never have given the time of day to. So I flirted a bit, she flirted back, and that was the end of it. I told her I was about to bumble across the country on my motorcycle, and I'd see her in a few months. That was when I was writing *Bumbling and the Art of Motorcycle Maintenance*."

"Right. I read it. Great stuff."

"Thanks. Anyway, Lucille told me that sounded like a lot more fun than slinging hash, but she guessed she'd still be doing that when I returned. It was fun to talk to her. I told myself I must be over Francesca, because what could be more unlike her than this unpretentious waitress? Fran was always—well, you remember Fran."

"Oh, yeah." Fran was petite but muscular, the kind of woman who looks like she's wearing an elegant designer outfit when she's sprawled on a sofa in jeans and a thermal undershirt. I had spent lots of time successfully not thinking about her, and I wasn't about to start dwelling on her now.

"I don't know why, but somehow just flirting with Lucille, I felt pleased with myself," Ted continued. "As if I had tried some exotic dish I'd heard rumors about."

"You sampled her dish?"

"No, no. We just talked, but I thought about it."

"And?"

He sighed. "Once I got on the road I started to get this obsession with her. That hair, those eyes, those breasts."

"Okay, okay, I get it. Turn your motor off."

"Sorry. Anyway by the time I'd got my material, and was settling down to write, I told myself I was creating an ideal woman out of a wild fantasy. Still, I could write anywhere, so why not down here on the peninsula near that charming mom and pop restaurant?"

"So you came back here."

"I found a place, and started writing. I took my meals at the restaurant. Lucille was still there. She seemed glad to see me, but I noticed she was nice to everyone. It was like I was a kid again. She wasn't wearing a ring. She didn't seem to be going out with anyone. But I just couldn't get up the nerve to ask her out."

"What happened?"

"It came to the point where I couldn't stand it anymore. I found out when she got off, and rode over there on my motorcycle just before quitting time. I asked if we could talk. I told her how I felt, and she agreed to go out with me."

I sighed. "Well, that's good, Ted, what happened then?"

"We were great together, amazing. One thing led to another." He smiled in a way that made me distinctly uncomfortable. "I sampled her dish, as you put it. We were so happy." I nodded. Ted leaned forward, gazing past me into that earlier time. "I was writing; we moved in together. We even talked about her maybe taking some night classes. She was fascinated with my work. She was a great reader. But her family owned the diner where she had worked since junior high school. No one ever told her she could go to college. I would have been delighted to support her in anything she wanted to do. It turned out what she wanted to do was lose weight."

"That wasn't your idea?"

"I believe on that memorable night when you and I talked, I got an earful of your views on that subject." He looked up at the ceiling and recited, " 'Long-term studies show that all but a tiny fraction of the people who do lose weight gain back every pound, some gain back more,' et cetera, et cetera."

I blinked at him. "Gosh, I don't even remember telling you any of that. It's true, but I can't imagine how the subject came up."

"You don't even remember how you told me off?" He stared at me, incredulous.

"Sorry. Don't take it personally. Remember what a crazy night it was. I gave you a hard time, huh?"

"I was pompous, I deserved it." He looked a little sheepish. "I made some casual remark about losing weight, and you told me what an ignorant ass I was in a rather dramatic fashion."

I shrugged. "Okay, I can imagine my saying something like that. A lot of the details of our conversation were driven out of my mind by the sight of Griff giving Francesca a pelvic exam along with a farewell kiss in the lobby."

"That was a shocker, wasn't it? But I got the impression you were more surprised at what Griff did than I was at Fran. It just confirmed what I'd suspecting for months. She was always looking for a higher mountain and Griff was it. Poor bastard." He shook his head. "Anyway, I told Lucille what you said about the futility of dieting. Maybe it lost something in the translation. She said it sounded like sour grapes to her. All I could say was I loved her, and I would still love her no matter what. I went on an assignment for a travel magazine to Costa Rica. I was gone for a month, did some book promotion along the way. When I got back to Bremerton, Lucille had lost forty pounds. In the next year she lost another sixty. I had never been around anyone on a serious diet before. It was like she had PMS for a bloody year. Both of us were nervous wrecks."

"And?" I was wondering if I should even bother to go back to the center. We had finished our lunches and I'd had a refill on the coffee. It was getting late.

"The more weight Lucille lost, the more hyper she got. Her doctor had her on some prescription diet pills. She lost a hundred and fifty pounds in a year and a half. I scarcely recognized her, but I still loved her. I was worried that she was having some kind of breakdown, she was so anxious. Then she just disappeared. I think she left town. Her family refused to tell me where she had gone."

He handed me a piece of pale blue stationery. The handwriting on it was large and rounded but very clear:

Dear Ted,
    It's not that I don't love you, because I do. I always will. But I have to love myself more and try to be the best Lucille I can. Maybe it's because of my

*weight that you haven't gotten divorced even though
you said you loved me."*

"Ted!" I looked at him.

He gazed at me sadly, "I don't know what to do."

"Well, how about getting a divorce, Ted? I'm with
her on that one."

"I know, I know!" He threw up his hands. "The web
around Francesca is harder to untangle than it should
be. We've got some small property that I should get
half of. Maybe I should just let it go, but I think I've
persuaded her. If only I could contact Lucille, I could
explain what I'm doing."

"Ted," I reached out and patted his hand. "I like you.
We suffered together on a very dark night of the soul,
but you can't expect a sensible woman to stay with a
married man, even if he is separated and working on a
divorce."

"You're right. But I'm married in name only, and
even that will be over soon. I love Lucille. Losing her
is driving me crazy. She told me she was getting so
much male attention nowadays that she was afraid there
was too much temptation there. Maybe she already had
another man." He looked so miserable that I put aside
my exasperation.

"Were you guys getting along otherwise?"

"I thought we were. I adored her. We made love several times a week, and she came like a freight train. Is
that what you wanted to ask?"

"Gosh, Teddy, mince me some words, would you?"
I laughed, but now he was making me very nervous.

"Well, you wanted to ask didn't you?"

"Um, well—okay, thanks for sharing." I knew in his
way, he was paying me back for the crack about the sex

change operation. Fair enough. That was another thing I remembered about Teddy—he kept track of who made fun of what. I could almost see him mentally chalking one up for himself.

I had felt so comfortable with him during that long night of soul-sharing. It took a minute to see what was different. He wasn't shy about looking at me now.

I decided to try the man-to-man approach. "You need to clean up that unfinished business, Ted. That might go a long way toward mending things with Lucille. Otherwise—how shall I say this? If you have broadened your tastes to include large women, there are even more wonderful ladies out there than you ever imagined."

He sighed. "You think I'm not serious about finding Lucille."

"It's not that. But she doesn't seem to want to be found right now."

"I was a sucker for an ambitious woman. Again."

He looked so stricken that I reached out to offer another comforting pat, but he captured my hand and squeezed it. I pulled free as soon as I could without being rude. I didn't know much about Francesca Benedict Etheridge. I had purposely kept it that way. Now Teddy told me she was still married to him, even though she was living with my ex-husband. I didn't waste any energy feeling sorry for Griff. Francesca might be a black widow spider, but I suspected my very resourceful ex kept a packed suitcase in the closet for those sudden escapes.

I started gathering my things to go. Teddy gestured for the check. "I'm begging you to trust me here, Jo. You know I'm harmless, and I am worried about Lucille. Even if she never wants to see me again. If you have any way of getting a message to her to let her know that I need to talk to her, just for a few minutes, just to make sure she's all right."

"I can't give you any information about the center's clients, Teddy. Even if I had access to it, which I don't, it would a breach of ethics. But I'm just a receptionist and you saw the way Delores looked at me before we left. I think today's my last day."

"I'm sorry if I contributed to you losing your job," Teddy said, looking at the floor like a bad puppy.

"It was only a matter of time anyway. Now I have a long weekend," I said.

We walked out of the restaurant and I took the ferry back to Bremerton. Ted said he wanted to walk around Port Orchard and think about things. We parted with an exchange of phone numbers.

I was almost looking forward to being fired.

A CONVENTIONAL CORPSE

A CLAIRE MALLOY MYSTERY

JOAN HESS

Farberville, Arkansas, is playing host to its first-ever mystery convention with five major mystery writers—each representing a different subgenre of the mystery world—making the trek to the local college for "Murder Comes to Campus." Bookseller Claire Malloy is looking forward to meeting some of her favorite writers. But when one of the conference attendees dies in a car accident, it's evident that in Farberville the murder mystery is more than a literary genre.

"Hess goes about things in a lively style. Her heroine, Claire Malloy, has a sharp eye and an irreverent way of describing what she sees."
—*The New York Times Book Review*

"Blends humor, eccentric characters, familiar emotions, and plot twists into an enjoyable lark." —*Nashville Banner*

AVAILABLE WHEREVER BOOKS ARE SOLD
FROM ST. MARTIN'S PAPERBACKS